The Blacksmith's Widow

Dr Hamish Hart Mysteries - Book Five

Karen Thurecht

Karen Thurecht

Also by Karen Thurecht

Dr Hamish Hart Mysteries
Book 1: Murder at the Dunwich Asylum
Book 2: Plantation Murders
Book 3: Murder at Frog's Hollow
Book 4: Death at Deepwater Point

Karen's books are available from: https://karenthurecht.com.au

The author acknowledges the Gubbi Gubbi (Kabi Kabi) and Batjala (Butchulla) people, who are the traditional owners and custodians of the land where Maryborough is now located, and pay respect to their Elders, past, present and emerging.

To all the women who swim against the tide.

Chapter One

"A wife should be something above a mere menial. She ought to be a helpmate and no wife can be that, in the higher sense of the term, unless she is a companion. Many an otherwise excellent woman, perfect in the ordering of her household and capable when necessary of working heartily herself, drives her husband to the company of the public house companions because she is no companion for him.

We do not say that a doctor's wife should study medicine, or a lawyer's wife study law, or a mechanic's wife should learn his trade in order to become a companion to her husband. But every man, even the most illiterate, has his peculiar tastes and sympathies, and it should be the business of his wife to discover them, to interest herself in them and to be able to talk appreciatively about them.

The poorer a couple are, the more they are thrown together and the more need there is of this companionship. With the very rich, society occupies much of the time of the wife, if not the husband, and there is perhaps less absolute need of this companionship. But even for the very rich a capacity for companionship could add to the mutual happiness of husband and wife and often prevent sad family tragedies."
The Albury Banner and Wodonga Express Friday 20 August 1886

Nelly

A warm yeasty smell swelled to fill the tiny room, while an iron stove occupied the kitchen with such determination there was little opportunity for anything else to assert itself. The oven was the only thing of note Nelly owned. She didn't care that it occupied two-thirds of the kitchen, or that in the summer, the heat it generated was suffocating. She could make bread in this oven to rival that of the baker in Kent Street. And Mrs Windermere and Mrs Bentley brought their mounds of yeasty dough to bake in her oven. In this, as in no other thing, Nelly could hold claim to superiority over the other wives in the street.

She brushed sweat from her brow and stared across her oven and through the open window adjacent. Light came through the small hole glanced off her eyes and made her blink. Banana leaves rustled against a liberty sky.

The depth of colour caught her attention, then, for no reason she could discern, a shiver ran down her spine.

Something was wrong. Something world shattering, life altering was wrong. Nelly fought against the nausea and rising panic. What could be wrong on such a beautiful day? She racked her brain. She was used to momentary fits of anxiety gripping her chest and threatening to suffocate her. The feelings usually preceded bad news. Then she heard it, as deafening as any sound could be – the empty space normally filled with the blacksmith's tap, tap, tapping. Isaac had been at work since daylight, hammering away in his workshop attached to the back of the house. But there was no sound of hammering.

Nelly patted the flour from her hands onto her apron and rushed through the side door. She pushed the lolling banana leaves aside and entered the blacksmith shop. It always took her eyes a few moments to grow accustomed to the darkness. Isaac always told her it needed to be dark to judge the colour of the iron. Cherry red, ideal for bending the metal to his will. On this morning, the fire in the forge glowed, but little else could be seen. As Nelly's eyes became used to the darkness, her mind made sense of the details before her. She recognised the familiar shape of the anvil and the heavy wooden block that supported it. Clusters of long iron tongs hung listlessly from the rafters, and Isaac's favourite hammer languished carelessly in the dirt.

Nelly blinked hard before her eyes settled on a mass in the corner, to the left of the main door, the public entrance to the shop. A large figure lay slumped forward on the ground. She swallowed and clutched her arms to her chest. She was struggling to breathe. An intense desire to run away from the sight overcame her, but with shuddering legs she moved forward one slow step at a time.

She ducked around the anvil, almost hitting her head on the hanging tongs in her haste, leant beside the figure and placed her hands on each side of his head.

He was lying face down in the dirt. Gently, she turned his head to one side. Eyes stared cold and empty outward, his skin still and thick. The energy that makes a body tremble with life, was missing. Isaac was gone.

Nelly draped herself over her husband's body and sobbed. How had the life in him been drawn away? Where was this strongest of all, most vibrant of lives now? She cried as though her love alone could be poured into the empty space and return Isaac to her. When the sobbing finally ceased, she heard bird calls outside and recalled the existence of a wider world. A world in which Isaac no longer existed.

She was still trying to wrap her mind around the space Isaac no longer occupied when she realised her fingers had sunk into an oozing gash at the back of her husband's head. The sticky substance slipped between her thumb and her first finger. Isaac's substance, the essence that gave him life no longer travelled through his veins. A blinding realisation came to her, one of those moments that feels like time skips a beat, the sudden inescapable knowledge that life is nothing more than movement. A pumping heart, lungs heaving with oxygen, blood travelling through the veins. But Isaac was still. That is all death is. Stillness. Nelly caught sight of her husband's favourite hammer on the dirt beside his body. The iron head was covered in dried blood. How had Isaac's hammer conspired to kill him? With a rush of fear, she peered around the room looking for any sign of movement. Could the killer still be lurking in the shadowy corners of the shop? Nelly climbed to her feet and ran. She ran without stopping while her neighbours watched in shocked surprise.

***

Within twenty minutes, the local Police Constable returned with Nelly to the blacksmith shop. She watched him write careful notes describing the scene before him. She knew the young Constable Williams was well out of his depth. There had been no sergeant at the station since the previous man moved on four months earlier.

"Did you hear anything, Mrs Brown?"

Nelly shook her head somewhat ashamed she had allowed her husband to be bludgeoned to death without noticing a thing.

The constable looked around. "Nothing seems to be amiss. I suppose he was working here when the intruder entered. He might not have noticed. He was unlikely to be expecting an attack. If he came through the main door, you wouldn't have seen him either."

The constable stood before the forge which was now reduced to embers. A set of tongs still lay balanced precariously at the edge of the forge. He picked them up.

"The assailant could have picked up the hammer and belted him with it.

The constable made the movement with his arms. Then he played out Isaac turning, staggering, and falling.

"Isaac didn't go down right away – he turned to face his attacker. Then the intruder ran and left Isaac to stagger a few steps before he fell forward and died."

The constable looked at Nelly as though something had occurred to him.

"Where were you this morning, Mrs Brown."

Nelly swallowed hard. "I was in the kitchen," she said.

At the very moment of saying it, the smell of smoke reached her. Her eyes widened and she ran from the shop and into the house. With a tablecloth wrapped around her wrists she grabbed a burning loaf from the oven and flung it onto the stove top. It was ruined. This, on top of everything else, made her slip to the floor crying. The world had shifted beneath her feet within the space of an hour.

Constable Williams left her where she sat. He needed help with this situation. The news of a murder within the small town would travel fast. Already, people were gathering outside the blacksmith shop trying to peer into its dark recesses.

Chapter Two

"A Perfect Wife for 25 Pounds: Such is the advertisement that has come into our delighted hands. It is issued by a lady who is going to start a school for wives. In these days of garish accomplishments – the practical side of women's nature is neglected. In the new academy it will be developed. Girls who go there will be instructed in housewifely duties. The classes will consist of cookery, dressmaking, physiology, book-keeping, elocution and debating. The book-keeping will be very useful.

The perfect wife, who keeps her husband's choice editions instead of lending them to casual acquaintances is far above rubies. But debating is the housewifely duty that requires cultivation. When a little debate occurs in the domestic circle (on milliner's bills for instance) it is lamentable to think how unfairly women are handicapped by the deficiencies of their education. It is the universal opinion of married men that debating power is the point at which their wives are weakest." **Clarence and Richmond Examiner Saturday July 1887.**

Bellamy

A hot wind slapped Bellamy as he stepped from the train carriage onto the platform. He shook one leg and then the other, stretching from his knees and rotating his ankles. The station was impressive given the town was 160 miles north of the capital and had held the title of town for barely two decades. A scraggly collection of passengers, tired and worn from the journey gathered on the platform further down. Mostly men, they carried rolled up tarps on their backs and stacks of tools tied with rope. As Bellamy scanned their faces, they looked bewildered at having found themselves in such a place. Still, they would only be in town long enough to purchase supplies and more equipment before heading on another train back to Gympie to work the claims. The peak of the Goldrush was over with most of the alluvial gold taken, but there was still work for men willing to do it, on the large sites, underground.

For men hungry enough to spend long hours down the deep shafts that followed underground veins through the mountains, the valley was still a place where fortunes could be made, even if they didn't reach the heady heights of the early days.

Bellamy had been assured a constable would pick him up from the station, but he could see no one who seemed a likely candidate. He took his one bag from the porter and walked through the station building into the sun. Looking back, he saw a central clock tower and a large station clock that confirmed his train had not arrived early. The constable must have been detained. He ran his fingers around the inside of his collar and felt the sweat that had gathered there. It was warm this time of year in Brisbane, but it seemed worse this far north. He hadn't been enthusiastic about his secondment to the Maryborough region to investigate this killing. He had enough to do at home. And Agatha wasn't happy to have to endure his absence either. She was nervous in their home alone, unjustifiably so, according to Bellamy. But still.

The station building had the look of newness about it. Bellamy could almost smell the paint, even though the numerals above the clock said 1882. He was impressed by the work involved in extending the railway north, as well as the additional line that went to Gympie, the new mining town. Queensland was springing to life along the railway tracks snaking northward opening up new pastoral and commercial opportunities. In Bellamy's mind the railway simulated the serpent that carved out creation in the stories told by the Indigenous people. Only the railway was a new kind of serpent, fired by steam and carving out a new landscape. A voice startled him from behind.

"Sergeant Bellamy, is it?"

Turning, he was met with the face of a young man, his pale skin liberally spotted with fine brown freckles, and he had neatly cut hair and large eager eyes. He didn't look old enough to be a police officer.

"Constable Williams," he said, holding out a hand that felt too soft when Bellamy took it in his own.

"Sorry, I'm late."

"No apology required," said Bellamy. "I've been admiring the building. I didn't expect anything so grand."

"There's a lot of traffic through here," said Williams picking up Bellamy's bag and walking toward a waiting carriage.

Bellamy followed, a little embarrassed about not carrying his own suitcase.

"There used to be even more traffic, with the rush at Gympie. It's petered out a bit now – but still busy. All the food and other supplies for the miners come by ship to our port on the Mary River. And then there's the banking. The miners bring their gold to be weighed and deposited into the banks here. Most of them catch the train in and out."

Williams placed the suitcase carefully behind the driver then both he and Bellamy climbed in.

"We'll go directly to the Police Station if you don't mind. The Detective Inspector is keen that we begin investigating as soon as possible. He wants me to bring you up to date then take instruction from you from there on. We don't get many murders around here and he doesn't like this one hanging over the town. The murdered man was well liked, a local, and until the killer is caught people will be edgy."

"I understand," said Bellamy. "I'd rather get right to work myself. Who was the victim?"

"Isaac Brown, a blacksmith. We have at least nine of them in town, but he was the best. Everyone went to him, miners, agriculturalists, even Walkers Engineering sent him work."

"Who found the body?" asked Bellamy going through the preliminary questions in his mind.

"His wife, bless her. He was lying dead on the floor of his shop at the back of their house. He seems to have been hit over the head with his own hammer. It was found lying beside him, all covered in blood and muck. This was yesterday morning."

The constable's face was as dry and innocent as an infant and Bellamy felt a pang of nostalgia for a time when his mindset could be so light and free from the impact of decades of death and violence.

"Superintendent Scratchley said your sergeant is away at present." Bellamy's tone indicated it was as much a question as it was a statement.

"He's not away, he's gone." Williams corrected him. "All the way back to England. His wife couldn't abide the place. She wasn't too bad in

Brisbane apparently, but when they were sent here...well, it was the last straw. Having said that, I don't think the sergeant was happy to be here either. He was hoping for a promotion, and instead they sent him to this backwater."

Bellamy chuckled.

"It looks like a nice town, and a large one," he said, taking in what he could through his window.

"Second largest in Queensland," said Williams, proud now that Bellamy had offered the compliment.

"Lived here all your life, have you?"

"Indeed, I have. Born and bred."

Williams looked straight ahead for a few moments as they rattled through town toward the police station.

Bellamy wondered what the young policeman thought of being lumbered with a senior officer from Brisbane to take over his case.

As if he had heard his thoughts, Williams spoke. "I couldn't do it myself," he said. "Not without help."

He turned toward Bellamy with such a face of admiration it made the sergeant's heart melt. "I'll look forward to learning from you, sir."

Bellamy smiled. He was going to like Maryborough. He returned to his mental list of preliminary questions.

"There is no doubt about the cause of death?"

"The body has gone to the undertaker. But no. There is no doubt."

***

They stopped in front of a substantial red brick building and again Bellamy found himself surprised by the facilities in this rural town.

How long had it been? Surely, only forty years since the first men settled in the area. In that time the town had grown from nothing to a bustling city, second only in importance to Brisbane. Constable Williams took the sergeant's suitcase and headed into the police station with Bellamy following.

Bellamy was led into a small room with timber walls and a wooden desk pushed up against the one window that let in natural light. There were three mismatched chairs in front of the desk, which was covered in papers and ledgers. Bellamy thought how like it was to his own office in Brisbane right down to the shelves along the walls holding various leather-bound books and dusty documents. The air was tinged with the scent of ink and aged wood.

"Is the superintendent waiting here?" said Bellamy looking around.

"No, sir." Williams hesitated. "He is further north. Some trouble with natives. A homestead has been assaulted. There is a family connection, I believe, and he has a personal interest in tracking down those responsible."

Bellamy felt a pang of nausea in his stomach. He knew the carnage that would be likely to result from such a hunt. He had his own troop of Native Police in the south-east and he struggled with the morality of using these men to hunt down their own. In fact, he struggled with the morality of hunting down men who were fighting for their land and their freedoms, at all. He wondered how many innocent lives would be lost based on the perceived attack on a homesteader. In his experience, those involved spent little energy investigating the evidence in these cases though they had a great deal of energy for retribution against those they assumed to be at fault. But these were complex problems and better men than he, presumably, made the decisions.

"He wanted me to get you up to date." Williams looked worried the visitor might be disappointed the superintendent was not present.

"He must have a lot of confidence in you," said Bellamy. "What have you done so far?"

"Yesterday I spoke to Nelly."

The constable took a notebook and pencil from the top drawer of his desk. He flipped the pages until he found the entry he was looking for. "She was upset, as to be expected. Came as a shock. Finding him that way. But she says she didn't see or hear anything until she went out there."

"Why did she go from the house to the workshop?"

"That's the thing." Williams looked up from his notebook. "She said she had a feeling."

"A feeling?"

"Yes, sir. Nelly has feelings…Like she knows when something is wrong. One time…"

"All right. I understand. Go on. Did she say anything else that might be helpful?"

"No, sir. But I spoke to the neighbours. They all speak very highly of the deceased and they said that Nelly was devoted to him. He was, by all accounts a hard worker and a good husband. Makes you think, doesn't it? I mean, going the way he did?"

Bellamy said nothing and the lad refocussed.

"The neighbours say Nelly is a bit of a loner. She doesn't mix much. But she isn't unkind, she lets some of the women use her oven to bake bread. They say she is different. German. She used to go to the Lutheran Services with her family. But not lately, I don't think Isaac Brown went in for religion. But they are certain there was never a harsh word between husband and wife – although they did say Nelly had a bruise on her face a few weeks back. She says she fell. I'm not sure if there's anything there."

"Does Nelly Brown have any close friends?"

"Yes, sir. Folks say she's close to Ruth Gowan, the woman who owns the White Swan Inn."

Bellamy's face remained blank.

"That's where you're staying," the constable hurried to explain. "The owner, Ruth, is a formidable woman. She took over the license and the running of the inn when her husband died.

She's a competent businesswoman and takes no nonsense from the patrons. We have very little trouble from the inn with her there to keep customers in line."

Constable Williams took a breath. He was talking fast, as though he wanted to get out all this local knowledge quickly before the new sergeant grew tired of listening to him.

"She has a manager, Arthur Kane, who is also well respected in the town," he went on. "Anyway, her and Nelly got on well by all accounts. I interviewed Ruth and she said the same as everyone else."

The constable flicked open his notebook.

"No problems in that marriage," he read from his notes.

"I asked her about the bruise, and she said she thought Nelly had fallen. But she assured me that, if it was not the case, it was not Isaac who had hit her."

Bellamy looked up with interest. "Her best friend isn't convinced the bruise came from a fall?"

Williams hesitated. "No. I mean, I don't think it's that." He stared at his notes as if hoping for inspiration. "I don't think she questioned it. I believe she simply wanted to reassure me that it wouldn't have been the result of an assault from her husband."

"She didn't dismiss the idea that Mrs Brown could have been assaulted by someone else?"

Williams put the end of his pencil to his lips. "I didn't ask that," he said.

Bellamy nodded for him to go on.

"I've been able to make a list of some of Isaac's clients. The biggest contract was with Walkers Engineering. They have a contract with Queensland Rail, and they have sub-contracted a significant portion of the blacksmithing to Isaac. He has a longstanding relationship with one of the directors, Mr Hawking.

The current lead engineer doesn't see the agreement as efficient and wants to bring all the work into the company's own shop. But the director insists that the quality of work provided by Mr Brown could not be matched in-house. Of course, now they have no barrier to taking that step."

Williams appeared to have finally run out of air.

"Well done, Constable," said Bellamy.

Williams blushed.

Bellamy recalled his constable back in Brisbane. Why can't Pennyweather be as appreciative as this fellow?

Encouraged, Williams continued.

"There're also the miners who come into town for equipment. Isaac Brown was well known and respected for his craftsmanship. He was the preferred supplier for many of the independent miners. The difference between a well-made tool and a second rate one could be the difference between life and death on the fields. I have a list of names to show you."

He tore a page from his notebook and handed it to the sergeant.

"Excellent," he said taking the neatly written list.

"Then, there's the local agriculturalists who require tools and equipment all the time. Isaac seems to be the busiest of all the blacksmiths in town, on account of his reputation for providing quality products at reasonable rates. It's a shame to see such a thriving business come to an end."

Bellamy looked up at Constable Williams. "What will happen to his wife now?" he asked.

Williams looked confused. "I don't know. I suppose she will inherit the house but how she will support herself, I'm sure I don't know."

"I'll talk to her first," said Bellamy. "Tomorrow."

He picked up his bags and the constable took them from him.

"I'll take you to the White Swan," he said.

***

When Bellamy first set eyes on Ruth Gowan he had to agree she was indeed a formidable woman. She was both tall and wide, though more muscle than fat. She had a waist a grown man could barely get an arm around and a bosom that was pushed high beneath double chins. Salt and pepper hair was pulled back tight from her face out of which grey eyes took in the world with suspicious consideration.

Nonetheless it was a pleasant face that may have been considered pretty in her youth. She was still a handsome woman, in her own way. She had a presence that could not be ignored.

"Bellamy is it?" she said taking the man's suitcase from the constable. She swung it to her hip as though it weighed nothing. Constable Williams was jolted by the force of the transaction.

"I'll show you to your room."

Bellamy turned to thank Williams, but he was already heading out the door. The sergeant followed the innkeeper up a narrow staircase, and it seemed to him that her hips only just missed the sides as she swayed from right to left up the stairs.

"I'm happy to take the suitcase myself," he suggested, but the woman climbed upward without acknowledging him. She wasn't struggling.

She opened a door to the right of the staircase just as they reached the top and Bellamy followed her in. The room was small and sparse with a cast iron bed, a single side table of silky oak and a plain wardrobe being the only furniture. Faded green wallpaper made the room seem darker than necessary. There was a decent sized window opposite the bed with thick drapes that took on the colour of the wallpaper.

"This will be fine," said Bellamy as the woman put the suitcase down beside the bed.

"You can have dinner downstairs," she said. "But you'll have to hurry. Cook goes home at seven."

With that she left Bellamy to his own devices. He couldn't decide whether the dizzying sensation in his head was attributable to hunger or fatigue, but he decided it would be wise to eat before retiring to give himself the best opportunity for a decent sleep. He ventured back down the staircase as soon as he'd hung his suits in the wardrobe.

The dining room was bustling. It was dark and had the smell of old wood and smoke. Men in rough working clothes crowded around every table. Most were finishing up their meals and preparing to leave. No one took any notice of Bellamy. These men were strangers in a strange town. And they were there with a single focus. Gold.

A thin young woman brought Bellamy a passable stew which he ate with all the gusto of a hungry man. An older man with a twinkle in his eye brought him a glass of cold beer.

"You'll be the detective come to investigate the unfortunate death of our blacksmith," he said.

"That I am," said Bellamy. He drank his beer in one long mouthful.

"Arthur Kane," said the man, holding out his hand.

"Bellamy." The man had a strong grip.

"I wish you well," said Arthur Kane. "Isaac was a good man."

With that he pulled down the towel he had swung over his shoulder and returned to the bar where he continued to polish the red cedar to a fiery glow.

Bellamy was happy to return to his room. It had been a long day of travelling. He fell immediately into a deep sleep.

Chapter Three

"The stars visible to the naked eye forming the several constellations, and the groups of transfigurations so familiar to astronomers and star gazers generally, have apparently retained the same relative position to one another from time immemorial, or at least from the earliest times when they were grouped into imaginary figures called constellations by ancient historians; and if Hipparchus could now look upon starry heavens he would see constellations and stellar groups just as he saw them thousands of years ago. Fixed stars are popularly regarded as immovable in space.

The more exact astronomy of modern times, however, has shown with regard to a very large number of these so-called fixed stars, that they are by no means so relatively immovable as they appear and they have movements in the heavens which are measurable from year to year, and even month to month. Some of the movements are regularly and continuously in one direction; others are in curves or even circles, as if moving around some centre in the heavens." **The Naracoorte Herald Friday 2 October 1885.**

Nelly

Moonlight filtered through banana leaves creating intricate patterns of light and shadow across Nelly's face as she lay staring at the ceiling in her small bedroom. Dappled light played upon every surface it touched, illuminating the soft outline of her jaw, while the silver halo of her hair spread across her shoulders. She let her eyes wander around the room and noted that the furniture cast elongated shadows across the floor bringing a dreamlike quality to the room.

Nelly stretched her hand out to the spot on the bed where Isaac should have been, and pretended she could feel his warm body there. She imagined she could feel his chest rising and falling beneath her fingers. She imagined the spicy scent of Isaac replacing the fruitiness of the ripening bananas. Rolling onto her side, she tried to pretend she could see him there, his long body stretched out the full length of the bed, his head tucked safely on the pillow.

But there was nothing. She could trick herself into believing she could touch him and breath in his presence, but visualisation was a step too far.

In the tranquillity of night, her heart was heavy with grief and longing. His passing had shattered her world into fragments of sorrow, the moments since his death like splinters, time seemed disconnected, her life no longer whole. During the day she felt like a ghost moving around the house they had shared together. Then at night, when blissful peace might soothe her in her sleep, respite would not come. Memories of cherished moments with Isaac came like relentless waves crashing against the shore.

She heard the persistent ticking of the carriage clock by the bed, one of the few possessions she'd brought from Germany. Now the sound seemed only to echo Isaac's absence, a stark reminder of the passing seconds.

Nelly threw herself onto her back and turned her head so she could see through the open window. A breeze wafted in on the summer night providing relief for what would have otherwise been a suffocating humidity. She knew she could usually calm herself by staring into the night sky, linking the stars in her mind's eye, recognising some constellations already well known and imagining others. She recalled stories she had been told since childhood and made the characters come to life. She imagined a sense of interconnectedness across the ages as she thought about the countless generations of women who had looked at the same stars seeking guidance, solace, or something else they couldn't define. The stars had witnessed history unfold. In this land, European history was short. But the land itself was ancient and the original inhabitants had been searching the stars for meaning for tens of thousands of years. She imagined the First People observing the same stars long before Europeans set foot on their land. She imagined the profound sorrow of these people when the strange newcomers kept coming, when they brought guns and unknown diseases; when they fenced off the land

and the waterholes; when they built their towns and cities and dug mines on sacred land. Her body shuddered. The sorrow was overwhelming, the problems too big for her to take on.

She forced herself to think instead about the science of the stars. She loved reading about female astronomers like Caroline Herschel, Mary Somerville, and Maria Mitchell, trailblazing women who defied societal norms to follow their passion. These women inspired her to consider the universe a boundless realm of knowledge waiting to be unravelled and told. They proved that women were a central part of that telling. That women were able to contemplate grand questions, that women could be accepted by an establishment dominated by men, through their professional standing, their scientific research, their publications, and their awards. She yearned for a world where women could explore not just the constellations but also the depths of their own minds and desires without barriers. No sooner than Nelly's mind had been distracted by thoughts of science, an ominous heaviness settled on her, a feeling of impending tragedy. She recognised the sensation. It had happened before. A haunting chill crept up her spine while she listened to the feint whispers of unseen messengers. She couldn't make out words, but the message was always tragic. It felt as though the universe stopped to hold its breath while time unravelled. The unfathomable sorrow of the future was presented to her as though it was current and tangible. The weight of the unknown crushed her, she felt vulnerable, exposed, and powerless. The sensation had never failed to produce tragedy.

But what more could go wrong? Her husband had been killed. Did someone want to harm her? She couldn't believe that to be true. But she couldn't believe anyone would want to harm Isaac either. She struggled to fight off the profound sense of dread that had gripped her, however there was no denying the feeling was the same one she experienced throughout her life. In every case, tragedy followed. Who else could she lose?

Chapter Four

"The attention of ladies is specially solicited by the official report just published by Doctor Ogle on modern social and sanitary improvements as a means of lengthening life. It shows that among the privileges that are to be a woman's when she obtains her full rights will be that of dying sooner. Though Doctor Ogle has found it hard to reduce the softer sex to statistics, his report points to the conclusion: If women want to live long, they had better remain as they are. At present their mean average of lifetime is 44-62 years as compared to men's 41-55 years, and all because they do not know the "feverish excitement and reckless expenditure of energy" that wears and tears men to pieces." **The Brisbane Courier Monday 4 January 1886**.

Bellamy

Bellamy felt the back of his eyelids warming up before he was aware of the sharp light piercing them. He opened his eyes and blinked several times to block out the early morning sun. A narrow gap between the curtains directed the rays unswervingly onto his face. He groaned and lifted his head, forcing his body to come to life sufficiently to climb off the overly stuffed mattress. As his left foot touched the polished floorboards, he heard a sudden, jarring thud from under his window. He was startled, but more so when a blood-curdling scream followed, piercing the dawn like a dagger.

Bellamy threw his right leg onto the floor and grabbed his dressing gown. He rushed to the window and threw it open peering down to the street below. The glow of the early morning sun cast eerie shadows. A woman's figure was slumped against the wall of the building. Even though the figure was partially obscured from this vantage point, he knew from the dimensions that it was Ruth Gowan. Two housemaids stood by the figure with their hands clasped to their mouths, staring at her in horror. One of the housemaids Bellamy recognised as the thin waitress who brought him his dinner the night before. Adrenaline surged through his veins as he ran from his room, down the stairs and out to the scene. The thin housemaid had by this time knelt to the ground and was about to take hold of the lifeless figure.

"Stop!" cried Bellamy. The maid looked up and froze.

"Don't touch her," said Bellamy more gently as he knelt beside the body of the Innkeeper.

"Go and notify Constable Williams," he said.

The thin housemaid rushed away. The more ample housemaid stood frozen, still.

"You continue your duties," said Bellamy. "The guests will be wanting their breakfast."

She hesitated staring for a moment at her lifeless boss, then she followed the sergeant's instruction.

Ruth Gowan, still in her nightdress, stared up blindly from a face that was blistered and raw. Bellamy's fingers hovered over her neck, but something stopped him from touching her. He could tell she was dead without needing to search for a pulse. Blisters had broken out down her neck and disappeared under the collar of her nightgown. The sergeant went to lift her cotton neckline, then hesitated.

"Give me your gloves," he said to the maid. She removed frayed woollen gloves and handed them to Bellamy. He stretched the gloves onto his much larger hands and carefully lifted the neckline between two fingers. Peering beneath, Bellamy saw that the damage continued across her chest.

He examined one hand after the other. The blistering was present on the backs of both hands and for about four inches up her arm. It looked as though she had raised her hands to protect her face. Her legs and feet were unaffected.

It wasn't long before Williams arrived on the scene, and when he saw Ruth's body slumped as it was, he stopped as if struck, gasped and took a step backward.

"What happened to her?"

"I don't know," said Bellamy. "It looks like burning to her skin, but I don't know. It seems unlikely she would die from the burns, as severe as they appear. And I can't see any sign of a fire. There is an unusual odour that troubles me as well."

Bellamy looked around and Constable Williams instinctively did likewise.

"Perhaps she came from somewhere else. Before she died," said Williams.

"Maybe. You go and check the outbuildings. Try the stable first. See if you can find any sign of fire."

The constable was about to move away to carry out his orders when Bellamy stopped him.

"Before you go, arrange for the body to be taken to the morgue, insist that it be preserved as well as is possible. And make sure the attendants wear gloves, for their own safety as well as the preservation of evidence."

Williams nodded but hesitated to move. Bellamy wondered if he were gathering the courage to ask a question.

"What will you do?" the younger man asked.

"I am going to send a telegram," said Bellamy.

Bellamy returned to his room and quickly changed from his dressing gown into his day clothes. As he did so, a plan was taking shape in his mind.

***

This was an unusual death. He needed someone he could trust to carry out the autopsy. He had no doubt there was a doctor in town who could do it, but there were strong ties in this community. How could he know the alliances of anyone local? He was convinced the two deaths were connected. Didn't Williams say that Ruth Gowan and Nelly Brown were friends? Too close to be a coincidence. He needed an outsider. Someone with an interest in investigation that went further than the medical examination.

The police cab arrived to pick him up and he travelled into the centre of town. From there he sent an urgent telegram to a doctor he had worked with in Brisbane, Doctor Hamish Hart.

He'd worked with the young doctor on several tricky murder investigations over the past couple of years and found him diligent and committed. Doctor Hart had proved himself willing to become involved at a deeper level than the regular medical examiner, even if he tended to become too personally involved in some instances. The doctor's one weakness, if it can be properly called that, was that he wore his heart on his sleeve, not a characteristic common within his profession. Bellamy admitted to himself, that he and the doctor had become friends and he looked forward to working with him again.

He then sent another telegram to Doctor Rita Cartwright, an exceptional woman, sharp, professional, determined, and skilled at interviewing women. Most significantly, Hamish was better when Rita was around.

Hamish

Hamish breathed a sigh of relief as he stepped onto steady ground. He felt like he'd been travelling for a decade. He'd secured a cabin on the first ship he could manage after returning from investigating a difficult case at Deepwater Point on the Queensland coast. He had received word of his father's deteriorating health and travelled to Melbourne intending to assist his mother and his ailing father. But things had not gone to plan. The journey by sea from Brisbane to Melbourne and back again took place within the space of less than a fortnight. His parents had not welcomed his offers of assistance resulting in a stressful and exhausting experience. But it was better to know.

He recalled his father's face as he ordered him to leave his house, his eyes bulging and the veins on his forehead swollen. Hamish hardly knew this man. Any more than the man knew himself. Dementia had robbed his father of his connection to his only son, as tenuous as that connection had always been. And his mother was clearly struggling. But neither of them wanted his help. They were too caught up in each other to have had any emotional energy left for him. It was the way it had always been. It seemed to Hamish that they took pleasure in their own despair.

Hamish shook off the feelings of self-pity that threatened to de-stabilize him. It was a clear day with a light breeze to take the edge off the late summer heat and he was finally off that ship and back in Brisbane, his home for some four years now. He looked about to see if his bags were ready for collection and a boy with more spots on his face than clear skin tugged at his sleeve.

"Are you Doctor Hamish Hart?" asked the boy.

"You know I am Tom," said Hamish recognising the boy from previous encounters. He had often delivered his telegrams to the house in Wickham Terrace.

"Yes. But I'm s'posed to ask, sir." The boy held out his hand. "A telegram, sir," he said, then ran off as fast as he had appeared.

Hamish unfolded the piece of paper.

Reboard immediately. Required in Maryborough. Passage booked and paid for. BELLAMY

Hamish held his hand to his forehead where a throbbing headache was emerging. He read the words again. Reboard that bloody ship? Not a chance in hell. He looked around at the other passengers scurrying away with their luggage and yearned to be among them. He caught sight of a porter out of the corner of his eye.

"When does this ship sail again?" he asked.

The Porter shuffled backwards a step or two and shot Hamish a dazed look.

"Four hours," he said when he had recovered. "We need to clear this lot and take in a whole new load."

The fellow shook his head and struggled on with two bags balanced precariously under each arm.

Hamish stood in the bustle, cargo, passengers, crew scrambling back and forth around him. He could neither move himself forward or back. His head was spinning.

Four hours to decide. Decide what? There's no question of getting back on that ship. How much longer to Maryborough? Good Lord, there's a practice to maintain. To establish. Perhaps establish is a better word.

There's little to maintain after being away for weeks already. All the more reason to get back to it. The purpose in coming to Brisbane was to establish a nice steady general practice. A steady life. A life where the risks are low and easily managed.

He took one last look at the telegram.

What is he involved in now? In Maryborough, of all places.

Hamish looked back at the ship. During the voyage to Melbourne, the ship was a snare in his mind, a trap he couldn't escape, carrying him to his inevitable confrontation with family, disappointment, and emptiness. Every swell, every fall a nauseating reminder of his never having been good enough.

But strangely, when he looked at the ship from the freedom of the wharf, readying for the last leg of its journey to Maryborough, the hulk trembled with anticipation. The funnels were bright against the sky with the promise of the unknown. Stories of adventure seemed to be embedded deep into each of the planks and ropes. Hamish stopped himself with the thought of Rita. He had missed her terribly during the long weeks travelling to and from Melbourne.

Damn Bellamy.

Hamish caught the eye of another porter. "Can you leave my bag aboard?" he said. "I'm travelling on."

"I know," said the porter, "the captain received a telegram. Your bag's still on board. You should go to the galley and have a drink. It'll be a while before we set off again."

Hamish turned around to glare at the ship before he lifted heavy legs to trudge back on board. Required in Maryborough. What does that mean? He'd do well to remember I don't work for the Police Department.

Hamish headed for the galley.

Once aboard and comfortable in the ship's galley, Hamish took a swill of cold beer and calmed himself. If he was honest, it was seeing Rita he had been looking forward to most. His relationship with the beautiful female doctor was complicated.

He admired her enormously. Rita graduated from the London School of Medicine for Women, but unable to register as a doctor in Australia due to her gender, she worked as a pharmacist at the Lady Bowen Lying-In Hospital. Rita was the most highly skilled doctor Hamish knew, and an inspired diagnostician. It was a terrible shame she couldn't practice in this country. A second terrible shame was that Rita preferred intimacy with women, and Hamish was in love with her. He told himself daily he was not – but his emotions betrayed him whenever she was in his presence. When he was away from her, he felt a part of himself missing. Rita loved him too, like a brother. He knew this. The relationship was complicated.

Hamish finished the last of his beer and headed toward his quarters. He supposed he could finish the book he'd been reading on the way from Melbourne.

He was making his way from the galley to his cabin when he noticed a slim woman in a neat skirt and plain white blouse striding toward him. She reminded him of...

"Hamish! There you are. I've been looking everywhere. The porter told me your cabin number. I think he was quite suspicious of my motives for asking." She laughed.

Hamish was staring at her in disbelief. "What are you doing here?"

"I've taken passage to Maryborough. What do you think?"

"Why?"

Rita took a telegram from her purse. It was from Bellamy, similar to his own, summoning her north.

"What's going on?"

"I was hoping you would know."

Chapter Five

"The subject of interest is the very pretty little town of Maryborough, one of the best known places on the southern coast of Queensland, and the centre of an industrious and thriving population. It is situated some miles inland from Wide Bay on the Mary River, on the banks of which, with its many tributaries, are some of the richest scrublands in the colony, and abounding in valuable timber, the export of which led to the first trade and settlement of the district. On this, followed a settlement of hardy pioneers who tilled the soil, cultivating principally maize which grew most luxuriously and grew crops in abundance.

Then came the introduction of sugar cane and the district is now developing into a splendid sugar growing country, and within a short distance from the town are some of the largest and finest plantations in the colony, whereby the judicious investment of capital, all the new mechanical appliances and processes are used to produce from the juice of the cane the snowy sugar now becoming so well-known and appreciated in the southern colonies. Besides the advantage of choice land, the district has likewise an abundant supply of coal. Maryborough has also been known for many years as the gateway to the rich goldfields of Gympie, the road from Brisbane being oftentimes impassable.

In the town several valuable industries have been permanently established, notably an extensive foundry and iron works where several steam vessels and barges have been, and are being, made for the Queensland Government. These advantages together with the settlement of a large number of bona fide selectors and agriculturalists have caused the town to flourish. Maryborough offers startling proof of the superiority of the Anglo race in the work of Colonisation." **Australian Town and Country Journal Saturday 25 September 1880.**

Hamish

Bellamy was waiting at the wharf on the Mary River when Hamish and Rita stepped off the ship the following morning. It was a busy port catering to immigrants from all over Europe and Britain seeking their fortune at the Queensland frontier. Two paddle steamers were lined up along the two-mile wharf and another was churning up the waters of the river as it headed seaward. A railway track ran the length of the wharf carrying logs to the sawmill while men darted back and forth like ants shifting cargo to and from the ships. Vendors were hawking goods from wooden stalls, offering fruits, spices, and trinkets. The aroma of freshly caught fish mixed with the scent of the sea, strangely out of place this far up the river.

Hamish looked back the way he had come, down river toward its mouth. The Mary River curled away amidst lush green vegetation, shimmering silver in the sun. Despite the bustle, this was a beautiful place.

On the way to the police station Bellamy got immediately to the point.

"There have been two murders, a blacksmith and an innkeeper," he said, "and we don't know if they're connected."

"What is your instinct?" said Hamish.

"I think they are connected. But to be perfectly honest, there's no concrete evidence that Mrs Gowan, the innkeeper, was murdered at all."

"I need to see the bodies."

"I thought you might be eager. The blacksmith has already been buried, I'm afraid. But Ruth Gowan's body is in the morgue."

Hamish stopped fiddling with the clasp on his carry bag and stared at the sergeant. "What do you mean...already buried?"

Bellamy shifted uncomfortably. He knew the doctor well enough to know this information was not going to be taken well.

"The cause of death was obvious," he said. "He was hit over the head with his hammer. There was a massive great gash in his head. We have the weapon if you want to see it."

Hamish settled back into his seat with an audible huff. He looked across to Rita and saw the corners of her mouth crinkle upward. Hamish shook his head and relaxed his shoulders a little. The lax disregard for maintaining a murder scene and protecting the integrity of the corpse in situ was a constant irritation to him. He had counselled the sergeant and his underlings enough times about its importance. He sat, going over in his mind the potential significance of lost evidence for some minutes, his lips pursed as he stared blankly at the town going by outside the window.

"We can take you directly to the morgue, if you like?" offered Bellamy, by way of compensation. "I'll take your cases on to the inn."

Hamish nodded resignedly.

"Would you like to wash before you join the doctor?" Bellamy asked Rita.

She shot him such a venomous look he decided to keep his head down for the rest of the trip. He had now offended them both. But it was Hamish's turn to smile. Bellamy failed to understand the depth of Rita's difference from other women.

The cab rattled on along the straight road that ran two miles from the centre of town to the new hospital. Hamish watched the misty purple top of Mount Bauple ahead of them until Bellamy spoke.

"There it is," he said.

Hamish looked to the left to see an impressive two storey brick building perched on high ground.

"The constable tells me the hospital is built on about eight acres of land," said Bellamy. "The locals are understandably proud of it. Apparently, they began with a hut in Fort Street thirty or forty years ago."

The buggy turned in through handsome iron gates set in stone pillars. Ahead of them stood the main building with broad verandas flanked on either side by adjoining wings.

Hamish was immediately struck by the wide stairs leading up into the building. The hospital was grand, suited to a town aware of its importance and eager to not only care for its populace with the best that medial science could offer, but to impress them as well with stately architecture and the promise of comfort.

"We'll let the Matron know we're here," said Bellamy. "Then I'll take you to the morgue. It's brand new, an addition to the hospital after completion of the main building."

Hamish, Rita and Bellamy entered the front hall, central to two large cedar doors.

Beech floors were perfectly tongued and grooved. On one side of the hall was the matron's room and on the other the dispenser's space, in the centre was a cedar staircase with an elaborate balustrade. Rita was running an appreciative glove along the bottom of the handrail when the matron, a tall woman with thin hair tucked beneath a veil, emerged from her office. Hamish suspected no one entered the building without her knowing about it. Initial introductions were made, without even a hint of an eyebrow raised in response to the female doctor.

"Would you like to inspect the wards?" the matron asked.

Hamish would have preferred to go immediately to the morgue, but it seemed impolite to say so.

"There are seventeen beds on the ground floor in this central building," she said.

"These are for female patients. There are the same number on the second floor for men. These are the only beds filled presently, the additional beds in the wings are vacant. The south wing is furnished superbly for the paying patients. We'll provide exceptional care for those patients once we are fully open."

"I would hope all the patients receive exceptional care," said Hamish. The notion that there was a 'special' wing for patients who could afford to pay jarred on him. It wasn't so much the superior furnishings, as the suggestion that they received a different level of care that offended him.

The matron flashed him a sideways glance.

"Indeed," she said.

Hamish noticed an elevator to transport patients to the upstairs wards and he was about to examine it when the matron put her hand on his arm.

"Follow me," she said. "I'm sure you'll appreciate the operating room, here on the ground floor."

His interest was piqued. He and Rita followed eagerly into a room that was pristine as though it had never been used. Well-lit and containing the latest equipment, Hamish noticed a nickel-plated sterilising bath and the large antiseptic spray pump.

"Look at this," he cried. "Lister's carbolic spray pump."

Rita joined him to examine the instrument.

"What is it?" asked Bellamy.

"It's for aseptic surgery.

Bellamy stared blankly.

"There are particles in the air, on the patient's skin, on the doctor's skin, everywhere, that cause putrification of a wound," said Hamish. "This contraption is filled with a mixture of carbolic acid and water which is sprayed continuously during the procedure. See this steam boiler, it keeps the spray going while the surgeon works. The carbolic spray purifies the air. The results in terms of reduced infection are amazing."

Hamish moved on to the modern cabinet stocked with the latest medical instruments.

"All steel," he said to Rita.

She grinned.

"Steel can be easily cleaned in the carbolic solution," she explained to Bellamy, "whereas wood can't."

Bellamy nodded tentatively. "The wonders of modern science," he said, unable to disguise the sarcasm in his voice.

"I know!" cried Hamish. Then he saw something more impressive.

"My Lord," he said. "It's a portable oxygen device."

He walked around the apparatus as though it had divine powers. The apparatus consisted of a polished mahogany box, divided into two compartments, one containing a copper bottle of compressed gas, the other fitted with a dilatable India rubber bag. When in use, the gas passed by a tube on opening a stopcock to the bag. Another tube which also opened into the bag allowed the admission of common air to dilute the gas. The air could be propelled into the bag by squeezing a handball. A third tube leading from the bag would deliver the gas to the patient. The apparatus had a wide tube terminating in a glass face-piece to cover the mouth and nostrils.

"I've read about the use of this system for oxygen therapy," said Hamish in awed tones. "But I've never seen one."

Rita ran gentle fingers along the mahogany case. "This will revolutionise the treatment of respiratory ailments," she said.

Bellamy gestured to the matron to move them on out of the surgery as quickly as possible before Hamish found any other strange apparatus to distract him.

To the rear of the building, they were ushered through a modern kitchen with a large cooking range and a modern water tank that looked like it might require an engineer to run.

Hamish thought how much his cook, Wallace, would like to see this kitchen. He had befriended Wallace during his first murder investigation at Dunwich on Stradbroke Island, three years earlier. Wallace had been a ship's cook all his life until he settled into work at the Dunwich asylum kitchen. Hamish convinced him to come to Wickham Terrace to work for him by purchasing a modern gas range. The old cook couldn't resist the opportunity to live a life of relative luxury after years of hardship. Hamish had come to depend on Wallace for much more than his cooking and began to wonder if he could justify bringing Wallace and his little terrier, Red to Maryborough. He thought if he was expected to stay more than a week, he would craft an excuse, the real reason being he missed having them around.

Behind the kitchen was another building that served as a washroom and laundry with two massive boilers set in concrete. It looked far more efficient than the laundry at the asylum had been.

Finally, they emerged from the main service buildings into the grounds where the matron pointed to a square brick structure that stood separate to the hospital building.

"That is the morgue," she said. "I've had the caretaker prepare it for you. You'll find Mrs Gowan waiting. I'll let you get on with it."

She turned on her leather heels and left them.

After the presence of the other buildings, the morgue seemed unremarkable but when they entered it, Hamish was delighted to find it light and airy. Mrs Gowan was laid out on a gleaming marble examination table. She was covered by a cotton sheet. Hamish had conducted examinations under worse conditions.

He and Rita went immediately to the corpse. He took in the full view of the body pressed up against the sheet. Ruth Gowan had been a large woman, but she was well accommodated on the extensive table. They stared at the red and blistered skin on her exposed face and fell instantly into a world of their own, one in which they operated with a synchronicity that required few words. They knew each other's thoughts and anticipated each other's movements.

"I'll let you get on," said Bellamy, always eager to remove himself from the presence of death, although neither of them heard him. "I'll find somewhere in the shade to write up my notes and wait."

Hamish and Rita both winced at the raw skin stretched across Ruth Gowan's face.

"What's that smell?" asked Hamish, leaning into the body.

"Acid," said Rita. Those are acid burns. I'd say hydro-fluoride."

Rita took out her notebook and pencil and looked around for gloves. A pair of new thickly padded cotton gloves lay on the workbench along the wall.

"You had better wear these," she said, handing them to Hamish.

Rita prepared to take notes while Hamish put on the gloves and ran his eyes across the body.

"Autopsy after one day," said Hamish in a slow and considered tone. "No sign of decomposition. Body has blisters over face, neck, and anterior chest."

Rita wrote.

Hamish leant over Ruth's head and examined her face closely, then he picked up each hand and checked first the front, then back.

"Burns to the back of the hands, as though raising them to protect her face," he said. "Can you help me tip her on her side?" he asked Rita.

She folded a towel to place over her hands.

"Large area of irregular peeling of the skin on the head, neck, chest, upper back, periumbilical region, lower back, right upper arm, left elbow, right and left hands."

Rita scratched it all down in her notebook.

"Could it have been an accident?"

Hamish shook his head.

"See how the blisters are spread. She's been splashed with acid. It looks purposeful to me. If she had fallen into the acid, or even poured it on herself, the coverage would be different. How would she get acid on her own lower back, for example?"

"True," said Rita.

Hamish poised a scalpel at a central point in the woman's chest and made his first incision. He followed a line down the centre of her upper body.

Hamish took a small saw and parted the ribs. He cut the heart away from the aorta and pulmonary vessels.

"The burns haven't affected the full thickness of the chest," he said. "There is no direct burn to the heart."

He held the organ up for Rita to see.

"There is hypertrophy."

Rita nodded.

"Can you unpack the microscope and set it up?" Hamish asked.

Rita unpacked the equipment Hamish's mother had gifted him when he graduated medical school and prepared a slide from a skin sample.

Hamish peered into the eyepiece.

"There's peeling of the epidermis," he said, his eyes squinting.

"Coagulative necrosis of both the epidermis and subcutaneous tissues, and the normal arrangement of elastic fibres has been disturbed."

"All consistent with hydro fluoride burns," said Rita, who had returned to her notebook.

Hamish took a sample from the heart and examined it.

"There is myofiber breakup. A checked pattern."

He stood up straight.

"Conclusion: acid toxicity with direct toxic effects on myocardial damage. Could have taken anything from twenty minutes to three hours to take effect."

"What does that mean?" came a voice from behind him. Hamish hadn't realised Bellamy had entered the room. He turned around to answer him.

"Heart attack as the result of being splashed with hydro fluoride acid," he said.

"And you can't narrow down the time of death?"

"Not really. It happened in the early hours of the morning, but as I said, the actual incident and death may have been anything up to three hours apart."

Hamish went to the washbasin to wash his hands.

Rita slipped her notebook into her pocket and walked over to Bellamy.

"What's next?" asked Hamish when he joined them.

"We have two murders and no certainty they are connected," Bellamy responded.

"What do they have in common?" Rita asked the sergeant.

He tapped his chin with his middle finger. "Ruth Gowan and Nelly Brown were close friends."

"Then we begin with Nelly Brown," said Hamish.

Chapter Six

"Back in the revolutionary days [American Revolution 1775-1783] there was a girl munitions worker who became popularly known as "Betsy the Blacksmith." For she did not merely assemble parts of standardised equipment. She actually stood at the forge, and so skilled was she that her expert knowledge on several occasions saved for the colonists many munitions that would otherwise have been discarded.

Betsy Hager was an orphan who was taken into care by a farmer who was also skilled in the forging of metal articles. He secretly worked in the smithy refitting and repairing old matchlocks and muskets. Betsy was his 'right hand man'. She helped him in grinding, filing, polishing and assembling, and she put together pieces as fast as he could turn them out. Together they repaired hundreds of firing pieces, and it was not long before Betsy became an adept blacksmith and knew every part of any gun and musket." **The Evening News Pennsylvania Tuesday September 24, 1918.**

Hamish

They travelled back toward town, each in their own thoughts. Hamish's mind was racing. Acid had been thrown at Ruth Gowan, but by whom? Where did the killer get the acid? Did they bring it with them to use as a murder weapon? It seems an unlikely weapon. It seems more like something that might be to hand, in the heat of an argument.

He shivered at the memory of her peeling, blistering skin knowing that the woman would have been in a great deal of pain in the minutes, or hours it took for death to bring relief. He wondered if she had struggled or crawled to the spot where she was found trying to get help. Had there been no evidence of the acid being thrown in the vicinity of her body? She must have been attacked somewhere else.

"We need to see the crime scene," said Hamish out loud.

Rita and Bellamy blinked simultaneously, both jolted out of their thoughts.

"We don't know exactly where she was killed," said Bellamy. "I can show you where we found her. But there is nothing to see. Williams and the men conducted a thorough search."

"She can't have come far in that state," said Hamish. "We need to go to the inn and search again."

Bellamy gave an order for the driver to stop at the White Swan Inn.

When the driver pulled the horses to a stop in front of the building, they climbed out and Bellamy led them along the frontage to the right-hand corner where the brickwork turned down the lane.

"This is where we found her," he said.

Hamish and Rita glanced around. They were on the main street with the lane behind them. Bellamy was right. There was nothing to see. They headed down the lane, keeping the wall of the inn a foot or so to their left. They scanned the ground and the rough brick wall for about fifty meters but saw no sign of acid or confrontation. At the end of the lane, they came to a weatherboard storage shed behind the inn, with the stables to the right. They decided to investigate the shed first. A heavy sliding wooden door bolted with an iron rod secured the building. Hamish tugged at the rod and found with some effort he could shift it from the casing holding the doors shut. He pulled back the door and waited for his eyes to adjust to the darkness inside.

He saw chairs stacked clumsily in one corner, and an old buggy leaning on one wheel at the back. The missing wheel lay on the dirt floor. At the opposite corner he made out a stack of hay bales, the uppermost of which balanced precariously off centre, looking as though it might fall at any minute. There was an old harness on top of that and a riding crop leant against the hay. Hamish breathed in the smell of hay and dust. He also registered a scent of horses even though there were no animals present at the time. He crinkled his nose and was about to sneeze when he detected a caustic odour, out of place in the dusty shed. He stepped closer to the haystack and noticed the bottom bale had been disturbed. It had been shifted about eight inches, sufficient to cause the upset of the bale at the top.

There was a straw broom resting against the wall behind the haystack, so Hamish took it up and began pushing the loose hay back into alignment. A cloud of hay and dust surrounded him, and the caustic odour became overwhelming. The movement of loose hay revealed a glass jar, the lid of which was missing.

Hamish called out to Rita. "Do you have gloves on you?"

"They're in my bag in the cab," she said, peering over Hamish's shoulder. "Don't touch it," she cried.

"I think we've found the acid," said Hamish.

Bellamy joined them. "What would it be doing here?" he asked staring down at the glass jar.

"People use it for cleaning old boilers, sometimes soaking carriage parts," said Rita.

"The glass will be lined with wax. I'll be back in a moment. For Lord's sake Hamish, don't touch that bottle."

"This is the murder site," said Hamish. "The killer threw the acid at Ruth Gowan here."

"Why didn't Williams see this?" said Bellamy staring hard at Hamish. "I told him to investigate the area thoroughly."

Hamish sighed. "It's probably for the best that he didn't," he said. "He and the other constables would have stomped all over the area and destroyed the site, if they had found it."

He added, "And they'd have burned their skin handling the container."

Hamish and Bellamy looked around the shed.

"Why would Ruth be out here in the middle of the night?" said Bellamy.

"I don't know," said Hamish. "Does this shed belong to the inn?"

"Yes. It does."

Hamish shrugged his shoulders in resignation. "To be fair, Williams wouldn't have known what he was looking for when he searched here."

While they waited for Rita to return, they searched the shed for any items the killer might have left behind, but they found nothing more.

When Rita hurried back into the shed, she pulled on the double thick cotton gloves and carefully picked up the bottle. She motioned for Hamish to pass her an old hessian flour sack and wrapped the bottle in it. She handed it to Bellamy. "Evidence."

He looked at her nervously but took the parcel with the offending container safely inside. They returned to the cab, where Hamish took charge of the acid bottle while Bellamy went into the inn to request a padlock and key from the inn manager, Arthur Kane. Hamish and Rita watched from the cab as Bellamy locked the shed securely, checking the integrity of the lock twice. He then joined them in the cab.

"We need to visit the blacksmith's widow next," said Hamish. "Since her husband's body is no longer accessible for examination," he added.

***

When they arrived at Nelly Brown's residence, a small worker's cottage, they knew without entering that there would be a hall running from the front door to the back of the house with two rooms off each side of the hall. These cottages were all constructed to the same plan. They didn't need to knock because they could hear the tapping of Nelly's hammer in the workshop out the back. They made their way around the house to the Blacksmith's Shop.

Hamish saw Nelly for the first time in heavy overalls and a calico shirt, sleeves rolled up past the elbows, her blonde hair tied back in a brightly coloured scarf, although much of it was left hanging down each side of her face, a complementary frame to her beautifully shaped green eyes. Her skin was tanned to golden brown. She didn't look like any woman he had ever seen.

Most memorable, was the posture they caught her in as they entered, bent over the anvil, one arm held high in the air, wielding a heavy hammer. She looked back over her shoulder when she heard them enter.

"Sorry to disturb you, Mrs Brown," Bellamy said.

She let the arm holding the hammer drop to her side. The muscles in her forearms glistened with sweat and charcoal providing definition to every muscle.

Hamish felt himself strangely attracted to this woman, dressed like a man, posturing as a man, but at the same time inescapably feminine.

Rita shot him a glance and groaned.

Hamish ignored her.

"This is Doctor Hamish Hart and Doctor Rita Cartwright," said Bellamy.

Nelly gestured to a bench in the waiting area where she herself sat down on a sawn-off stump used for pounding metal.

Hamish's eyes shifted to the massive brick forge and the chimney that went right through the roof. Built off one side of the chimney was a box like structure into which was set the hearth. Air was pumped into the hearth from a giant leather bellows about eight feet long and four feet wide. Near the corner of the forge was a heavy wooden crane with a travelling carriage and a pulley for lifting heavy pieces of iron in and out of the fire.

"Doctors Hart and Cartwright came up from Brisbane to examine Ruth Gowan's body for us," said Bellamy. "We would like to ask some questions, if we may."

"About Ruth?" she asked.

"About both murders, in fact."

Nelly tried unsuccessfully to retie her scarf and capture her hair. More hair fell over her shoulders. She wiped her face with the back of her hand smearing the charcoal that was already there further across her cheeks. Tiny beads of sweat glistened on her fair eyebrows.

"I'm a mess," she said. "But this is how I look when I'm working."

Hamish thought she looked delightful.

"What do you want to know?"

Bellamy opened his mouth to speak but Hamish cut in.

"I see you are a blacksmith yourself?"

"Yes. I worked with Isaac for seven years before we could afford to take on an apprentice. Jakob has been with us for nearly two years. But I haven't seen him since my husband passed."

"Was Jakob working on the day of the murder?" asked Bellamy.

"No. My husband gave him the day off. He said he had a family commitment. But I doubt that was true. Isaac doubted it too, the lad doesn't have any family living, but he gave him the time off anyway. Isaac thought him a good worker and there wasn't much on. I often helped when Jakob was not in the shop, but Isaac said he didn't need me that day."

"How was your husband's relationship with the apprentice?"

"Jakob adored my husband," said Nelly, "and Isaac thought him worth the effort he put into training him. I found him lazy, but young people are now, aren't they? They haven't had to work as hard for survival as our generation."

"I don't know about that," laughed Hamish. "Have you seen the youths playing Australian Football. That's a fight for survival if I've ever seen one."

Bellamy glared at him.

"Do you know where we can find the apprentice?" he asked.

"I can tell you where he lives," said Nelly. "I know nothing of his movements beyond these walls, but he rents at Mr Bennett's. In the building out the back. It used to be a stable, I think. Opposite the sawmill, down near the wharf. The house is green."

"Thank-you," said Bellamy, writing the information down.

When he had finished, he looked again at Nelly Brown.

"About Ruth Gowan," he began.

Nelly waited for a question.

"Tell us what you know about her."

"I was devastated to hear about her death," she said quietly. "We were close friends. She was my only friend, really. She took over the inn when her husband passed, and it wasn't easy for her. But I relied on her support. I don't know how I will manage now."

Rita stood close to Nelly. "I have respect and admiration for you both, as women struggling to run businesses," she said.

Nelly's face allowed her a small smile.

"It's hard," she sighed.

"Yes," said Rita. "Yes, it is."

Hamish coughed.

"Is there anyone who had a grudge against Ruth?" he asked.

Nelly shook her head slowly. "I can't think of anyone," she said. Then something seemed to occur to her. "Was she robbed?"

"Why would you ask that?" said Bellamy.

"She was always wary of being robbed. She talked about it. She often had a lot of money at the inn overnight and she worried that someone would try to rob her. It was no secret that she held her takings there. She did the banking at ten every morning. That was another time she worried. She was anxious about someone robbing her in the street on her way to the bank."

"Where did she keep the money?" asked Rita.

"In a safe in her bedroom."

Hamish and Rita glanced at one another, and Bellamy stared up at the ceiling. Hamish assumed he had no prior knowledge of this safe.

"She sometimes asked Arthur to follow her to the bank, if there was a large taking to deposit. But she insisted on taking the money herself."

"Arthur Kane?" asked Bellamy.

"That's right. Her manager. He has been with the family for decades."

Bellamy went through his list of routine questions.

"Did anyone ever threaten to rob her? Or to harm her?"

"Not that I'm aware of."

"Did anything ever happen on the way to the bank?"

"No."

Nelly's eyes had become moist for the first time during the interview.

"Thank you," said Rita gently and shot a glance at Bellamy defying him to ask another question. "We'll talk again soon. Let's leave it at that for now."

Rita nodded to the door and Hamish and Bellamy began to follow her, but Bellamy turned back.

"People have mentioned a bruise on your face recently," he said. "Can you tell us about that?"

"I fell," she said flatly.

Bellamy watched her closely.

"Clumsy, that's all," she added and turned back to her anvil.

Bellamy joined Rita and Hamish outside. They were glad to be out of the dark.

"I have more questions," said Bellamy.

"Of course, you do," said Rita. "But they can wait. That woman is strong, but she's about to break down. She doesn't want anyone to see that. We have enough to get on with. Like why no one asked yesterday about the possibility of robbery?"

Sergeant Bellamy had the decency to blush.

"And we need to visit Jakob's accommodation. Talk to his landlord, Mr Bennett."

"Let's do that on the way back to the White Swan Inn," said Hamish.

Bellamy directed the driver to stop and collect Constable Williams on the way to Mr Bennett's house.

"I need you to interview the two housemaids when we get back to the inn," Bellamy said to Williams. "You know them. They will feel more comfortable with you."

"Clora and Edith?" asked Williams. "I have known them all my life."

"That's what I mean. I want you to find out what they know about Mrs Gowan. I want gossip. I want to know how she got on with everyone. What was she like to work for? What did the patrons and guests think of her? Did she have any friendships, other than with Mrs Brown. Did she have any relationships..."

"Relationships?" Constable Williams was shocked.

"You know what I mean," said Bellamy.

"We'll talk to Arthur. He should know something of her personal life. See what light he can shed."

"We need to find out whether a robbery occurred," said Hamish. "That places a different perspective on the whole reason we are here. If Mrs Gowan's death was a robbery, it might have nothing to do with Isaac Brown's murder."

"I have two murders in one town and the victims are well known to one another. They are connected," said Bellamy.

"Everyone in this town is well known to the others," said Hamish.

"We still need to investigate the possibility of robbery," added Rita.

"She was outside in her nightgown, for pity's sake," said Bellamy. "How was she robbed?"

"The thief might have come into her bedroom while she was sleeping to access the safe. She may have woken up and disturbed him and he ran. She chased him, there was a confrontation in the lane, and he threw the acid on her, then continued running," Hamish said.

"He ran into the shed to get the acid, and then came back, did he?" asked Bellamy.

"Why are we assuming the thief is male?" said Rita.

They all looked at her. Constable William's brow furrowed as though he were struggling to imagine any alternative.

"I would have thought a woman equally capable of throwing acid over someone," she said.

"Maybe so," said Bellamy. "Then when did she get the acid?"

They were all quiet for a moment.

"What if he ran into the shed to hide and she caught up with him. Then he saw the acid and threw it on the spur of the moment?"

Bellamy shook his head. "Theft is still not sitting right with me. Why would Ruth chase the villain into a dangerous situation?"

"What about blackmail?" asked Rita. "What if she went outside to pay someone money, secretly?"

"If she had the money, why would the blackmailer want to throw acid on her. In my experience blackmailers return time and again for more money."

"True," said Rita.

"But if she refused him, or her," Hamish looked pointedly at Rita, "he might respond in temper."

Chapter Seven

"Three villains were found in Maryborough on Saturday, and on Monday they were tried and remanded for further evidence. On the Saturday morning following, one of them was found to be missing. The leg irons were left, as was a large hole in the brick wall of his cell. Rather a creditable arrangement I can assure you we consider our new lockup to be. Search was made in all quarters, but he could not be found. To give you an instance of the earnestness with which the people entered into the search, I may mention that one of the water police walked about all day with a rifle in his hands and looking daggers at every human being.

Monday, Tuesday and Wednesday brought news of the runaway being in the neighbourhood, and on Thursday night he was caught in a house at the old township. On Monday night he robbed the pantry at Mr Aldridge's. On Tuesday he entered the White Swan Inn while in the house they were playing at cards and pilfered from a bedroom money and a coat. On Thursday night he came into town and bought sardines, bread and jam and took a bottle of soda water from right outside the courthouse. We may thank the wet weather or he would not have been caught again so soon." **The Courier Brisbane Tuesday 15 March 1864.**

Hamish

"Is this the house do you think?" said Bellamy. Hamish, Bellamy, Rita and Williams sat in the cab staring out at a small worker's cottage just taller than the overgrown grass surrounding it.

"It's green," offered Hamish.

They all looked to the constable for local knowledge. "I don't know for sure," he said. "I know Bennett, of course, but he keeps to himself. This must be it though – opposite the mill, and green, as you say."

"We don't need to all go in," said Bellamy. He turned to Hamish. "You come with me and talk to the landlord while I search the lad's room."

Hamish and Bellamy climbed out of the cab leaving Rita and Constable Williams to wait.

Bellamy knocked while Hamish peered through the dusty window beside the door. The house was small enough for him to see Mr Bennett come in through the back door and make his way to the front. He opened the door with a scowl.

Bellamy introduced them.

"We are looking for Jakob, the apprentice to Isaac Brown," he said. "We believe he is a tenant of yours."

Mr Bennett gestured for them to follow him around the outside of the house to a small shed at the back where he explained the boy had stayed for the last twelve months. He opened the door and Bellamy entered while Hamish stayed at the door with Mr Bennett.

"Have you any idea where we might find him?" he asked.

The old man shook his head. "Left without a word," he said. "He's taken his belongings, so I don't expect he'll be back." Hamish could see from the doorway that there was nothing in the room but an iron bed with a worn horsehair mattress and a woollen blanket. There was a small handmade wooden cross hanging on one wall and a newspaper print of a tall ship at the wharf in Maryborough. There were no cupboards or personal belongings.

Bellamy lifted the mattress and searched in the corners of the room, but it was clear there was nothing to find that would give them a clue as to the lad's whereabouts.

"Does the boy have any relatives he might have gone to?" asked Hamish.

The old man rubbed his beard. "Couldn't say. His father died six month' ago. I know that much. He said when he moved in that his mother lived in Sydney, but I hear she passed last year as well, a few months before the father."

"Reliable lad?" asked Hamish.

"Paid his rent, didn't drink as much as some."

"How'd he get along with Isaac Brown?" said Bellamy.

Mr Bennett took a grubby handkerchief from his pocket and blew into it. A trumpet blast filled the air.

Hamish took a step back instinctively.

"Apologies," he said, stuffing the crumpled square back in his pocket. "I didn't talk to the lad about his work, or his relationships. I couldn't tell you what his thoughts were. I imagine he was glad to have a job."

"Thank you," Bellamy said. He nodded to Hamish.

Hamish shook the old man's hand and smiled. "Thank you for your assistance," he said as they returned to the others in the cab.

"Anything?" asked Rita.

"Nothing," said Bellamy.

Bellamy gave the nod to the driver and the cab trundled on to the White Swan Inn.

***

When they arrived, Williams went off to find Clora and Edith, while Hamish, Bellamy and Rita went to the bar to find Arthur dragging a weighty keg from the storeroom. For a wiry man of at least sixty years, he was remarkably strong. Taught muscles flexed beneath his torn shirt sleeves.

"Let me assist you," said Hamish rushing forward.

"Don't bother, I'm right enough."

Hamish stepped back as Arthur swung the keg into place below the bar. His white hair stood outward from his ears, wispy like spun cotton, his blue eyes as pale and clear as glass.

He wiped his brow with the towel he had been using to wipe down the bar.

"We need to ask you some questions Mr Kane," said Bellamy "Is there somewhere we can sit for a moment?"

Arthur Kane gestured toward a wooden table and bench in the corner of the room.

"No one will bother us at this time of the day," he said.

They assembled on each side of the table.

"As you know, I'm Sergeant Bellamy and these are my colleagues, Doctor Hamish Hart and Doctor Rita Cartwright," he said. "The doctors carried out the autopsy on your employer."

Arthur scanned them with his pale eyes.

"How long have you worked for Mrs Gowan?" Bellamy asked.

"Not long, since her husband passed two year' ago. Before that I worked for Mr Gowan."

"And how long for Mr Gowan?"

"All me adult life. Started as a stableboy in the sixties. Maryborough was no more than a collection of huts back then. Further up the river, Mr Gowan's father, the senior, had a small business hiring out horses to the early miners. I looked after the horses for him. When he passed and Mr Gowan built this place, I came with him. That was before he married Ruth."

"What was Ruth Gowan like as an employer?"

"Ruth was a gem of a woman. I've never met a woman as worked so hard. She could do the work of ten men. And she was fair. She didn't throw anyone out who didn't deserve it."

"Did she throw anyone out recently?" asked Hamish.

Arthur ran his hands across his chin. White stubble shifted as he did so. "No. no. I don't reckon she did. Not recent, like."

"How did she get along with the other staff?" asked Bellamy.

"Everyone respected her. No one got away with shirking the work, but like I said she was fair. No one could say ought against her on that score."

"Did others make comments against her?" asked Rita.

Arthur tossed his ample nose toward the ceiling.

"Those girls upstairs complained a bit. Don't like to work, that's the trouble. Sometimes Ruth, Mrs Gowan that is, had to chastise 'em, get 'em moving, like. But it weren't never serious. Like I said, they respected her."

Bellamy changed tack.

"Mr Kane, we heard you often accompanied Ruth Gowan to the bank with the takings because she was afraid of being robbed..."

Arthur cut in, "Ruth Gowan weren't afraid of no one! That's for starters. I didn't accompany her, I followed behind. Just to make sure there weren't any trouble, like. There're some desperate men about these parts, with the gold petering out for independent prospectors."

"She must have been worried if she asked you to follow," said Hamish.

"She covered all contingencies, did Ruth. She were always a step ahead."

"Was she ever robbed?" asked Rita.

"Over my dead body," declared Arthur.

"What about the other night, the night of her death?" prompted Bellamy.

Arthur looked surprised. "Robbed?" he said. "She weren't robbed, she were bloody murdered."

"Yes, but was anything missing, from upstairs or anywhere in the place?" Bellamy pushed.

"Have you checked the safe since?"

Arthur stared.

"We are told there is a safe in her room?"

"There is, right enough," said Arthur. "But she weren't attacked in her room."

"Even so, have you checked the safe?"

It was clear from his expression that Arthur had not. They went upstairs together.

Arthur removed a shabby painting from the wall in Ruth's bedroom and slid it onto the bed, revealing a hole where a small iron safe was nestled. Arthur fiddled with the lock until it released and swung the door open. Neat piles of cash were stacked in bunches held together by paper bands, alongside several small nuggets of gold gathered in a paper bag.

"That's quite a lot of money," said Bellamy.

"I haven't been to the bank," said Arthur. "Normally Ruth would go every day but with everything going on, I didn't go yesterday, and I haven't been today."

"I suggest you get that money into the bank as soon as possible," said Bellamy.

Arthur nodded and gathered the money into a cotton bag also stored in the safe.

"We'll have Williams accompany you, if you like," said Bellamy. "Just to be sure."

Arthur nodded in silence.

"It's clear you assisted Mrs Gowan to run this place," said Hamish, "did you have much to do with the business side of things?"

"I did not. I did the slog. Ruth was the brains. I don't know what's to become of the place now she's gone. I don't know how I'll keep those lasses in line or manage the financial side of things."

"Won't the inn be sold now that Ruth is gone?" asked Rita.

Arthur looked surprised at the question.

"Ruth left the inn to me," he said. "I'll not be selling it."

Hamish, Bellamy and Rita exchanged glances.

"Did you not know? It were never a secret."

"We didn't know," said Bellamy.

Just then Constable Williams appeared in the doorway with Cora and Edith. The two young women bowed their heads lightly and scurried down the corridor.

"Can you accompany Mr Kane to the bank?" Bellamy directed the constable. "Then return to the station. We'll meet you there."

***

Thirty minutes later, they gathered at the small office in the police depot.

"Any problems?" asked Bellamy as the young constable walked in.

"None at all, Sir."

"Sit down and tell us what you learned from the housemaids."

Constable Williams sat. "Edith and Cora didn't have much to say. They said Mrs Gowan could be hard, she made them work, but they weren't afraid of her. They said she was fair."

"That's the word Arthur used," said Bellamy. "We are no closer to knowing why Ruth Gowan was killed," he went on.

"We know it wasn't a robbery," said Rita.

"There is still blackmail," suggested Hamish.

Bellamy blinked slowly. "Blackmail over what? We haven't found anything to suggest Ruth Gowan has any secrets worthy of blackmail."

"And what about Isaac?" asked Hamish. "We can't afford to lose sight of his murder in the light of Ruth's.

Bellamy chewed his pencil.

"Isaac Brown was a popular tradesman, loved his wife and was respected by his neighbours. Ruth Gowan was a strong widow running her own business, respected by her employees and her customers. What do we have to link them?"

"Nelly," said Rita.

"Do you think this has something to do with Nelly?" asked Hamish.

"No. But you asked what they have to connect them."

"I can't imagine Nelly Brown thumping her husband over the head and splashing acid over her best friend," said Hamish.

"Don't be indignant," said Rita. "Really Hamish, you're not becoming infatuated with Nelly Brown, are you? You do this every time..."

"I'm not infatuated, I just can't see it, that's all. And what do you mean every time?"

"There was Charlotte, then Celestine..." Rita had begun to run off a list of names of women Hamish had become smitten with during their investigations.

"Can we stick to the case at hand?" cut in Bellamy.

Hamish and Rita exchanged sidelong glances but dropped the subject.

"Is there a relationship between Nelly and Arthur?" asked Bellamy.

Rita almost choked on her tea. "Arthur Kane is old enough to be her grandfather!"

Hamish became protective. "Nelly is a fine young woman. I really don't think..."

Bellamy stopped chewing.

"There might be a relationship," he began waving the pencil in the air, "they each inherit a strong business. Maybe there is a relationship. Maybe Arthur is her grandfather."

"Isn't that a bit of a stretch," said Rita. "What makes you suggest that?"

Constable Williams spoke hesitantly.

"Sorry to interrupt," he began. "I have lived here all my life and so has Arthur Kane. Nelly immigrated from Germany only ten years ago and almost immediately took up with Isaac. They have been married for seven years. Arthur Kane never married and has no children. He worked for Mr Gowan senior, then Mr Gowan junior and then for Ruth."

He looked like he might add something then stopped himself.

"There might be something between Mrs Gowan and Mr Kane," said Bellamy. Since the death of Mr Gowan."

Again, Constable Williams looked as though he wanted to say something but stopped himself.

"What is it?" demanded Bellamy.

Williams stuttered. "I don't know. Idle tongues. People hear rumours and see things that don't mean anything, but make something of it in their minds..."

"About Ruth and Arthur Kane?" asked Bellamy.

Williams seemed frozen and incapable of speaking.

Bellamy assumed he didn't wish to gossip about the affair.

"Who would know for sure?" asked Bellamy.

The constable shook his head.

"Only Arthur Kane would know for sure. His affections are surely his own business."

"Then we must ask him," said Rita.

"No one is passing judgement," Bellamy said to the young constable. "But this is a murder enquiry. We need to know."

Williams blew air through his lips and dropped his shoulders.

Hamish caught himself wondering at why the lad would be so concerned about a discreet relationship between a widow and her manager. Was Maryborough a town particularly attuned to moral offences? Or was constable Williams a young man with a substantive dislike of gossip. He would need to get over that if he were going to become an effective detective.

Bellamy was already moving on.

"We need to interview others who knew Isaac as out next step. We'll begin with his clients. Nelly has given us a list to begin with. We'll start with those miners who owe him money. They may believe they no longer have to pay now that he is dead."

"Both Tom Barnes and Ed White are in town," said Constable Williams looking at the list.

"Were they in Maryborough the morning Isaac was killed?" asked Bellamy.

"I believe so. And according to Cora they were both drinking at the Swan Inn the evening before Mrs Gowan was found."

"Good work," said Bellamy. "Bring them in."

The constable's face glowed, not only because the sergeant had complimented him, but also out of relief that they had shifted from ruminations about Arthur Kane's romantic affections. "Together or separately?" Williams asked.

"Are they to be found together?"

"They share the same lodging."

"Bring them in together then. It will save time."

Chapter Eight

"Much of Maryborough's prosperity is no doubt due to the industry of those who earn their daily bread at the anvil, and throughout the town may be heard the cheerful clang of the hammer. Mr James Nicol has been plying his trade in Maryborough for the last sixteen years, and from small beginnings he has now established an extensive business in Kent Street, where he undertakes to carry out every kind of work pertaining to the blacksmithing, farriery, and coach building trade. There are seven hands consistently employed and in the blacksmith's shop, horses are constantly being shod and in addition all ironwork required for the manufacture of vehicles.

A large number of spring carts, drays and buggies are being turned out and they are entirely made on the premises. They reflect the greatest credit upon Mr Nicol and his employers for their neatness in finish, strength and durability. Just now a buggy is nearing completion which has been designed in quite an original manner. It is a double seated trap, but the back seat working on a privet, shuts up onto the front seat in such a manner as to entirely hide its existence and convey the idea it only has one seat. A convenient concern when you don't want to give anyone a lift.

Not content with a trade, Mr Nicol also practices as a veterinarian, with much success and is often in request as a skilful castrator of horses. Mr Nicol's enterprise finds another outlet in running a regular four-in-hand coach to Pialba every Sunday and back on Monday. Mr Nicol's Smith has that stability about it which will ensure its healthful progress." **Maryborough Chronicle Monday 16 May 1887**

Hamish

Tom Barnes and Ed White were ushered into the office by Constable Williams. He stood over them as though they were his greatest achievement. Hamish watched as Bellamy basked in the attention he was awarded by Williams.

"I'm Sergeant Bellamy, from Brisbane. This is Doctor Hamish Hart and Doctor Rita Cartwright. They performed the autopsy on Ruth Gowan."

The two men looked nervously from one to the other of the doctors.

"We are interviewing you in relation to the deaths of Isaac Brown and Ruth Gowan," Bellamy went on.

Tom shuffled his feet while Ed remained still and defiant. "There's nothing we'd know about that," said Tom.

"I believe you both owe money to Isaac Brown for products he manufactured and sold to you."

Tom looked to Ed for reassurance, but Ed's face could not be read.

"What of it?" said Tom.

"I heard there was an altercation over the money owed," went on Bellamy. "I understand Isaac was refusing to provide further service until the debt was settled."

Neither man spoke.

"That seemed to make you angry, according to those who observed the argument."

"He'd of got his money," said Tom. "We've been needin' a bit 'o' luck, is all. Bastard was too tight."

"What happens to the debt now?" asked Hamish.

Tom grinned.

"We don't owe it anymore, do we. That's it. He's dead."

He chuckled and looked at Ed, who remained steadfastly silent, but whose lips did turn upward slightly at the corners.

"Actually, you owe the money to the business, not to Mr Brown personally," said Rita.

"There ain't no business now though, is there," said Tom with satisfaction.

It was Rita's turn to smile.

"Mrs Brown intends to continue the blacksmith workshop herself," she said sweetly.

The grin fell from Tom's face.

"She can't. She's a woman. Whoever heard of a lady blacksmith? It's a contradiction it is."

"An assault on nature," added Ed, speaking for the first time.

Rita's eyes went dark, and Hamish braced himself.

"What about a lady doctor?" she asked. "Would that also confront your sensibilities Mr White?"

Ed looked confused for a moment and Tom shifted in his seat. "What's that got to do with the price of fish?" he asked.

Hamish leant across the desk and articulated his words clearly.

"Rita is a lady doctor," he said.

The two men grimaced. Ed's eyelids dropped and he raised his chin. A moment passed before either man spoke.

"We thought she was yer wife," said Tom at last.

Rita rolled her eyes.

"The fact remains, you still owe the debt. You now owe it to Mrs Brown."

"So, if that was your intent in murdering..." Bellamy didn't get to finish his sentence.

Tom was beginning to sweat.

"Wait on...we didn't murder no one. Who says we did?"

"Where were you early on Tuesday morning?" asked Bellamy.

"How early?"

Bellamy tapped his pencil on the desk.

"Before eight."

Tom turned to his partner.

"We was up at five, weren't we Ed? We had to get out to the pineapple farm. We had a bit of work on that day. We walked out there. Plenty would have seen us."

"What about overnight when Ruth Gowan was killed?"

"Home. In bed. Asleep by midnight," said Tom.

Bellamy waited before asking his next question while Hamish watched the men closely for a sign they might not be telling the truth.

When Bellamy finally spoke, he changed his tack.

"Do you know of anyone who would want to harm Mrs Gowan and Mr Brown?"

Tom's jaw dropped.

"Why? You think it was the same killer for both? What's them two got to do with one another?"

"Good question," said Hamish.

"Do you ever speak Mr White?" Bellamy dared the taller of the two to answer.

Ed's eyes moved slowly to meet the gaze of the detective.

"How did you get along with Ruth Gowan?" he asked.

Ed's eyes shone with defiance. "I had nothin' to do with the woman," he said. "Save drinkin' at her pub."

"We'll be checking your story about where you were at the time of each murder," said Bellamy.

"Do as you like," said Tom. Ed's expression remained defiant.

Bellamy let out a sigh and told the prospectors they could go, at which they shot from the room as though they'd been fired from a gun.

"There's nothing to tie them to Isaac Brown, other than the fact that they owed him money and there's no connection to Ruth Gowan that I can see," said Bellamy.

"I think we should find out more about them at least," said Hamish.

Bellamy agreed. "Williams, get out to the pineapple farm and ask around. Check that they were there Tuesday and ask what is known about them. Talk to the owner about Isaac as well while you're there. He is on our list as a client of the blacksmith."

"I'm going to talk to the neighbours about Nelly and Ruth," said Rita. "They might reveal more to me than to your men."

"Good Idea. Hamish and I will go to Walkers Engineering."

***

It was a pleasant day, so Hamish and Bellamy walked to the foundry. It was a short walk from the police station in Kent Street to the riverfront. The Foundry consisted of one enormous building that ran along the river, as well as several workshops in Bowen Street.

Upon entering they located the offices up a staircase and found the Senior Engineer, Percival Wellington. Hamish reached out to shake the engineer's hand and noticed it was soft. He also noted the delicate features of his face. He was a small man with fine bone structure. Hamish thought he looked agreeable at a superficial glance, but there was something that didn't ring true about him. There was an unpleasantness that seemed to lurk beneath the perfectly put together exterior.

Eager to show visitors the expansive works of the business Mr Wellington leapt into an account of the machinery and the creations in progress at the Foundry. Hamish looked around. The whirr and buzz of machinery filled his ears and there was nowhere a machine that was idle. As Hamish and Bellamy stared in amazement, the workshop was in full swing. Walker's Limited had the appearance of a busy, successful enterprise.

They began the tour with the shipyards which had lately produced five hopper gunboats for the Government, according to Mr Wellington.

"We have girder bridges and coal wagons underway down there," he said pointing to an area further along the river.

"A ferry punt for use on the Burnett River at Bundaberg has been on the slips for some time, but it was launched on Monday," he took them to see a large new punt floating gently on the water. "Sixty-five feet with a twenty-foot beam. The machinery is stowed away in the hull of the vessel and comprises a boiler driving a ten horse-power double cylinder engine to work the friction driving wheels, all of which were turned here at the foundry."

Hamish and Bellamy looked duly impressed.

"What are those for?" Hamish pointed to a pile of handsome logs of hardwood already trimmed and bolted together.

"They are to become the frame for winding gear, to be transported to Mt Morgan Mine," said Wellington.

They turned back toward the inner factory. "This work fulfills the contract with the Government for supply of fifty railway hopper coal wagons. They're putting the trucks together in the shipyard."

They moved further down the long shed. "Here they're working on the contract for the supply of steel girder railway bridges for the Cairns Railway," said Wellington. "We've already completed two bridges and shipped them north. These two should be completed in a short time. This Foundry shed is to be lengthened by about one hundred feet and fitted with travellers and cranes for lifting. And we're acquiring a hydraulic rivetter and cutting machines for the bridges."

Hamish pushed his fringe from his eyes. The amount of industry taking place was overwhelming. There were over one hundred men working on various types of machinery and the noise in some parts of the building was deafening. The smell of sweat and grease and steam from the boilers threatened to choke him. He needed air.

"Over at the workshops in Bowen Street we have various projects in progress," said Wellington. He kept talking without taking a breath.

"In the moulding shop we are casting enormous cylinders to support a new crane for Government Wharf. Already five of the cylinders have been cast and the sixth is being moulded as we speak. They'll be the largest cylinders in the colony. Would you care to go over to Bowen Street to see the works there?"

"Yes," said Hamish, eager to get out of the building they were currently in. He thought he would pass out if he didn't get some air immediately.

"No. Thank-you," said Bellamy, and Hamish's hopes sank.

"We need to get on," he said. "We have some questions for you."

"As you like," said Wellington but he was unable to shift his mind from the wonders of his machinery. "There are several boilers being turned out over there. A considerable number of cages, trucks, gold retorts, and other appliances being made. Gympie claims are having their needs attended in the way of winding engines..."

Bellamy cut in. "Is there somewhere quiet we can talk?"

Wellington went silent and nodded. "Yes. Yes, sorry."

He led them to a small office at the corner of the shed. There was a desk, but it was covered with plans and papers. He cleared two chairs, one for each of the visitors and perched himself on the front of the desk.

"We are here to talk about the killings of Isaac Brown and Ruth Gowan," began Bellamy, hoping he could steer the engineer away from his machines.

"I believe Walkers have a contract with Mr Brown for the tools required in the railway manufacturing side of the business."

"Yes, we do, I mean did," he said.

"The contract has been ceased?" said Hamish.

Wellington stared. "Well, I thought...I mean he's dead."

"Mrs Brown intends to continue the business," said Hamish.

Wellington frowned. "A woman?"

"I believe she has worked alongside her husband in the business for seven years," pointed out Hamish.

"Yes. Of course, but she could hardly meet our requirements...To be honest I was never in favour of the contract. We have our own blacksmiths here in-house. I have never seen why it was necessary to have Isaac Brown contracted, but one of the partners has a great deal of respect for his work and insisted on the quality of it, above our own tradesmen, for certain items. I will review this arrangement now."

"Is this your decision to make?" asked Bellamy.

Wellington puffed out his chest. "Since the untimely and unfortunate passing of our previous Lead Engineer, I have been elevated to the role," he said. "Yes. It is my decision to make.

Though it is an obvious transition. I would not expect any uncertainty."

"How did you get along with Isaac Brown?" asked Bellamy.

"I hardly knew the man. He carried out the work required of him as expected. He was paid well for his work."

"What about Mrs Brown?" asked Hamish.

"Mrs Brown? Why would I have knowledge of her?"

"She was active in the business," said Bellamy. "I would find it strange if you did not."

"I have met the woman," said Wellington. "She's German, I think."

Hamish blinked. Why was that detail relevant?

Bellamy changed the subject. "What about Mrs Gowan? What do you know of her?"

"I know of her," he said. "Just as you say. Some of the workers drink at the White Swan Inn – most prefer the Engineer's Arms across the road from here. But some have been thrown out by Mrs Gowan for brawling in her hotel. I don't drink myself."

"Would any of them harbour a grudge?" asked Bellamy.

Wellington chuckled. "Detective, if these men murdered women for objecting to their brawling there wouldn't be a female left in the Mary-Burnett region."

Chapter Nine

"The following are particulars of the case Edward Ford was alleged with having on Monday last, committed a rape on Elizabeth Currie at Stockyard Hill. The police took Mr Ford to the girl's place where he was identified by her as the boy who had assaulted her. He was arrested the same day about thirteen miles north of where the offence is said to have taken place.

Elizabeth deposed that she and her next younger sister were gathering mushrooms on Stockyard Hill when Ford came along. He suggested to her that better mushrooms could be got some distance off the road. She did not comply with his suggestion about going far from the road to look for mushrooms, but very soon he took her by the arm and throwing her, committed assault upon her. This she swore most positively giving all details, which were, of course, unfit for publication.

The actual carnal part of the assault lasted about five minutes. She screamed during the whole time and her sister ran away, also screaming and calling for help saying her sister was being killed. Meanwhile two men came along, and seeing them, he let her go and ran away. The prisoner had pulled her behind a bush to assault her. She did not go there herself, nor had ever before had any such connection with anyone else.

The girl's younger sister by two years corroborated her evidence as far as the assault was seen by her. She ran away screaming for help, and before returning, the other men had arrived, and the assailant had left. Neither of the sisters knew Ford, but they had seen him before. A labourer working near Stockyard Hill heard the younger sister calling out, "Oh my poor sister." Thinking she was in distress he and another man went to the top of the hill, from where they saw Ford rise off the other girl who was making a noise as if she was being strangled.

The man ran away, with his trousers half down. He ran down a gully and into the scrub. The witness pursued him for about 250 yards then lost sight of him. The girl could not speak for five minutes and looked as if she had been half strangled. The witnesses took the girl to her mother and explained what had happened. Mrs Currie said she was the girls' mother, and that the victim was thirteen years old. She at once reported the matter to the Police when she was told about it. She also took the assaulted girl to Doctor Stuart in the evening, and he examined her. She did not examine the girl herself but examined the clothing and found nothing wrong. The clothes were passed to the police.

Doctor Stuart stated that he examined the girl and found an actual rape had not been committed upon her; he examined her carefully and minutely and could affirm most positively that internal penetration had not taken place. Nor were there any sexual marks whatever on the girl's clothes. The girl must have mistaken external for internal contact. Ford pleaded not guilty." **Illawarra Mercury Tuesday 20 April 1886.**

Rita

Rita had intended to call on the women living adjacent to the blacksmith shop and ask them about Nelly Brown. She hoped to gain more insight into the friendship between Nelly and Ruth because this was, after all, the only connection they had between the two murders.

But as she was passing Nelly's house, she noticed the open door and Nelly sitting at her kitchen table, surrounded by open ledgers. It felt impolite to walk past without checking on her.

"Good morning," Rita called from the door.

Nelly looked up, golden hair framing a face pinched with worry.

"Good morning. Please come in."

Nelly rose, took another mug from the bench, and filled it from a kettle swinging on a tripod in the fireplace. Rita admired the gas range that took pride of place in the small kitchen, more an extension of the living area than a room.

"Why not use the range to boil the kettle?" asked Rita.

Nelly smiled at her modern range. "I only use it to bake," she said. "This oven is my pride and joy, Isaac bought it for me when we married." Her smile faded at the memory that her husband would no longer scoot around her as the tantalising smell of hot buns turning golden sent him mad with anticipation.

Rita accepted the mug offered to her and took a sip of the warm tea.

"Thank-you," she said, sitting with her hands cupped around the mug. "How are you feeling?"

Nelly's eyes grew soft, and her lips curved up into a small smile.

It seemed more out of gratitude for the kindness than any sensation of real happiness.

"You look worried," said Rita nodding toward the journals.

"I'm afraid the accounts don't look promising," said Nelly. "I've been over these ledgers several times. Isaac always managed the accounts, and I had no reason to doubt his ability to do so. There was always sufficient for expenses and our needs were modest. But I see now there are large sums of money owed to the business and I don't know how to retrieve it."

"Ed White and Tom Barnes?"

"You know them?"

"We interviewed them this morning," said Rita.

Nelly nodded. "Then you know I have little chance of retrieving the money owed. They are prospectors, nothing more. They've had little luck on their claim and live day to day doing odd jobs to keep food in their mouths and lodging over their heads. I would never have provided them with credit. But now it has been done..."

"Your husband confronted them about the debt recently, did he not?" asked Rita.

Nelly sighed. "He did. At the White Swan Inn. I know of it because Ruth told me. Isaac didn't mention it. He wouldn't have wanted to worry me. Or perhaps he was ashamed to have trusted them in the first place.

He told them he would supply them with no more until the debt was paid. But it mattered little because there are plenty of other blacksmiths in town. Their work is not a patch on Isaac's, but sufficient to the needs of those two."

"Surely they cannot have run up so much debt as to threaten the business?"

"It is not only them. Isaac was too kind. He let the agriculturalists run up credit as well. I fear no one will be in a hurry to pay now he's dead. They'll simply take their business elsewhere. I've heard many of them have already done so. Even the engineering company owes him money."

"What about your husband's apprentice? Has he spoken to you since Isaac's passing?"

Nelly looked up surprised. "Jakob? No. I haven't seen him. He would have heard about the death and moved on. He was close to Isaac. A strange boy. Insular. He rarely spoke to me unless I addressed him directly. I think he resented my presence in the workshop. My work is of a higher quality than his, and I'm faster at it. If we had to produce a lot of work in a hurry, or fine work, Isaac preferred to have me do it. He was always attentive to Jakob's learning. But Jakob wouldn't have wanted to learn from me. I suspect he's working with one of the other blacksmiths in town as we speak."

Rita waited a moment before asking her next question. "Tell me about your friendship with Ruth Gowan."

Moisture gathered in Nelly's eyes. She licked her dry lips.

"Ruth was my only friend," she said. "The women in this town have...alliances. They belong to the Temperance League or the Salvation Army. Or they are wives of the Oddfellows.

I've been something of an outsider since coming from Germany a decade ago. When my only relative, my brother decided to immigrate here with his wife, there would have been nothing left for me at home. So, I came with them."

"How did you come to settle in Maryborough?" asked Rita.

"We sailed directly to the Port here. This is where we first stepped onto Australian soil. We didn't think of travelling anywhere else."

Nelly's eyes grew moist.

"I soon met Isaac and have been happy here ever since."

She fiddled with the gold band on her ring finger.

"Isaac taught me to assist him in the workshop. We couldn't afford an apprentice at first. I proved myself to have an aptitude for the work."

Her face lit up at the thought of her work as a smithy.

"It excites me to see something so cold and hard as metal become malleable when fired, so that it can be moulded into any shape. There's something magical, spiritual about it."

Rita thought Nelly had lost her thread for a moment because she went silent.

"Anyway," she went on, "when Isaac put on an apprentice two years ago, I continued to assist him as often as I could. But my interest in the business set me apart from other women. That and my Lutheran background."

"Are there not others who follow the German faith?"

"Oh yes, quite a few. But not in this street. My brother mixes with them. But Isaac is not a churchgoing man, and to be honest I preferred to spend my time with him."

Nelly again, glanced down at her hands resting on the table and the ring, dulled by years in the blacksmith shop. She didn't remove it, even when in the workshop.

Rita appreciated the beauty of the strong hands that worked iron, the slightly swollen knuckles, the blackened tips of the nails. No amount of scrubbing would remove every tell-tale sign of the smithy. But they were hands that created, contributed. Nelly moved her hands to hide them underneath the table, self-conscious beneath Rita's gaze.

"I suppose I have no one to blame for my isolation but myself," she went on. "I loved our work, our life together, and I didn't seek the company of others."

She lifted her mug and swallowed the remainder of the contents.

"Except for Ruth. She was my rock. She socialised so much within her work she had few interests outside of it. But she was a strong woman and her and I got on well."

"Were there confidences between you, as is often the case between women?"

Nelly stared into her empty mug. "Would you like a fresh tea?" She picked up the cup from in front of Rita.

"Thank-you," she said.

Nelly sat back down when they both had another steaming hot brew before them.

"I did share a confidence with her," she said. "I was assaulted once. It was not long after Isaac and I were married."

Nelly's pale green eyes locked with Rita's. Wisps of blond hair fell from the bun at the back of her neck. She looked truly vulnerable for the first time since Rita had met her.

As she told her story, Nelly's eyes became absent, transported back to a time when she was younger and naïve.

Nelly - 1878

Sweat gathered in beads on Nelly's eyebrows and pricks of moisture collected along the top of her lip. A length of yellow hair, the colour of the gold men scrambled for in the mines, fell across her forehead and over one eye. Instinctively, she blew from the corner of her mouth, but the hair didn't move. Bands nor pins could be relied upon to contain her hair. Nothing about her was constrained. The man's shirt and overalls she wore when she was working barely touched her skin. Her body was free to move, to breathe, Muscles in her arms flexed and bulged, also moist, glistening with the buzz of life and effort. Life is energy, and life pulsed through every cell of Nelly Brown.

She was lost in the musical rhythm of the tapping as metal hit metal. Tap. Tap. Taptaptap. One arm swung the hammer effortlessly over her shoulder toward the roughhewn rafters above and drew down against the cherry red of the rod sizzling against the anvil. Again, and again. Nelly watched the metal flatten and spread, elements once cold and hard were made soft and malleable and reconstituted into something entirely new. She never tired of watching this process, taking part it in, orchestrating it.

She had married Isaac in November and now six months later she was as much in love with blacksmithing as she was with the man himself. She loved the heat of the fire on her skin, even in the summer months, which had been her first taste of the trade. She loved the glow of the metal and the smell of burnished iron. She even loved the black ash that covered her face and arms by the end of the day. She loved the way the muscles in her arms had grown and the strength she felt course through her veins with every swing of the hammer. She loved that she was helping Isaac build their business, their livelihood, and that Isaac loved her for it.

Intent on her work this day, Nelly didn't notice someone entering the workshop. At the sound of a man's voice, the hammer stopped mid-air, she turned and let the hammer fall to her side.

"It's risky, creeping up on someone who's wielding a hammer," she said.

Nelly recognised the intruder. The man was a prig. He stood before her in his gentleman's clothes, soft leather shoes, his hair waxed and waved. He was not unpleasant looking by some standards, but not by any criteria of interest to her. His hands were pale and soft. Not the hands of a working man like Isaac. He smiled in a way she supposed was meant to denote charm. Nelly was impervious.

"I'm here to see your husband," he said.

"I didn't think you were here to see me," said Nelly.

"Is Isaac here, then?"

"I'm afraid he is not."

The fellow stood there, with that artificial smile spreading his face and displaying teeth too straight to seem real. This was not a man who had ever worried where his next meal was coming from.

Nelly was aware of the young man who worked for Walkers Engineering. She had seen him in town when she was buying supplies and he had come to the workshop to speak with Isaac more than once. He'd always looked at her in a slightly discomforting way. Even when he was speaking with her husband, she could feel his eyes on her, his stare burning into her skin. It was an unfamiliar sensation for her then. But he had never spoken to her, and she had never been alone with him. She had not thought much about why, but she knew she would avoid him if she could.

Nelly turned back to her anvil. The interaction had reached its conclusion from her perspective. Questions asked and answered. She lifted the iron rod, cold now and needing the fire.

"When do you expect him?" said the intruder.

Nelly turned again to find he had taken a few steps closer. She frowned wondering why this man was still in her workshop.

The man relaxed his shoulders, and his tone became quieter.

"You know, I could help your husband enormously."

The words were thick like syrup.

Nelly's green eyes darkened.

"Let me introduce myself properly."

Her guard was up. She could see he wanted to place her at ease, but his manner was having the opposite effect.

"I'm afraid we have never been properly introduced. I'm Percival Wellington," he said holding out a pearly hand with flawless pink nails. "Engineer at Walkers."

Nelly balanced the iron rod carefully across the anvil. The last thing she wanted to do was to touch this man's skin, but it seemed churlish to refuse to shake his hand now that he had offered it. She removed her thick leather glove and took his hand in her own feeling his powdery dryness against her own moist skin.

"I know who you are, Mr Wellington," she said. "Exactly what is it you can do for my husband?"

"Oh, I don't think we need to go into detail." He straightened the collar of his jacket.

"Let us say that the Lead Engineer is older and has become unwell of late. If he should retire, as he surely must in the coming months, I will become Senior Engineer and take charge of procurement. That is, the contracting of external work will fall within my responsibilities. The railway extension project will be most lucrative."

The man had taken two more steps toward her while he was talking.

"What is that you want, Mr Wellington?" said Nelly.

"Are you expecting your husband to return soon?" he asked as he continued to move closer.

Nelly felt a prick of anxiety but controlled her breathing. This man was objectionable, but surely harmless. He was a professional man, after all, a representative of the largest business in the region, the most important foundry in Queensland. And the contract with Walkers was important to Isaac. It would do her no good to antagonise him unnecessarily. Still, her women's intuition continued to prick at her skin as he moved closer.

"You are an exceptionally beautiful woman Nelly Brown," he said.

She held her breath.

He placed his hands on her waist, and she jumped backward, but the anvil was in the way, and she tripped. Like lightening he was at her side and caught her before she fell into the ash. One arm held her around the shoulder and the other hand kept her head close to his own. Nelly was in shock, trying to understand what was happening when he pressed her face toward his, and his lips against hers. She tried to struggle but he manoeuvred her onto the soft sawdust on the workshop floor. At the same time his hands were moving quickly to unbutton her overalls.

When one side was free, his hand slid down the front of her shirt to cup her breast. She didn't wear the restrictive underwear of other women when she was working because it constrained her movement. She had never appreciated the safety such garments might provide.

Nelly struggled to push him away. He was not a large man; she should have been able to push him off her. But his strength was relentless. He was working fast. His hands were everywhere, and a raging fire was suddenly lit in her.

As she came to fully understand what was happening a determination rushed through her veins. She found the strength to unbalance the man on top of her, now alight with his own fire. She struggled until she had one hand free, and she pushed his chest with all the power she could muster. It was useless, his body was too close to hers and she had no leverage. Her head fell back against the sawdust, and she let out a gasp of exhaustion. She took in a breath to scream but he slapped one hand across her mouth and held it there, all the while still working at her with his fingers. Desperately looking for a means of escape she began to scan the floor. The iron tongs had fallen from the anvil when she tripped and lay just within arm's length. She reached out quickly and grabbed the handle, swept it up in a single movement and thrashed it down on her attacker's skull, careful to hold back so that she didn't kill him. He shrieked and jumped to his feet holding the back of his head with both hands.

He crouched with his head hung low for a few minutes bracing himself against the dizziness that was threatening to immobilise him. Nelly also got to her feet and grabbed her hammer. She held it in front of her, a clear message of what she intended if he approached her again. He glared at her with intense emotion, whether it was desire or hatred, Nelly couldn't tell. Then he turned and left the workshop.

Nelly straightened her clothing and secured her hair, ran into the house and locked the door. She sat down and hid her head in her arms on the kitchen table where she remained crying until there were no more tears. She was not a woman who cried often, but the shock of the attack and the physical energy involved in repelling it had completely disarmed her.

She knew the importance of the railway contract to her husband, and she knew that if she told him about the assault, he would want to kill the engineer. She also knew the man would deny it ever happened and no one, apart from Isaac would believe her. She made up her mind to never tell anyone.

Nelly brewed a fresh pot of tea and sat drinking it.

Rita

Rita's toes curled in her soft leather boots while she listened to Nelly tell her story. She'd heard too many stories of violence against women since she'd been working on these investigations with Hamish. Poor Emily Avery had been battered and abused until she was cast aside in an asylum by her husband. Another young woman, Kate had been sold into prostitution by her mother and frequently assaulted until she found her way out of her mother's influence, and Hilda, a young hard-working maid had been murdered to protect a man's secret. Rita thought about all the women that stayed in the house she maintained in Milton who had been abused by their husbands. She paid for a Governess to take care of the women and their children, to keep them safe until they were strong enough to find work and return to the world free of abuse. Many returned, time and again to their abusers, because they couldn't find the strength they needed after years of being told they were not enough. Rita wondered what it would take to stop the cycle.

She took Nelly's hand and squeezed. "Has he ever approached you again?" she asked gently.

Nelly swallowed.

"Not in the workshop," she said. "I haven't allowed myself to be alone in the workshop after that incident." She sighed. "Until now. Now that Isaac is gone and Jakob has left, I'm alone all the time."

Rita patted her hand. "You'll be ready next time," she said.

"That I will," said Nelly. "I keep a hammer and tongs close by the anvil and another set by the fire. Wherever I am in the workshop I know where the tools are, and they are never out of reach."

Rita grinned, then a thought came to her.

"Do you think Isaac found out about the incident, recently?" she asked.

Nelly's eyes widened. "I don't think so," she said. "Only Ruth knew. She wouldn't..."

Rita patted Nelly's hand, thanked her for the tea and left her to her journals.

Nelly – New Year's Eve 1887

Nelly sipped her champagne slowly. She had already had more to drink than was usual. She came to the celebration to support Isaac. The contract with Walkers Engineering was the mainstay of his business and he was thrilled when Mr Hawking, one of the two Directors, invited him and his wife to the annual New Year's Eve celebration. It wasn't that Isaac enjoyed parties, he didn't. It was the recognition that his business was an important part of Walkers industrial progress that lured him to the celebration. They had had a profitable year, with several new government contracts including barges and steamers, and the extension of the railway. Walkers' success translated to success for Isaac. And Nelly's primary purpose in life was to support the business. She didn't see herself as a dutiful wife so much as a partner in life and in the business.

Walkers had erected a grand marquee by the river and decorated it with garlands of flowers and streamers. Gas lights shone throughout bringing glittering brilliance to the women's frocks and the decorations. There was a lively dancefloor and men in tailored suits swirled women in sweeping gowns in time to the melodies of the band. Nelly looked on as they danced waltzes, polkas and reels.

As the clock neared twelve a chorus of voices counted down the seconds. Then at midnight a brilliant display of fireworks lit up the night sky. The partygoers rushed from the marquee to watch rockets soar creating cascades of coloured lights that were reflected in their eyes as they gazed upward. Jubilant toasts to the New Year rang out. Champagne glasses clinked and the fizzy elixir flowed.

Nelly looked around for Isaac, seeing him at last, still under the canvas roof chatting with a smithy who worked internally for Walkers.

She would have liked to join in the conversation, but she knew her input would have been unwelcome or worse offensive, to the men at the table. She watched the other wives gather in a cloud of pastel fabrics. They were happy to be together and Nelly envied them. She wished she was able to enjoy the company of other women, but she didn't know how to fit in.

She reached for another flute of champagne as the waitress passed with a fully laden silver tray. She had already enjoyed several glasses and was feeling no ill effects, so she felt no hesitation in taking another. But the first sip made her light-headed. She decided to leave the crowd for some air. Struggling to maintain her dignity, she pushed through the revellers, concentrating carefully on each step. As soon as she set foot in the open air, an overwhelming heaviness swept over her. Certain she was going to pass out, she leant back against a pole to steady herself and closed her eyes to stop her legs from folding beneath her.

Suddenly, there was warmth on her cheek. What was that? The world around her was swirling. She opened her eyes to see Percival Wellington's face close to her own. His hand was on her face. In shock and panic she pushed him hard against his chest and he stumbled backward. But the force made her fall as well. She slid down the pole grazing her face on an iron peg holding the ropes that tethered the marquee. She blacked out for a second and when she opened her eyes again, Isaac was helping her to her feet. Percival was nowhere to be seen.

"Hold on to me," said Isaac gently. "You've had too much to drink." He kissed her forehead.

"I'll get you home. We've done enough."

Nelly didn't recall the walk home, but she woke up in her bed late the next morning. Isaac came in from the workshop to bring her tea in bed. He was smiling.

Her face was sore, and she ran her fingers across her cheek feeling the roughness of her skin where it was grazed. She grimaced.

"You seem to have hit your face when you fell," Isaac said.

Nelly recalled the interaction with Percival and her brow furrowed.

"Was there anyone with me when you found me?" she asked.

Isaac shook his head.

"You were alone when I came out to check on you," he said. "Why?"

Nelly shook her head.

"It doesn't matter. "It's all so confusing," she said.

Isaac laughed.

"It's the alcohol," he said. "You've never had so much before. This is what happens. My wife the drunk," he laughed.

She punched him in the arm. "Stop it!" She laughed also.

Chapter Ten

"So many talents are wasted, so many enthusiasms turned to smoke, so many lives spilt for want of a little patience and endurance, for want of understanding and laying to heart that it is not the greatness or littleness of the duty, but the spirit with which one does it, that makes one's doing great or mean. Perhaps it may be of comfort to you in moments of fatigue and disgust to know how I came to this understanding.

I had gone with my husband to live on a little estate sixteen miles distant, on every side, from all the conveniences of life, shops and even post office. Further we were very poor, and worse, I was an only child brought up to expect great prospects. I was sublimely ignorant of every branch of useful knowledge, though a capital Latin scholar and a very fair mathematician. It behoved me, in these circumstances to learn to cook, no capable servant choosing to live in such an out of the way place, and my husband having bad digestion, which complicated my difficulties dreadfully. So, I sent for 'Cobbett's Cottage Economy' and fell to work at a loaf of bread. But knowing nothing of the process of fermentation or the heat of an oven, it came to pass that my loaf went into the oven at about the same time as I ought to have gone to bed.

One o'clock struck, then two, then three, and still I was waiting there in solitude, my whole body aching with weariness. That I, who had been so coddled at home, my comfort studied by everyone in the house, who had never been required to do anything but cultivate my mind, should have to pass all the hours of the night watching a loaf of bread – which might not turn out bread after all – maddened me. Then somehow the idea of Benvenuto Cellini sitting up all night watching his Perseus in the furnace came to my mind and suddenly I asked myself, what is the difference between a statue and a loaf of bread, so that each be the thing one's hand has found to do? The man's determined will, his energy, his patience, his resource, were the really admirable things. If Cellini had been a woman with a dyspeptic husband, sixteen miles from a baker, all the same qualities would have come out as fitly in a good loaf of bread." **Weekly Times Melbourne Saturday 5 May 1883.**

Rita

Once Rita left Nelly contemplating the debts owed to her business, she continued down the road to the house of her closest neighbour, Mrs Bentley. Constable Williams told her to be wary as Mrs Bentley was the biggest gossip on this side of town. But Rita thought that might serve to her advantage under the circumstances. She was searching for information, and it would be helpful if Mrs Bentley was inclined to provide it.

She knocked on the door and waited until it opened, at which point Rita found herself looking into blue eyes tucked into a face the shape of the moon. Mrs Bentley's hair was rolled loosely away from her face, creating a dazzling ginger halo.

The shock of tangerine hair clashed with a large amount of tan fabric, stretched extensively across her ample frame. The non-descript shade of brown sucked what little colour the poor woman may have had from her face. She didn't greet Rita but stood staring at her suspiciously.

"I'm Doctor Rita Cartwright. I'm assisting in the investigation into the murders of Isaac Brown and Ruth Gowan," said Rita beaming her widest and most friendly smile.

The woman's demeanour changed immediately. She greeted the visiting doctor enthusiastically.

"Come into the drawing room," she said, stepping aside. Rita followed her into a room to the left of the hallway which showcased sophistication and colonial charm.

Rita scanned the room making an instant assessment of atmosphere and hence the woman. A large, ornately carved mahogany table was adorned with delicate lace doilies and surrounded by upholstered chairs in rich fabrics that complemented the furniture. Intricate floral motifs adorned the wallpaper on all four walls of the room. Further complicating the pattern of the wallpaper were several framed landscapes and a richly patterned rug. At one end of the room a large fireplace was set off by a mantle decorated with a few carefully arranged porcelain figurines.

Large windows with lace curtains allowed light to flood the room on this summer morning. Three gas lamps with decorative glass shades would provide a warm ambience in the evenings. Two wooden plant stands stood watch in opposite corners of the room holding up porcelain planters painted in Chinese designs and holding two flourishing sword ferns that cascaded over the sides. It was a room pretending to be more important than it was, a small room, crowded with pattern, texture and objects d'art, in a moderately sized house. The contrast to Nelly's simple home next-door was marked.

"Tea?" asked Mrs Bentley.

"No, thank-you," said Rita, sitting in one of the upholstered chairs at the table.

"I wanted to ask some questions about Mrs Brown's friendship with Ruth Gowan, if I may."

"Of course," said Mrs Bentley eagerly. She squeezed herself into the chair opposite.

"Nelly and Ruth were great friends. Indeed, Ruth was the only woman Nelly was close to. Mrs Windemere and I have always tried to make Nelly feel welcome. But she isn't really…warm. I mean, she can be rather…cold. Well, we put it down to her being German, you know."

Rita did not know, but she tried not to flinch.

"I understand you and Mrs Windemere regularly make use of her cooking range?" said Rita.

"Oh, that? Well, yes, occasionally. We do take our dough round, but it's just an excuse to visit. Check up on her, you know."

Mrs Bentley smoothed her hair with one hand, pulling the orange fizz tight. As soon as she released her hand, the strands sprang back into individual coils, fighting one another for prominence.

Rita thought she did know. Nelly's neighbours were happy to take advantage of her oven, the latest in technology, while simultaneously looking down upon her and gossiping about her behind her back.

"Did Isaac know Ruth very well?" she asked.

Mrs Bentley's eye widened.

"I don't believe so, dear," she said. "Of course, they both grew up here in Maryborough, so they may have known one another when they were young. My husband and I only came here to settle about ten years ago. About the same time as Nelly and Isaac married. Isaac paid little attention to Ruth, to my knowledge. He was always working, that one. He kept Nelly working too. Improper, for a woman. I was saying to Mrs Windemere only the other day..."

"Indeed," Rita cut in. "Getting back to Ruth Gowan, do you know if she had any relationships with anyone other than Nelly?"

"What type of relationships?" asked Mrs Bentley suspiciously.

"Friendships," suggested Rita.

"Ruth Gowan kept herself to herself. That's why she and Nelly got on. Always about the work, those two."

Her eyes narrowed.

"There's always that deviate, the manager at the White Swan," she added in a half-whisper.

"Arthur Kane?" asked Rita.

Mrs Bentley nodded, and her chins wobbled.

"Why do you say deviate?"

Mrs Bentley sat back in her chair and folded her hands on the table. With her lips pursed, she said, "Not for a lady like me to say, dear."

Rita immediately concluded that she was referring to an affair between Ruth and Arthur Kane. But the idea still didn't quite sit right.

She changed the subject. "Is there anyone you know who had a grudge against Ruth Gowan?"

"Not specifically. But she did serve some unsavoury characters in that hotel. A woman who mixes with lowlife types, brings trouble on, I say."

Rita felt the hairs rising at the back of her neck. "But nothing specific?" she forced herself to ask.

Mrs Bentley shook her head.

It suddenly occurred to Rita that she wasn't going to access any more useful information from Mrs Bentley and that if she remained she would have to endure a considerable amount more sneering and judgement. Perhaps she was still irritable after hearing Nelly's story about Percival Wellington, but whatever the reason she couldn't abide another minute with this Mrs Bentley.

"Thank-you," said Rita. "I must get on." She stood and brushed down her skirt. She was experiencing a desperate need to get away from this woman and the suffocating little room.

Mrs Bentley pursed her lips again. "Very well, if you must," she said, standing. She brushed past Rita a little too weightily and opened the door for her.

Rita gave one last forced smile to which she received an icy response and left. As she came back out onto the street, she considered her plan to visit Mrs Windemere as well but couldn't face it. She thought there would be little the woman could add, and it wasn't worth the strain on her constitution.

Ruth – Three weeks earlier

Ruth tried to concentrate on her work, but Nelly's story rung in her ears. Percival Wellington represented the type of man she hated. It was his firm belief that his position in society, his education, and his money entitled him to anything he desired. Nelly showed him otherwise, but he was unlikely to accept her rejection permanently.

Ruth thought about the bruise on Nelly's face and wondered if that had been the result of another of his advances. Nelly and Isaac had been at the Walkers celebration on New Year's Eve and Percival would also have been there. Her blood boiled. She wiped the bar counter with such force she knocked down a counter display.

"What's the matter?" asked Kane rushing in to see what the noise was.

"Nothing," said Ruth throwing the cleaning rag onto the clean glasses and stalking from the bar. She felt Arthur's gaze on the back of her head as she left through the front door.

Ruth stormed down Kent Street with a driving determination to put a stop to the Percival Wellington's bullying. She found him at the Bowen Street foundry inspecting a new machine.

"I need a word," she said. Percival looked up at her and blinked.

"Certainly Mrs Gowan," he said. "Have some of my men been creating trouble at the inn?" He led her to a small makeshift office where they could talk. He took one seat and gestured for her to take the other.

Ruth remained standing.

"I want you to cease your attentions toward Nelly Brown," she said flatly.

Percival's face reddened. "I don't know what you mean," he said.

"You know exactly what I mean," Ruth went on. "If you don't cease, I will tell Mr Hawking about your true character. Nelly might not want to upset the applecart, but I certainly will. Mr Hawking is a gentleman. Do you think he will accept a rapist as a senior manager in his employment?"

"You don't know what you are talking about," said Percival. He turned away to dismiss her, but not before she noticed that his face had gone from red to ghostly pale.

"I will not be silenced," said Ruth and left the office with a determined stride.

Chapter Eleven

"'I dare you to dress up in girl's clothes and wear them to the masquerade ball tonight,' cried Caroline Boyd, the prettiest brunette in the city addressing a midshipman who had just come on shore from the Frigate Constellation in the harbour.

'A midshipman dares do anything that is not dishonourable,' replied the young officer, not yet out of his sixteenth year. 'If you lend me the garments, I'll wear them or perish in the attempt.'

'Oh mamma!' cried the lively girl. 'Will he not make-up just lovely? You and my maid shall dress him. He is just my height, has such small hands and feet, and his complexion is lily and rose combined. His long hair, almost like new gold, can be curled around his white neck. Oh, he'll be too sweet for utterance.'

As it was planned, so it was carried out.

That night on the great dance floor, there were no other girls to compare with the blonde and brunette under the watchful eye of the brunette's widowed mother. They were masked, but their figures exquisitely robed in snow white muslin, were as near perfection as a sculptor could wish for in a model. From the very first waltz they were surrounded by officers who aspired to the pleasure of a dance with them.

Captain Renshaw of the Constellation became literally infatuated with the blonde, the more so when he learned from her low tones that she was American and staying with friends. He sought to get her away from the crowd where he could pour out all the passion of his soul in words of love, and after repeated failures at last gained her consent to take some cake and wine in the refreshment arbours in the rear of the great ballroom. There, over a glass of champagne he declared that his love, though sudden, was as boundless as the sea which he made his home.

Sighing softly, the lovely blonde acknowledged that she loved sailors and could be happy with him on the ocean's wave. 'Love of my life, wear this in token of this happy hour,' he whispered, and he pressed on her first finger a large solitaire diamond ring, which he took from the little finger of his left hand.

She trembled with excitement, and he felt the conquest was sure. 'When will we meet again?' he asked, when his fair companion insisted on returning to the hall. 'Tomorrow – I cannot think where now, but you will surely hear from me.'

'I must be content with that promise, fair angel,' he said, and he pressed her hand tenderly. He went on board his ship at a late hour, exultant, almost too happy to sleep.

In the morning, rising late, he did not feel like breakfasting alone, so ordered his steward to invite his aid, the midshipman to join him. The young man came in looking pale and weary. He pleaded a headache said he had been up all night and asked to be excluded.

'No. A cup of strong coffee will do you good. I'll drop a little cordial in it,' said the captain. 'Sit down.'

The youngster could only obey. As he reached out his hand to receive the coffee, a ring sparkling on his finger caught the captain's eye. 'Where did you get that diamond?' thundered the officer.

'My lover gave it to me last night at the ball, as a token of his boundless passion,' said the midshipman with a blush.

'You, young devil!' he exclaimed. 'If you ever breathe a word of my folly I'll keel-haul you!'

'I would not, sir. To be honoured as I was last night is too great a joy to be shared.'

'You little rascal. You made up prettier than any girl in the room and danced as light as a fairy. Keep the ring as long as you keep your mouth shut.'

The midshipman kept the ring until he married, whereupon he gave it to his bride.

And this is a true story." **The Ballarat Star 16 October 1886**

Hamish

Hamish, Bellamy and Rita met back at the police station to compare notes.

"We didn't learn much from the visit to Walkers," Bellamy began. "The chief engineer Percival Wellington showed us around. It's a busy place and he seems proud of it. He's a bit of a prat but I don't see how he, or Walkers are connected to the murders."

"He's more than a prat," said Rita, her eyes wide.

"What do you mean?" asked Hamish.

"Nelly told me he tried to rape her. Very nearly succeeded. It was ten years ago, and she has never told anyone, except for Ruth Gowan. She confided in her recently."

"Good Lord!" cried Bellamy. "Ruth Gowan doesn't sound like the kind of woman who would stay silent about something like that."

"Nelly didn't tell Isaac for fear he would kill the man."

Hamish tilted his head to one side.

"Ruth might have told Isaac about it," he said slowly. "But there was no indication of a confrontation at the workshop. It looked more like the killer disturbed Isaac at his work. If Percival was there, for some unrelated reason and Isaac confronted him, a fight might result. But the scene would look different."

"What if Percival knew Ruth had told Isaac and decided to attack first. He kills Isaac and then Ruth to keep them both quiet," said Bellamy.

"What about Nelly? Surely, he'd need to silence her as well?"

Bellamy considered that.

"Maybe he thinks that since Nelly hasn't spoken out in all these years, she'll continue her silence."

Hamish thought about it.

"I just don't know," he said. "This fellow is all about his career. We know he wanted Isaac out of the contract with the Foundry. He certainly thinks he has that now."

"Perhaps he wants to see Nelly suffer," said Rita. "She told me there was real hatred in his eyes when she prevented his assault."

"How did she stop him?"

Rita blinked at Hamish slowly.

"She hit him on the back of his head with iron tongs."

"That would do it," said Hamish, touching his head instinctively.

"I'm not clear on the detail yet," said Bellamy. "But this is our best lead for a link between Isaac and Ruth. If they both knew Nelly's secret, they were both a threat to the engineer. I'm sure he wouldn't want the directors of the foundry to hear any such rumours of assault. And didn't Wellington tell us Isaac had a friendship with one of the directors?"

"Yes. He said one of the directors was insisting Isaac carry out the work for them. Should we confront Wellington about this?"

Bellamy looked thoughtful. "Not yet. Let's not play our hand."

Constable Williams joined them.

"Did you find out anything about the miners at the Pineapple Farm?" asked Bellamy.

"No," said Williams. "Only that they do work there from time to time, and they were working the day Isaac was killed."

Bellamy cursed.

"But they had some gossip about Jakob. They say he told them he was travelling to Gympie to look for work."

Bellamy's face lit up.

"That's the first lead we've had on the lad's movements," he said.

Hamish thought he wouldn't mind a train ride to Gympie, with Rita. He was about to say so aloud when Bellamy spoke.

"Who benefits financially from these two deaths?"

"Certainly not Nelly," said Rita.

"Are you sure?" asked Bellamy.

Rita stared back at him blankly.

"A lot of men buy insurance for their families these days," he said. "If Isaac was so fond of his wife as people are telling us, he may have purchased an insurance premium on his life, to be paid to her upon his death."

"If he did, I'm certain she doesn't know of it."

"What about Ruth Gowan?" said Hamish. "Who would have an insurance premium on her life?"

"She may have benefitted from her husband's death,' said Bellamy. "Even without an insurance policy she is likely to have been relatively wealthy at her death. Who inherits the Inn? That alone would be worth money."

"Arthur Kane says the Inn is his now," said Hamish. "But if inheritance or insurance are the motive then the two killings can't be linked."

"Maybe," said Bellamy. "Williams, contact all the insurance companies and find out if either party had a claim to insurance. And contact the solicitor, find out if Arthur Kane really has inherited the White Swan Inn and if there is anything else in the deal."

"How do I contact the insurance companies?"

Bellamy glared at the constable.

Hamish wondered if the shine was fading on the young officer's hero worship. He suspected the sergeant was missing Pennyweather, his constable in Brisbane. That lad was an expert problem solver. Whatever the sergeant asked of him he worked out a way to do it.

"There is a Mutual Life Insurance office in town, isn't there? Why don't you start there?" suggested Bellamy.

Williams scurried off while Bellamy, Rita and Hamish were left to ponder further possibilities.

"Perhaps I should have you insured," said Rita looking at Hamish.

He shrugged.

"Be my guest."

"You can't," said Bellamy. "You can only insure someone if you have a pecuniary interest in them."

"My life would be boring without him," said Rita.

"I said pecuniary," replied Bellamy.

"I'm sitting right here," said Hamish. "I'd rather you didn't discuss the pros and cons of my death in front of me."

"Fine. We'll continue the conversation when you're not around," said Rita.

Two hours later Williams returned to the office with buoyant self-satisfaction.

Rita had left Hamish and Bellamy to return to the inn. She was tired and needed time to process the information she had gathered from Nelly and her neighbour. Hamish was reading a medical journal and Bellamy was completing the monthly financial report, without sufficient data about what had gone on before his arrival in Maryborough. The figures he had been left with were sparse and didn't add up.

"I've visited every insurance office in Maryborough," said Williams. "There's no insurance policy in the name of Isaac Brown. But Ruth Gowan did receive a substantial settlement when her husband passed."

Bellamy put down the pencil he'd been using to enter numbers in the ledger. He used pencil so he could rub the numbers out and change them as need be. And he had to do so several times.

"It has not been twelve months since his passing, she is likely to have most of it in the bank when she was killed," said Bellamy.

"Correct. I visited her solicitor next. Arthur Kane inherits the White Swan Inn, and the lion's portion of the insurance money."

The three of them looked at one another.

"But why would Arthur want Isaac dead?" asked Hamish. "Are we now assuming the deaths are not linked?"

Bellamy looked thoughtful. "I still believe they are linked. What we need to do is find a link between Arthur and Nelly."

"I think we should speak with Arthur Kane again. Let's do it here, this time. Williams, bring him in here, will you?"

Constable Williams shuffled uncomfortably.

"What's the matter with you?"

"He'll not want to come at this time of the afternoon," said Williams. "The busiest period for the hotel will be kicking in. Without Ruth, they'll be short-staffed."

Bellamy was getting ready to bellow at the lad. He took a deep breath instead.

"Tell him we want to see him here, first thing in the morning."

Williams was half-way out the door when Bellamy called him back.

"On second thought, tell him we'll come to the inn," he said. "He might be more forthcoming in his own environment."

***

The next morning, Hamish, Rita and Bellamy entered the bar and dining area and made themselves comfortable in the cushioned booths lining the exposed brick wall on the left side of the building. Faded advertisements for Castlemaine

Brewery at Milton and a newspaper article about the soon to be completed Bundaberg Rum distillery adorned the wall. The counter was the focal point of the room, constructed from polished cedar with intricate carving, and featuring brass fittings to hold mugs and tankards. An array of bottles containing spirits, wines and liquors was multiplied in number through an ornate mirror that stretched the full length of the wall behind the bar. They saw Arthur Kane counting inventory. Apart from him, the bar and dining room were empty.

"Could we ask you to take a moment?" asked Bellamy when Kane greeted them.

"We need to ask you a few more questions about Ruth's murder."

Kane watched them closely before he sat.

"We are interested in who benefits from her death," Bellamy said. "Mrs Gowan's solicitor confirmed that you inherit the inn and hotel."

"I told you that, already," said Kane.

"How long have you known this?"

"Mrs Gowan told me not long after her husband died. She said she had no children and no connection to her brother in England. She said I had always stood by them and worked hard, and she intended to leave the business to me."

"How did that make you feel?"

Kane was surprised by the question.

"I was shocked to be honest. But I saw the sense in it. She was a woman alone, and without my help she couldn't have kept the business going. I suppose in her mind, she was making sure I looked after the business, since it might potentially be mine, some day. But it wasn't necessary. I would have looked after it anyway. I've spent my whole life working for that family. I wouldn't be looking to change now."

"Is the business going well?" asked Hamish.

Kane turned his attention to the doctor.

"Extremely well," he said. "Since gold was discovered at Gympie, this town has flourished. It's the port. It brings in supplies for the goldfields and all the financial business is carried out here. The whole region has come ahead in leaps and bounds."

"Were you aware that Mrs Gowan benefitted financially from the death of her husband?"

"What do you mean?" asked Kane.

"Mr Gowan had a large life insurance policy," said Hamish. "Mrs Gowan was the beneficiary."

"Life insurance?" said Kane. "I don't know anything about that sort of thing. It's wrong in my book, betting on a man's death."

"Quite," said Bellamy. "Still, there was one. And Mrs Gowan received a lot of money from it. Do you know how much she had in the bank when she died?"

"I do not," said Kane.

"A considerable amount. And now it's all yours."

Kane blinked several times quickly.

"The solicitor told me she left everything she had to me," he said quietly. "But he never mentioned a figure. He said a letter would come outlining the facts. I assumed the business was pretty much all she had. Maybe some operating funds."

"You are a wealthy man," said Bellamy.

Arthur Kane went pale. It seemed he'd lost the power of speech.

"Were you and Ruth becoming close, after the death of her husband?" asked Rita.

"What are you implying?" said Kane sitting forward in his seat.

"Did you think she might marry you?" persisted Rita.

"No!" cried Kane. "I'd known that woman for years. She was a girl when she married Mr Gowan! They were my family. There were no romantic notions."

Bellamy decided to shift to his real reason for the interview.

"What was your relationship with Isaac Brown?" he asked.

Kane took a moment to refocus his thoughts. "Isaac? None," he said.

Bellamy waited staring at him.

"I knew him. Course I did. He came into the inn sometimes, like any other man."

"What about Nelly?" asked Rita.

Kane didn't respond.

"Were you interested in Nelly? She is a beautiful woman," Rita went on.

Arthur Kane leant forward across the table and looked Rita in the eye. "What's wrong with you, girlie? You seeing romantic attachments everywhere you look? I wasn't interested in Nelly Brown. Granted she's easy to look at it, but she's a young woman. A young, married woman until recently. I had no desires on Mrs Brown."

As he spoke a woman swept into the bar with a flourish of her beaded purse gripped in one gloved hand, waving a small book wildly in the air above her head with the other.

"I declare I've not slept a wink since I laid eyes on this novel," she said. "Madame Bovary, a creature so morally corrupt she makes even my eyes water."

They all stopped to give her their full attention. She, in turn, stopped to stare back at them.

Hamish first noticed her dark eyes and impossibly long lashes. Second, his attention went to her cheekbones and chin, so finely defined they could have been cut from glass. She was striking. Not beautiful exactly. Something odd about her appearance rattled Hamish. Something was out of place. She was fine boned, yet her features were large.

"These people are detectives," said Kane, a slight tone of irritation in his voice.

The woman's face lit up when Kane spoke. Voluptuous lips curled upward exposing teeth the colour of milk. She swayed out from behind the bar toward them, wide hips accentuated by the smallest waist possible. Her breast appeared to be held tight in undergarments, though her neckline was low, there was no appearance of cleavage. It struck Hamish that there was something unnatural about her movements. Everything about her was larger than life.

She headed directly toward Hamish.

"Handsome," she said bowing her head and fluttering long eyelashes before him.

Hamish reddened. He noticed the over developed Adam's apple beneath her lace collar and realised his mistake immediately.

"Leave him be," said Arthur Kane, his eyes rolling back. "He's not available to the likes of you."

The woman, or man dressed as a woman, looked wounded. Liberally painted lips pouted. But her dark eyes remained fixed firmly on Hamish.

"If you say so," she breathed.

Hamish felt the blood rush to his neck and rise to his cheeks. He brushed his fringe back with one hand.

"Ziggy," said Arthur Kane, a note of resignation in his voice.

Rita thrust her small hand out. "Delighted to meet you," she said. "I'm Rita Cartwright."

Ziggy took Rita's hand in hers, and it disappeared in glossy white satin. A pearl bracelet shimmered on Ziggy's gloved wrist.

She then stretched her hand delicately toward Hamish, accompanying the gesture with a coy smile.

Hamish hesitated for a moment and Rita glared at him.

"Hamish Hart," he said hastily.

He held out his hand to the tall creature in the crinoline frock, and Ziggy shook it vigorously.

"This is Sergeant Bellamy," said Kane. "He's investigating Ruth's murder."

"Ooh!" breathed Ziggy as she sat in the remaining vacant chair at the table.

This was too much for Arthur Kane who placed his head in his hands.

"Ziggy," he said, looking up, "this is an official interview, not a gossip session. Go and set up the bar. Lord knows you are late in already."

Ziggy threw back her head and sniffed. She rose from the table, pecked Kane on the cheek then sashayed back toward the bar throwing a single backward glance toward Hamish as she went.

Hamish shuffled in his seat and Rita grinned at him.

"I apologise," Kane said. "She has no sense of restraint, I'm afraid. She worked in the theatre from when she was ten. A small boy with a pretty face, she played the feminine parts and continued dressing up even when the curtain came down. Most of the locals, who have known her all her life, accept her for who she is. Sometimes the miners coming and going give her a hard time."

"I like her," declared Rita.

Bellamy, who had avoided shaking hands with the strange woman, appeared sufficiently uncomfortable to take flight as quickly as possible.

"Don't apologise," he said. "We were finished anyway. Thank-you for your input."

He stood up and put his hands on the back of Rita's chair to pull it out for her. She rose, as did Hamish.

"So now we know why Arthur Kane is not romantically interested in Nelly," said Rita when they were out of earshot.

"Or Ruth Gowan," added Hamish.

Bellamy shook his head.

"I don't understand. Arthur Kane doesn't look the type."

"And what is the type?" asked Rita.

Bellamy faltered.

"The same type as Ziggy," he said.

"All homosexual men don't dress in women's clothes," said Rita.

"And all men who dress in women's clothes are not homosexual," said Hamish. "But I did get the impression that Arthur and Ziggy are intimate."

"They are a couple," said Rita emphatically. "It doesn't matter what you think about it," she said to Bellamy.

"It does, though," said Bellamy. "It matters particularly what I think about it. Because it is illegal for a man to dress as a woman.

I would never intrude on a person's right to do what they like in the privacy of their home, but public displays risk offending others. By rights I should be arresting her...him."

"Ziggy works publicly at the inn," said Rita. "If the town objected, Ziggy would have been arrested by now, don't you think?"

"It's common enough in the theatre," said Hamish. "I think Ziggy views the bar at the inn as the same category of place as a theatre."

"Getting back to the murder, what do we think of Arthur Kane as a suspect?" asked Rita.

"I'm not seeing him as a murderer," said Hamish.

"Nor me," agreed Rita. "He was genuinely surprised to hear you say he was a wealthy man,"

She looked at Bellamy.

"Could Ziggy have done it?" suggested Bellamy.

Both Rita and Hamish laughed.

Hamish noted the stony face on his friend and coughed back the laughter.

"I don't think so," he said. "But let's not discount either of them for now."

Rita said, "I can imagine Ziggy being mean if she were crossed, but she's not calculating. She wouldn't lure her victim into an alley in the middle of the night. She would throw the acid at her in a flare of temper in a crowded bar, with an audience."

"I need to think," said Bellamy. "Why don't you two head to Gympie on this afternoon's train, and I'll take the constable to Jakob's last place of residence. Maybe we'll find something to let us know where he is. I'll send a telegram if I do. I think it is important to find the apprentice as soon as possible. Apart from Nelly, he was the closest person to Isaac."

Hamish was delighted at the prospect of taking the train to Gympie. Judging by her grin, Rita was also enthusiastic.

"We have nothing to go on so far, apart from the suggestion he went to Gympie to find work," said Bellamy. "It may not be easy to find him."

"I don't know," said Hamish. "We'll try the blacksmith's first, obviously. Gympie is not as large as Maryborough. I'm sure a new lad will stand out."

"Perhaps not in a mining town," warned Bellamy. "Men of all ages come and go. But I wish you luck. Don't stay there too long. If there are no leads in twenty-four hours, the lad is probably not there."

Chapter Twelve

"The novel spectacle of a steam fire engine puffing and whistling, drawn through the streets by a score of stalwart firemen in uniform with lighted torches, was afforded the townspeople on Saturday night, and of course drew a large crowd. The procession was preceded by a band and on top of the engine were seated members of the Fire Brigade Board.

The engine, which is a beautiful piece of workmanship and cost over 500 pounds, arrived here on the barque La France from London, and being somewhat damaged by saltwater was taken to pieces in the Union Foundry and made right. From thence it was drawn to the Town Hall on Saturday night where a public exhibition was given of its powers.

Two horses were attached, and streams of water were thrown far over the Town Hall and other buildings in the vicinity. The mayor, having broken a small bottle of fizz on the machine, named it "The Progress" after which the Board and the Brigade adjourned into the Town Hall, where several toasts were drunk and congratulations made as to Maryborough possessing the only steam fire engine in the colony." **The Telegraph, Wednesday, 1 July 1885**.

Hamish

Hamish and Rita climbed aboard the rattling wooden carriage with the same enthusiastic anticipation with which they always met a new experience. Smoke belched out of the engine and their carriage lurched forward. At first, the sound of the wheels on the metal rails drowned out any attempt at conversation. Hamish remained content to stare through the window at the landscape sweeping by, a welcome sight after weeks at sea travelling to and from Melbourne with nothing to look at but endless Pacific Ocean. Still, after half an hour, the view of scraggly gums stretching as far as the eye could see seemed just as monotonous. Grey green leaves fell from papery trunks of white and beige, long grass filling the gaps between them, all set against a sky of relentless blue.

Hamish wondered how it was that when he watched for long enough, he had the impression of standing still. Nothing changed as the wheels rattled on.

Rita was the first to break the illusion.

"Tell me about your father," she said. "We haven't had a chance to talk about him."

Hamish brushed his fringe from his face. It felt like they had to shout to be heard over the noise of the train. Looking around the carriage, he noted the other passengers were either sleeping or reading.

"There's nothing to tell," he said. "My father has dementia, and my mother is determined to care for him at home. The steward picks him up in a buggy in the morning and takes him to the track then he brings him home in the afternoon. My father has spent his life at that track since moving to Melbourne and I expect he intends to continue in the same way until he dies."

Hamish sighed.

"As soon as they cashed in the gold from their time at Ballarat, father established his set price bookmaking business. All his shady deals are centred around the racetrack and that world. It's like his office."

Hamish glanced down at his hands. Doctor's hands. His expensive education had been paid for through his fathers' less than ethical, if not downright illegal, extracurricular business dealings. This was a cause of concern to Hamish.

"At least, it gives mother a few hours of peace," he said. "But goodness knows what he gets up to all day."

Rita smiled.

"He stopped a race recently," said Hamish chuckling. "He turned up on the track just as the gates were about to go up. It's lucky he wasn't killed. They had to drag him from the track."

Rita laughed. "Your father must be well liked, or they wouldn't have him there every day."

"He's probably gambling away the family fortune," said Hamish.

"What fortune? From what you've told me he did that years ago."

"That is true."

Hamish smiled.

They were silently enjoying the comfortable companionship when a loud scream of metal against metal startled them. They, and the rest of the passengers, were lurched forward in their seats. Rita's head banged against the wooden panelling in front of her. Hamish tucked his arm around her shoulders and pulled her toward him as the carriage screeched to a halt.

Loud exclamations of shock rose as passengers attempted to right themselves. Hamish made sure Rita was unharmed, then stuck his head out of the window. Looking toward the engine, he saw nothing but dust rising from the gravel at the sides of the rail.

"Why did we stop?" cried Rita.

Just as Hamish pulled his head back another train sped past. It was so close he felt the wind from it on his face. He turned toward Rita, whose eyes were wide.

"Obviously unexpected," she said.

When the train had passed, Hamish stretched his neck to look out again and this time he saw a guard walking beside the carriages toward him.

"What happened?"

The guard stopped and looked back the way he had come, toward the front of the train.

"A Special on the other track," he said. "We knew nothing about it. There's a curve up ahead and the tracks cross right after. It would have been dangerous to pass further on. We've no confidence in the men working the points currently. The experienced men are leaving in droves, and they're being replaced with inexperienced youths who don't know what they're doing. It's only a matter of time until something catastrophic happens."

The sound of a man yelling from the direction of the engine caught the guard's attention.

"Fire!"

The guard gazed toward the engine with a shocked expression then took off in a sprint to the front of the train.

"Did he say fire?" whispered Rita.

Hamish looked at the other passengers to see if anyone had heard. They seemed preoccupied recovering belongings and settling themselves.

He nodded.

"I'm going up front to see if there's anything I can do," he said. "Make sure everyone stays calm until we receive further instruction."

Hamish forced the side door ajar and jumped from the carriage landing on the hard dry ground with a thud.

Rita pulled the door shut, gripping the bottom of the window with gloved hands, she watched him stride quickly toward the engine.

When he came alongside the engineer's window, Hamish saw the fire burning in the cab. The Engineer was pouring water on it from a barrel, but the fire was spreading. Oil had spilled from the piston, and coal had scattered forward from the coal store in the sudden stop.

The fire was working its way toward the main store of coal.

Hamish heard horses approaching him from behind and turned to see two men with large hats and suntanned faces ride up.

"I live a half a mile from here," one of the men said. "We heard the train stop. Is there anything we can do?"

"There's a fire," cried the train's fireman, through the door. "Is there water around here?"

"There's a creek over the way," said the horseman. "A couple of hundred yards."

The fireman passed out four barrels to Hamish who passed them to the horseman.

"Ride into town," he called to his friend as he tied the barrels to his own saddle. One man galloped toward town while the other set off toward the creek.

While the fireman exhausted the water supply he had at hand, the fire continued to burn. Lumps of coal close to the main store were already alight. The Engineer was using a broom to gather the remaining coal and push it away from the flames. He looked up at Hamish with a face the colour of the coal.

"Can you help the guard get the passengers off the train," he said. "If this coal store catches alight the fire could spread to the carriages. If that happens, we won't be able to stop it. The wagons are all timber."

Hamish and the guard left him, climbed into the first carriage and instructed the passengers to leave the train. There was little resistance, although some of the women fussed about their belongings.

"Leave them," snapped the guard.

Hamish assisted a small boy from the train while his mother climbed down after them. Once out of the train the passengers were able to see the flames coming from the engine and word soon spread along the train. Hamish and the guard entered the second carriage as passengers were already climbing over one another to disembark. Rita, who was in the third carriage, had already begun to assist people onto the ground when Hamish reached her.

***

Within minutes one of the horsemen returned with barrels of water from the creek and some of the passengers formed a chain to get the water up into the engine and onto the fire.

It was hot dirty work and Hamish was now up inside the engine fighting the fire. He was black from head to toe.

Only twenty minutes after the fire had started, they heard the fire bell. A large steam fire engine was hurtling along the dirt road to the left of the railway line. A score of uniformed firemen sat on top of the fire engine. Within seconds they were shooting water from a hose across the fire. Within no time the flames receded.

The passengers gathered around the fire engine in awe of its power.

"It's fortunate we weren't far from town," said Hamish, his teeth white against his blackened face.

"It's fortunate we have in Maryborough the only steam fire engine in the colony," said the Engineer.

Hamish and Rita sat on the grass beside the train with the other passengers while the firemen and the railway employees assessed the damage.

Eventually, the guard told them that another train had been despatched from Maryborough and would continue their journey to Gympie. Night had fallen by this stage, and everyone was relieved to know they would not be sleeping in the abandoned carriages.

It was well after midnight when they reached Gympie.

***

Hamish and Rita climbed from the second train, exhausted and in need of a wash. They were surprised to find several buggies waiting in front of the station representing a half a dozen hotels in the area. Hamish found the one that coincided with the accommodation they had booked, and they climbed aboard. There was confusion and excitement among the buggies as overwhelmed passengers found their luggage and their transport.

Hamish breathed a sigh of relief as the horses moved forward. He was looking forward to a comfortable bed.

But they had barely left the station when the horses gathered speed. Hamish grabbed the door and held on while Rita caught hold of his arm.

"What on Earth?" she cried.

"Just hold tight," said Hamish, straining to see out the window while gripping the door.

The carriage lurched along Nash Street increasing the pace as it went. The other buggies did likewise. Hamish saw one buggy pull ahead of them, then it was passed by another.

At that moment their own driver cracked the reins and yelled to drive the horses forward. Hamish and Rita were thrown back against the upholstery.

"What's going on?" cried Rita. "Are we being chased?"

"I don't know," said Hamish trying to peer back the way they had come. "I can't see anything behind us."

Then it suddenly dawned on him it was a race. They lurched forward and regained the lead, but not without missing the carriage previously at the front of the group by a whisker. The wheels threw up dust and gravel as they careered dangerously close to another buggy to their left.

Hamish held Rita's hand tight. With the other hand he gripped the bottom of the window to steady himself. Rita did the same on her side. She glanced at him with eyes that conveyed more amusement than anxiety.

The drivers whooped and hollered, calling out to one another as they raced into town. When they reached Mary Street, they slowed down with a suddenness that jolted Hamish and Rita forward. They thrust their arms against the cab wall to avoid hitting their heads.

Each driver called out insults, each claiming to have bested his rivals. Hamish and Rita, who had been holding on for dear life, now released their grip on various parts of the carriage and each took a deep breath. Rita smoothed down her skirt then fixed her hair with pins that had worked their way loose during the jostling and scrambling.

"Are you alright?" asked Hamish.

Rita wiped her brow with a tiny white handkerchief.

"Perfectly," she said. "You?"

Hamish grinned. "We do enjoy an adventure," he said.

They both climbed down out of the cab and gathered their belongings. Rita had a single carpet bag and a shawl, Hamish his suitcase, his hat, and his coat.

They were rattled by the time they entered the hotel and glad to be shown their beds immediately.

But even when washed and laying on a reasonably comfortable mattress, Hamish still found it difficult to sleep. He wondered whether every arrival triggered a race into town. He wondered why the authorities didn't curb such dangerous activity on the road. Then his mind shifted to their task, and he wondered where he and Rita might begin their search for Jakob in the morning. He thought about the blistered body of Ruth Gowan and what the apprentice blacksmith could possibly know about that murder. And he wondered why the apprentice would kill his own boss putting himself out of work. Still, he knew they needed to speak with him. Jakob could know something that might explain the murder of his boss, at least. Hamish fell into a deep sleep at some point while his thoughts continued to race. It was a restless sleep punctuated by nightmares of carriages careering out of control at speed and a sensation of falling. Hamish had fallen into an old mine shaft as a child, where he waited, injured for twenty-four hours before being rescued. Every traumatic experience in his life resulted in dreams about falling.

***

The following morning at breakfast Hamish and Rita received a list of the six blacksmith businesses in town from the hotel owner. He knew of no young lad looking for work but wished them luck in their search. Hamish and Rita spent a hot, dusty day walking, and riding in cabs, from one blacksmith workshop to the next asking about Jakob. No one had heard of him.

Gympie was little more than a collection of ramshackle huts with a scattering of surprisingly elegant hotels. The population was clearly more itinerant than permanent. The streets lacked a sense of order, darting in one direction, then another, little more than dirt tracks. Everywhere was the reminder of its existence as a mining town that had grown up virtually overnight, from the hodgepodge of twisting streets to the rusted relics of abandoned machinery.

There were permanent houses on the hill overlooking the town, as well as the beginnings of what might become more sustainable industry. But at this point, Hamish could see the fortunes of Gympie going either way.

It wasn't officially a town, yet. Once the gold ran out, the place might diversify and manage to sustain itself with pastoralists and agriculturalists, or it might dissipate altogether.

Hamish and Rita were glad to see the gold rush settlement as they had heard so much about it, but as they trudged from blacksmith to blacksmith without any new information about Jakob they tired of the heat and the dust. By late afternoon, they were exhausted. The adventure of the journey south, coupled with the wasted day left them disillusioned. They stopped at their hotel to wash up and enjoy a drink prior to the journey back to Maryborough.

"You look much better," said Rita as Hamish joined her in the hotel garden, his face freshly washed and shaved.

He smiled.

"I don't feel much better. We have two hours to kill before the train back and we have nothing."

"Don't be disappointed," said Rita. "I think we can be pretty sure Jakob is not in Gympie. If he were looking for that type of work, someone from one of the workshops would have heard about him."

"Perhaps he is out on the mines," suggested Hamish.

"If that's the case, we wouldn't find him until he returned to town," said Rita. "It would take days to ride to each of the mines scattered across this region."

They were enjoying a thick cold brew when a grizzled man joined them. He had a nasty scar that interrupted the right side of his face, removing a portion of his cheek and culminating at his jaw.

"Mind if I take a load off?" he asked as he sat.

Rita smiled, "Be our guest."

The man took a long drink from his glass. It looked like whiskey.

"Are you the folk been asking around about young Jakob?" The man had a raspy voice that reminded Hamish of footsteps on gravel.

Hamish and Rita sat up straight. At last, some news.

"Yes", said Hamish. "Do you know where he is?"

"Nope," said the man, a liberal amount of whiskey dribbling from the corner of his withered lips. His long grey hair fell over his shoulders. Hamish wondered if the damage to his face effected his ability to swallow effectively.

He shot a glance at Rita, but she was watching the man intently.

"But I knew his father," he said. Small eyes of indeterminant colour looked out from beneath wrinkled eyelids.

Hamish waited.

"We were friends, Elijah and I, before his passing."

"We heard that Jakob's father was dead," said Hamish.

"He is. Died some six month' ago. Weren't that old either. Not like me."

Hamish's mind was racing to decide whether information about the apprentice's father's death might be important or not. Six months ago, Jakob was working for Isaac. He decided to take the opportunity to find out whatever he could and to make judgement about its relevance later.

"Did Jakob live with his father before his death?" asked Hamish. "Did Elijah die in Maryborough?"

The old man took his time to answer. It seemed two questions asked in quick succession were too much for him to process.

"I don't think the lad lived with him at the end," he said at last. "But they did both live in Maryborough. I visited Elijah there about twelve month' past."

"Can you tell us his address?" asked Hamish.

"Won't do no good," said the man. "Someone else residing there now. Elijah was a tenant. He never owned a place in his life. Been rented out to a young family now."

It seemed like another dead end. Jakob had been living close to the blacksmith shop prior to Isaac's murder, and he was no longer there. There was no reason to think they could track him by going to his father's old house.

The old man waved at the barman for another drink. He didn't appear to be ready to leave them.

"Are you able to talk about the accident?" asked Rita.

Hamish was startled.

The old man smiled with the good half of his face.

"Don't mind talkin' about it," he said.

"Happened at the old North Glen Mine. Reefs three and four. It's not many a miner reaches my age without being in sev'ral situations that threaten life and limb," he said as he swigged a fresh glass of whiskey delivered by the barman. It seemed he was well known, and the staff replaced his drinks as he finished them without him needing to ask.

It struck Hamish that the fellow had told his story many times, and indeed, probably came to sit with them with the express purpose of telling it.

"Me and me mate, Patrick had two shots, one for the upper reef and one for the lower," he began. "We decided to fire the lower one first and to put the other off separately, so it might have a better chance of doing its work. We waited for the smoke from the first shot to clear away then we went back to fire the remaining shot."

He looked at them with eyes like crystals, stopping a moment to be sure he had their full attention.

"Just as we got under it and were preparing to light the fuse," he said in his crushed gravel voice, "the shot went off."

His skinny arms flew into the air for effect.

Rita jumped.

"From our position at the time, it was a wonder we weren't both blown to pieces," he took a swig of the whiskey. Hamish wondered if he was finished, then he began again.

"But Patrick had the good fortune to get away unscathed. I wasn't as lucky. A fragment of rock struck me in the right cheek pen'trating the flesh and sticking in me jawbone."

Hamish and Rita both stared at the scar.

The old man tilted his face a little to the left and held back his hair to facilitate their view.

"Impressive," said Hamish. "Reduces my scar to shame." Hamish pulled back his fringe to reveal the scar that ran down his own cheek. "I've had it since I was small," he said. "I fell down a mine shaft in Ballarat. My friend and I played among the old shafts when I was a child. We lived in the mining camps. I grazed my face on the way down. It took them almost twenty-four hours to find me."

The miner looked duly impressed.

Hamish was a little ashamed that his scar had caused him to be self-conscious about his appearance all his life. When compared to the damage done to the old miner's face, it was insignificant.

What's your name?" asked Rita, holding out her hand.

"Ryan," he told her.

"It's a pleasure to meet you Ryan," she said, and they shook hands vigorously.

Hamish also shook hands with the miner, noticing the roughness of his skin and the firmness of his grip.

"How long have you been in the area?" he said.

The old man stared into his glass. "Near to three decades now."

"You must have seen some changes."

Ryan' eyes became moist. "That I have, and not all for the better."

"Tell us what Maryborough was like in the early days," said Rita. "The town is so new, and it has grown so quickly."

"I don't think you really want to know about those early days," he said, "although you ask it."

Rita's eyebrows came together. "What do you mean?"

"I came to the area in January of 1860," he began. "It wasn't much of a town then, but the settlers had a sense of entitlement to the place. They'd built houses, and pubs and a warehouse beside the river for moving wool. It was further upriver then."

Both Hamish and Rita watched the old man with anticipation.

"I'd only been in the area for two weeks when I had my first real taste of the place." His face crumpled into a grimace.

"It was a base for the Native Police," he said. "A man led them, going by the name of Bligh. He was a lazy sod, unpleasant altogether. The settlers were making noises about him and his troop lazing around drinking all day instead of protecting the town. 'Lazy and close to useless', they called him and his troop. So, one morning, on the third of February, he got together a party of the native police early in the morning and rode into town firing shots at a few Aboriginal men camping near Cleary's. Then they changed course across to east of the town and charged on a camp near Mr Melville's. They drove the Aboriginal families, men, women and children from the camps. They chased some of the men through the town, just to make sure everyone saw, and some of them jumped into the river to save themselves."

Hamish felt the grip of nausea in his stomach. Ryan had been right they didn't want to hear this story. But now that the old man had begun there was no way to stop him.

"One of the fellows, 'Darky' they called him, had been working in the town for years. If he'd done anything to deserve it, they could have arrested him at any time. But he hadn't and they didn't. Bligh shot him in the back that morning. Just to make a point."

Rita swallowed hard.

"A crowd had gathered at the river by then to watch the spectacle. Bligh climbed into a boat with a handful of native police, and they chased the poor devils trying to swim to safety. He perched himself at the helm of the boat and forty or fifty shots were fired in all. They shot men in the back, no charges against them, shot like mad dogs. One old man, blind in one eye, mind, was marched through the town in handcuffs and taken out to Six Mile Creek. That's where they shot that old fella."

Ryan took a long mouthful of whiskey.

"It was the foulest day Maryborough has ever seen."

Hamish and Rita were momentarily speechless.

When Rita did speak, her voice was cracked. "Was Bligh punished for what he'd done?" she asked.

Ryan threw his head back and laughed. It was a deep laugh with a dark edge to it. "Punished?" he said.

"The bloody town hailed him as a hero and awarded him a ceremonial sword inscribed with words of gratitude."

The sickness in the pit of Hamish's stomach threatened to rise to his throat.

Tears welled in Rita's eyes. "Did no one see that this was wrong?" she whispered.

Ryan looked her in the eye. "Some," he said. "There were murmurings of injustice and indignation. But in the end, the courts found Bligh's excuses sufficient. He made vague claims against the men who were shot, such that a dray had been robbed six weeks earlier, that settler's wives had been attacked, no specifics mind, and such like. For most people, Bligh was a hero and that was that."

They all finished their drinks in silence. There seemed to be no more to be said in the wake of this horrific story. Hamish reflected silently on how, as horrific as it was, the story was not unfamiliar. He knew of similar incidents, resulting in the death of hundreds of Aboriginal families and individuals throughout the country. It was jarring to be confronted with the recency of these events in Queensland. The colony was young and Europeans were still reaching out into new regions, taking over land for agriculture and pastoral pursuits in ever expanding numbers. The insatiable lust for gold was matched by a lust for land. The European expansion would not be stopped.

***

The train ride back to Maryborough was quiet in comparison to the trip in the other direction. Hamish and Rita were exhausted, disappointed they had found no sign of Jakob and upset by the story told to them by Ryan.

No matter how he rationalised it, somehow Maryborough and everyone who lived there seemed tainted by the story.

The conflict between those who settled new frontiers, and those who already lived their lives there constituted the fabric of the colony. It was a clash of ideas, though the European settlers justified their actions through their belief that the original inhabitants were incapable of ideas. That one group of values could differ so greatly to their own and yet hold equal value was too difficult a concept to comprehend. Hamish hated the sense of entitlement that allowed the kinds of incidents that had been described by Ryan, but at the same time he had to grapple with the knowledge that he personally benefitted, directly or indirectly, from these activities. His education, his home, his profession, his lifestyle, all dependent upon the displacement of the first inhabitants and the establishment of European institutions in this land.

After an hour's silence, Rita lightened the mood. "How do you think Wallace and Red are doing on their own?" she said.

Hamish was jarred by her voice and not ready to be jolted from his reverie, but he told himself firmly that the incident in the story happened in the past and there was nothing to be done now.

"I miss them," he said.

"I'm sure they miss you," replied Rita.

Wallace was an older man, of similar age to Hamish's father, but he had led a life of adventure on the sea as a ship's cook. His wisdom and steady character had proved beneficial to Hamish during his frequent attacks of self-doubt.

Wallace was inseparable from a wiry terrier who had been abandoned on Stradbroke Island from a ship held in quarantine in Moreton Bay. The terrier became a fixture at the Dunwich Benevolent Asylum where Wallace had worked as a cook in recent years. Wallace felt he had also been abandoned on the Island. The match was also no doubt facilitated by the fact that Wallace had access to the Island's supply of meat. No one knows what the dog's name was prior to meeting Wallace, but the old cook insisted people call him 'Red', not because of the fiery orange hue of his coat, but because the dog was a staunch socialist.

"Perhaps we could find some excuse to have them join us in Maryborough," suggested Rita.

Hamish laughed.

"They have not long been home from the stint at Southport," he said. "I don't imagine he'd be that keen to up sticks again so soon."

Hamish continued to contemplate the passing scrubland.

"I'm eager to be home myself."

Rita took his hand and squeezed it. "I don't imagine we'll be away much longer," she said. "You'll soon be back to examining widow's bunions."

Hamish feigned a look of disdain.

"There's nothing wrong with a stable life of general practice," he said. "Regular patients, regular income."

"Nothing wrong at all," agreed Rita. "If you're cut out for it." She glanced sideways at him, moving only her eyes.

Irritated with himself for allowing her to rile him, Hamish responded scornfully.

"Am I to take it you don't think I am cut out for a life of general practice?"

Rita's face softened. "Oh Hamish. You can do whatever you set your mind to. All I'm saying is, that if you had set your mind on becoming a general practitioner, you'd be doing it. Why are you still running around the state involving yourself in Sargent Bellamy's intrigues?"

Hamish pouted. He didn't know why. Since he couldn't answer the question, he chose to stare out of the window and cling to his irritation with Rita for asking it.

It was dark when they arrived in Maryborough, so they agreed to meet in the morning to speak with Bellamy.

***

Bellamy was at his desk with a mountain of paperwork in front of him when they entered.

"How can there be this much documentation when you have been here less than a week?" said Hamish.

Bellamy blinked slowly and tapped his pencil on a tiny patch of wood peeking out from beneath the papers.

"What did you learn?"

"Nothing," said Hamish. He threw himself down in a chair.

Rita sat beside him and pulled off her gloves one finger at a time. "Let me help you with that," she said, shuffling the mess on the desk into neat piles.

Bellamy appeared to have lost interest in the sheets and folders. He was focussed on their information on Jakob's whereabouts.

"We did meet a man who knew Jakob's father," offered Rita. "Though he is also deceased, so that is of little help."

Bellamy groaned.

"The boy could be anywhere by now."

He pushed the neat stack Rita had made away in a sweeping gesture of dismissal.

"It does seem odd that he's disappeared."

"He didn't think he had a job any longer," said Rita.

"I can't think of any reason he would have killed his boss and put himself out of work though, and I certainly can't see why he would kill Ruth Gowan."

Bellamy continued tapping the pencil on his desk. The tapping increased in pace and density until suddenly he left the pencil still.

"We'll put him aside for now. I'm sure he'll turn up." He didn't look as convinced as he sounded.

"Did you find out any more about the two miners?" asked Hamish.

"Not really. I asked around. Everyone knows them. They did owe a decent amount of money to Isaac, and they are bragging about town that they don't need to pay it now. It will be up to Nelly to take them to court to retrieve the money owed to the business.

But they owe a lot of people in town money. I can't imagine them murdering them all."

"What about the apprentice's place?"

"Nothing."

"Who are we left with?" said Hamish.

"Arthur Kane," said Rita.

"And Ziggy."

Rita rolled her eyes.

"Nelly?" said Bellamy.

Both Hamish and Rita shook their heads.

"Why would Nelly kill her husband and her best friend?"

"Percival Wellington," said Rita.

"Yes, my money is on him as well," agreed Hamish. "He's a thoroughly unlikable fellow."

"Hardly makes him guilty of murder, though, does it?" said Bellamy.

"Not of itself," Rita conceded.

She stood up. "I'm going to call on Nelly. See how she's getting on."

"Good idea," said Bellamy. "Press her for more information about Isaac. There must be some connection between the two murders we are missing."

"Or maybe, they're not connected," suggested Hamish.

Bellamy glared at him.

"I'm simply saying that if it is too difficult to contrive a connection, it may be because there isn't one in the first place."

Bellamy continued to stare for a moment before relaxing.

"There's something else I need to talk to you about," he said.

Chapter Thirteen

"What Business Men say of Women: They will tell you that a woman is never satisfied that she is being treated fairly; she is full of suspicion; cannot count a roll of notes accurately; will avail herself of the slightest technicality to cheat a creditor; will rush into litigation, and once there and in the witness box will swear to a series of contradictions and perjure herself with sweet unconsciousness. They say that in a suit instituted to recover money from a woman any jury will take the woman's part without considering either the law or the justice of the case.

One might reasonably reply that the defective business education of women is sufficient to explain their business ignorance; the espionage which is exercised by many men over the expenditure of their families, and the numerous frauds practised by sharpers upon inexperienced women explain, if they do not justify, the suspicions of women.

It is well to know what disadvantages women rest under in business; but all of them can be traced to the disadvantage of not being trained into careful business habits.

Every girl should be taught how to keep her accounts in an orderly and businesslike manner; she should be trusted with an allowance and be held responsible for its management and made to abide the consequences of its mismanagement; and every girl should be taught arithmetic in such a practical way that she can compute interest, buy and sell and depend, with perfect confidence on her own figures. The injustice that parents, rich and poor, do to their daughters by bringing them up in a state of infantile ignorance of affairs and by keeping them in a condition of pecuniary dependence even after they reach womanhood is hardly to be computed."

The Armidale Express Friday 8 May 1885

Rita

As Rita walked up to Nelly's home, she heard the usual tapping from the workshop so continued around to the back of the house.

Nelly was in her overalls, hard at work. The tanned muscles in her arms rose and fell with the large movements she was making, her hair escaping in every direction from a loose bun at the back of her head. She was focussed on her work and didn't see Rita come in.

Rita watched for a moment unwilling to disturb her rhythm. After a while Nelly stopped tapping and looked up startled.

"Good morning," said Rita. "I've come to see how you are doing."

Nelly brushed the hair from her grimy face.

"Would you like tea?" she asked. "It's time for a break anyhow."

Rita followed to a wooden bench at the side of the door where there were two chairs.

Nelly suspended an iron kettle over a small fire in a portable forge and brewed them two mugs of strong tea.

"What are you making?" asked Rita.

Nelly glanced over to the anvil. "Large nails for Mr. Watson," she said. "It's an order that Isaac was working on prior to...his..."

"Quite," said Rita.

"Has business picked up then?"

Nelly sighed. "No."

She held her mug in both hands and stared into the steaming liquid.

"I don't know what to do. There is a lot of money owing and everyone is slow to pay now that Isaac is gone. It's not only the gold miners, but everyone. Even Walkers is trying to say they didn't receive an order, that I know for a fact was completed and delivered to them."

"Why would they do that?"

"They don't intend to continue doing business with me, so they have no incentive to pay for what they've already received."

"I wish I could contact Jakob. He delivered the goods. He could corroborate that the order was filled."

"Do you have any idea where Jakob might be?"

Nelly shook her head. "As I've said to you. I had very little to do with the lad. He resented my intrusion into the workshop. I heard he'd gone to Gympie looking for work."

"We heard that too. Hamish and I travelled to Gympie to seek him out. But no one there had seen him. Or so they claimed. We met a man who knew his father."

"Yes. Elijah, is it?"

"That's right. Did you know him?"

"I met him once briefly. He came to see my husband, about six months ago, not long before he passed."

"Do you know why he came to see Isaac?"

Nelly shook her head again. "No." she said. "Though, I got the impression Elijah must have fathered Jakob when he was quite young because he seemed close to Isaac's age."

"Did Isaac tell you anything about him?"

Nelly puckered her brow. "I can't remember anything significant," she said.

"Are there any other visitors you can remember? People who came to see Isaac in the past few months?"

"Only customers," said Nelly sipping her tea.

"That devil Percival Wellington was here every other week with another order, the latest of which they are now refusing to settle," she said.

"Wouldn't there be records of the order and its delivery?"

Nelly made a sound that wasn't quite a laugh. "Isaac didn't keep good records, any order I was aware of, I wrote in a ledger and signed off once complete.

I told Jakob a hundred times to get a signed receipt from customers on delivery. But he didn't listen to me, and Isaac didn't pay attention to those details. I think Walker's was more than happy to get away with underpaying Isaac."

"Do you know exactly what was in the order?" asked Rita.

"I do," said Nelly. "I helped put it together myself. I wrote every item in the journal. But without proof that it was delivered I'm not sure what I can do."

"I think we should confront the directors," said Rita. "Surely, they wouldn't want it spread around town that the company is trying to steal from a widow."

Nelly's face brightened. "Do you think it will do any good?"

"It's worth a try," said Rita. "We should publicly confront the miners as well. They're probably not as concerned about public shaming as Walkers might be, but it will make you feel better to address it."

"I think it will," agreed Nelly.

"Good. Get the ledger and we'll go to Walkers after morning tea."

Nelly hesitated. "I need to finish the nails and send them out to the farm by lunchtime," she said. "Should we go this afternoon, Ed and Tom will be at the White Swan by then and we can see them after."

Rita agreed.

"Our first order of business is to recoup the money owed to you. But secondly, we need to think about how you will attract customers. Since the people in this town seem unwilling to accept a woman as a blacksmith."

Nelly's shoulders slumped again.

"Do you have family and friends we could begin with?" asked Rita.

"I have my family in town," said Nelly. "But I haven't spent a lot of time with them since moving here. I married Isaac almost immediately and have been distanced from them since."

"Is there a reason you stay distanced?"

Nelly considered the question. "No...I suppose it's because they are a deeply religious family, and I'm less so. Isaac was certainly not interested in a religious life. I might have continued going to church, but Isaac didn't want to go, so I just stopped."

"What about if you joined them again?" asked Rita.

Nelly screwed up her nose. "It's been so long. I don't know how to fit in. They might not welcome me."

"Tosh," said Rita. "They're Christian, aren't they? They must welcome you."

Nelly laughed. "In theory."

"Tomorrow's Saturday. On Sunday, Hamish and I will accompany you to church. That way if your family don't embrace you, you won't be alone."

Nelly looked startled at the suggestion. "I'm Lutheran," she said simply. "Have you ever been to a Lutheran service?"

"I have read many of the works of Martin Luther," said Rita.

"That's not the same."

"Hamish and I love a new experience," smiled Rita. "Don't worry."

***

Rita returned to the blacksmith's cottage after lunch. She had changed into a smart gown of burgundy, wore black lace gloves and a black hat and was looking professional and well-off. Nelly wore one of the only two dresses she owned, a simple frock of printed cotton, pinched at the waist and high at the neck. A little out of style, but clean and smart. She had tied her hair into a neat bun at the back of her neck. Her green eyes shone, reflecting the emerald print on the fabric.

When they arrived at Walkers, Rita walked directly up to the main offices, gave both their names and announced she would like to see one of the Directors, Mr. Hawking.

A neat man with a trimmed beard looked up at her from beneath hooded lids seeming irritated that two women were intruding into his space.

"Mr. Hawking is not available for consultation," he said, lazily.

Just as Rita was about to insist, Percival Wellington came from one of the offices.

"What a delightful surprise," he said, holding his hands in his pockets in case there should be any miscommunication that led to either of them wanting to shake hands with him.

Rita felt Nelly stiffen alongside her.

He nodded to the man at the desk and gestured for the ladies to follow him into one of the offices. The man showed his disinterest by returning to write in his journal.

Rita and Nelly stayed put and Percival turned back to see why they weren't following him.

"We are here to see Mr Hawking, said Rita smiling, but determined.

"As you have been told," he nodded to the man at the desk, now doing his best to ignore them all, "Mr. Hawking is not available. Surely, there is something I can help you with," he said.

"If you will join me," he gestured toward his office yet again.

Rita continued to stand where she was.

"Is he on the premises?" Rita demanded to know.

"Er...yes, but..."

"Then we will see him," said Rita.

Percival let out an exaggerated sigh. "Mr Hawking is a busy man," he said. "He is unable to see visitors without an appointment."

"Then we request an appointment," said Rita. "We will wait." With that she and Nelly sat down on the plush seats designed for visitors along the wall of the foyer.

Percival's head dropped to his chest. He walked over to where the ladies sat.

"Look," he said, "whatever this is about, I'm sure I can assist you..."

At that moment, a distinguished man with an impressive head of grey hair popped his head out of one of the larger offices.

"What's going on?"

Nelly stood up.

"Mrs Brown," he said, walking out to greet her. He held out his hand to shake hers vigorously. "I'm sorry for the loss of your husband," he said kindly.

Nelly smiled.

Rita stood and addressed the man. "I'm Doctor Rita Cartwright," she said. "I'm in town to assist in the investigation into the deaths of Mr Brown and Mrs Gowan."

"A lady doctor?" said Mr Hawking. "How impressive." He took her hand and shook it firmly.

"We were hoping to speak with you," said Nelly.

"Of course, Mrs Brown," he looked at Percival, who bowed his head and stepped away to return to his own office. He strode in slowly. Rita had a smug grin on her face as they followed Mr. Hawking.

Nelly and Rita scanned the office. It wasn't pretentious. It was a workspace with a large oak desk covered in ledgers and journals, a bookcase against the wall, and various small machinery parts on the floor. The walls were decorated with machinery plans. This was not a man who wanted to flaunt his power.

After initial pleasantries, Rita came to the point.

"Mrs Brown has been in correspondence with your staff in relation to payment owed to her husband's business," she began. "As this correspondence has not proved fruitful, she has decided to bring the matter to you, as you were known to Mr Brown as an honourable man."

Nelly looked him directly in the eyes. Rita was proud that the blacksmith's widow did not look intimidated or apologetic. She looked in every way a confidant businesswoman.

"What is the nature of the payment?" asked the Director.

Nelly handed him the journal where she had clearly listed the items delivered by her husband's apprentice with the costings alongside. There was a neatly written total at the bottom of the column.

His brow knitted. He examined the list and looked up. "And you are certain the items were delivered?" he asked Nelly.

"I am certain. The apprentice, Jakob, left the workshop with them on the date noted. He returned an hour later claiming to have delivered the items."

"Did someone in my employ sign for the delivery?" asked Mr Hawking.

Nelly wrung her hands. "I told Jakob many times to request a signature upon delivery, but no, in this instance he did not acquire one."

The Director considered the journal before him, then he called out to the man with the beard.

He came in swiftly. "Bring Mr Wellington in, will you?" he said.

Nelly and Rita exchanged glances.

A moment later Percival joined them, his head held high.

"Mrs Brown tells me there is money owed on the Blacksmith contract," he said. "Were these items delivered, or not?"

Percival scanned the list in the journal. He looked up at the women. He seemed to be considering his response. Finally, he said, "I cannot say for certain. I would have to check."

"Take the list and check, then," said Mr. Hawking.

Percival hesitated and the Director added, "Go on man. These ladies don't have all day, and nor do I."

The old man put an arm around Nelly's shoulder and led her gently toward the door. Rita followed.

"Grieve for your husband," he said. "He was a good man. Then soon enough you will remarry. You are a beautiful woman, Nelly."

Rita felt her blood go cold. She wanted to object.

She wanted to say that Nelly was a capable woman, a skilled blacksmith. Whether or not she remarried, she would remain those things. But Nelly was continuing through the door and into the foyer, where the man with the beard didn't even look up. This was Nelly's life. To speak for her would be patronising. She was already experiencing enough of that.

As they reached the top of the stairs, Nelly stopped and looked back at the Director. "I was hoping to continue the contract," she said.

Mr Hawking pursed his lips. "I maintained the arrangement with your husband out of my absolute respect for the quality of his work," he said. "But I am a businessman. It makes no sense to continue to outsource work that can be carried out more efficiently inhouse now.

Good day to you, ladies."

He turned into his office and shut the door.

Rita bit her lip and they continued out to the waiting buggy in silence.

"Let's hope Percival admits the mistake and tells his boss the products were delivered," she said when they were settled in the buggy.

"That won't happen," said Nelly. "Percival Wellington will never admit a mistake."

***

Hamish and Rita strode toward the church in John's Lane on the following Sunday morning. There was a breeze coming in from the river and the air didn't feel as close and warm around them as it had for days. They both enjoyed the early walk knowing the clammy humidity of summer's height would return later in the day. They had arranged to meet Nelly outside the church. As they were approaching, they saw people gathering on the lawn in front of the building, but they couldn't see Nelly. Hamish stopped to take in the building, a pine structure with a rectangular nave and a portico at the front. Gothic style windows down each side gave away the religious function of the building without being overly ornate. It was built to accommodate about two hundred people.

"It's not an impressive feat of architecture, is it?" said Hamish.

Rita agreed. "They're not trying to impress anyone," she said. "Lutherans take a more restrained approach to their religious architecture. The building is sturdy and simple."

She wrinkled her brow. "Although this building may not have been built for the German faith, I believe it is used for a number of denominations."

She had a twinkle in her eye. She loved knowing something Hamish did not. "Nelly told me that prior to building this place, the Lutherans used to meet in one of the parishioner's houses."

"Which parishioner?" he asked.

"Nicholas Thurecht, I think."

They waited outside, a short distance from the gathering crowd. The women were all dressed in the same modest fashion, heavy black ankle length gowns with high collars and long sleeves. Black bonnets were secured tightly under the chin and black gloves covered the hands. Practical leather shoes, flat for comfort during the prolonged periods of standing during the service completed the outfit. No glimmer of jewellery broke up the dense sea of black.

"Very sombre," said Hamish.

Rita nodded. Nelly had warned her, so she was also dressed in black, although she wore a split skirt that she generally used for riding and a black silk blouse that had a boat neckline and rather more lace than was worn by the Lutheran women. Her hat was wide and adorned with burgundy velvet roses, an embellishment that also set her apart. They watched as a group of men with brass instruments filed into the portico of the church.

"A brass band?" said Hamish.

Rita laughed, "not as sombre as you thought then."

Just then, Nelly walked up to them, wearing a gown undistinguishable from the other parishioners.

Rita and Hamish greeted her warmly.

"The congregation is larger than I expected," said Hamish.

"Over twelve thousand German immigrants have made the region home in the last two decades," said Nelly. "Most of them from the north. They come from a lot of different regions, and each had its own way of doing things."

Rita's eyes shone with curiosity. "How so?"

Nelly went on. "For one example, the order of service differs, even between the two Lutheran congregations here in Maryborough. Here, they always do Holy Communion on Sundays, although people are losing interest, debating the need for it."

She leaned in closer to Rita so no one could overhear.

"I wouldn't be surprised if communion falls off the service before too long," she said. She held her head up and looked around the gathered souls.

"And there will be baptisms if there have been any babies born to the congregation this week."

Hamish and Rita glanced around for babies.

"But one of the highlights today will be Confirmation. The children prepare for it for weeks."

Soon the pastor appeared in the doorway of the church and ushered the congregation in.

Hamish heard a man in the next pew grumbling to his wife. "I hope he's prepared this morning," he said.

His wife responded, "I don't know why he insists on using this hymn book."

"There are many hymn books," whispered Nelly to Hamish. "Each region uses a different one. When we came to Australia, the regional differences became a problem."

The man heard them whispering and turned to glare at them. Hamish stared back defiantly.

"There's my brother and his wife," Nelly pointed to the front pew.

They had not seen Nelly as she, Hamish and Rita came in behind them.

Hamish could only see the back of their heads, but it was immediately obvious that Nelly's brother was tall. He sat with a straight back, his head a good six inches above that of his wife. His wife had her hair pulled into a tight bun at the back of her neck in much the same fashion as Nelly wore. Only her sister-in-law's hair was neatly contained, whereas Nelly's was always escaping in wild tendrils that defied captivity. Even from this distance, Hamish could not imagine Nelly fitting in comfortably with her family.

Hamish shifted his attention to the interior of the building and admired the walls decorated with garlands and wreaths. Texts of scripture were displayed on the walls, and his eye was drawn to one that was prominent amongst them from Revelations, Hold that fast which thou hast, that so no man takes your crown.

"Interesting," murmured Hamish.

The service commenced with the hymn, Oh Holy Spirit Come to Thee. The congregation sang loudly in German, against the lively music of the brass band. It was a spirited reverberation within the confined walls of the church. After this the Service of the Altar followed, then the congregation sang Oh Stay with Your Grace. Hamish felt a headache coming on.

Finally, there was respite from the music as the minister began his sermon. He spoke from a raised pulpit taking his text from Hebrews Chapter Thirteen. The congregation listened with serious attention, spending much of the service on their knees, silently in prayer.

When the general sermon had been completed, the Minister reminded the congregation of the importance of Confirmation. He said it was necessary that the Lutheran Church uphold this tradition because in Baptism the parents and Godfather of the child swear to uphold their duties, whereas at Confirmation it is the child who takes the vows, thereby taking on responsibility for their own adherence to Christian values. In order to do so, he reminded them, the child must be taught thoroughly in the knowledge of God and in the Christian faith.

He requested that the congregation stand firm in their commitment to having their children learn the German language and the scriptures, as difficult as it may be in a strange country.

Young Christians were weak and easily led, he added, looking toward the back of the congregation.

This opened a floodgate of responses. Those who had been straining to remain composed throughout the service felt permitted to speak out. There was a flurry of loud comments causing Hamish and Rita, with the rest of the congregation to turn around and lay sight of three young women, resplendent in colourful gowns, perched confidently in the back row. One was in pastel pink, one in blue and one in sunny yellow. They looked striking with blond hair piled fashionably high on their heads. Bright jewels in a sea of black clad matronly piety. Rita smiled a broad appreciative smile.

"There's nothing you like more than a little deviance," Hamish accused her.

Her smile broadened even further.

"Absolutely," she said.

The girls exuded defiance as an older woman in the second from back pew turned in her seat to berate the girls. The priest stopped talking in response to the commotion. The silence caused the woman to face the front and sit, her face red with indignation.

The three girls seemed unashamed, even smug. Order was soon restored, and the Pastor described the long hours the children had spent preparing for their Confirmation exam. He invited them, fourteen in all, to come to the altar. The examination commenced and when the children had successfully provided all the answers asked of them, the candidates prayed the Apostles Creed and promised to be faithful to the Church.

The final hymn, A Pure Heart Lord Create in Me was sung and the service came to a conclusion.

Hamish felt a rush of relief. The confined space, combined with the sound of the band and the voices of the congregation raised in hymn, had resulted in a throbbing head. He pushed his fringe from his face as he, Rita and Nelly edged along their pew and into the stream of people making their way down the aisle and out into the sunshine.

Immediately, they saw the three shining gems in the crowd. Matrons tutted and whispered behind their hymn books. Hamish and Rita admired the girls for both their fortitude and their beauty.

"They look beautiful, don't they?" said Nelly. "I'm surprised to see them grown into women. Last time I saw the sisters they were skinny girls."

Nelly was distracted by the approach of a man whose considerable height was even more enhanced by a tall top hat. "I'm surprised to see you here after so long an absence, my sister."

Nelly's brother turned toward the three young women who had engaged the attention of the entire congregation. "I'm afraid they have scandalised the other women," he said. "It is disrespectful to come to church dressed in this frivolous way."

"Nonsense," said Nelly.

Her brother's face reddened but he did not pursue an argument with his sister.

"These are my friends, Doctor Hamish Hart and Doctor Rita Cartwright," said Nelly. "My brother, George."

Her brother's eyebrows went up. "A female Doctor?" he said. Rita smiled and shook his hand.

"They are in town to assist in the investigation of the murders," she said. "Of my husband and Ruth Gowan."

George looked surprised. "Is it entirely appropriate to befriend someone so close to a murder during your investigation?" he asked Hamish.

"Do you consider your sister a suspect in the murder of her husband?" asked Rita.

George faltered.

"Of course not," he said. "But perhaps you should."

At that moment a raised voice caught their attention. "Go home immediately and repent," the voice was saying.

"Repent on what?" said one of the young women.

"On being joyful, rather than dour and miserable," said another.

The original voice, a mature woman, was indignant.

"Go home. You are embarrassing the family," she said in an extremely loud whisper.

"We'll not go home," said the third girl, perhaps the most beautiful of the three, though Hamish felt it hard to choose.

The priest was making his way toward the group to intercede.

"Here is Minister Paul," said one of the young women when she saw him. "Ask him if we are embarrassing."

Minister Paul froze to the spot as it seemed the entire congregation was looking to him for a verdict on the shameful behaviour of the younger generation.

"I'm eager that the young come to Sunday service," he began slowly, "and grateful for their presence regardless of their costume."

Nelly whispered in Rita's ear, "That woman, is the girls' mother."

"What? All three of them?" asked Rita.

Nelly nodded.

"Oh, she has her hands full!" Rita laughed.

The mother of the girls tutted and scoffed. "Balderdash" she said.

The Minister's eyebrows rose.

"It's a matter of respect," she muttered, attempting to herd the girls from the congregation.

Hamish had been so focussed on the interaction he hadn't noticed Rita and Nelly edging their way closer to the young women. Nelly threw her arms around the beauty in yellow.

"I haven't seen you in years Daisy," she cried. "You look astonishing."

Daisy responded by hugging Nelly tightly. "Nelly Brown," she said. "You used to play with us on the ship."

The other girls gathered around Nelly and waited for their turn to hug her.

The older people began to move away, except for the girl's mother.

"This is my friend, Rita," said Nelly. "Doctor Rita Cartwright."

The girls held out their gloved hands politely, blushing slightly at meeting such a distinguished woman.

Rita held each of their small hands in her own and smiled.

"And Doctor Hamish Hart,' said Nelly. Hamish moved forward to shake their hands. They were blushing profusely now. Hamish thought it endearing.

Suddenly, a menacing voice broke through the greetings.

"You will return home immediately," said the mother of the girls, with an icy glare in Nelly's direction.

"You must be very proud of your daughters," said Rita. "They are beautiful in every way."

The woman clearly didn't appreciate having her authority undermined by an outsider, and the fact that Minister Paul himself, had not supported her position had weighed heavily. She swung around in search of her husband, tears of rage in her eyes. When she spotted him chatting casually with an acquaintance, seemingly oblivious to the disrespect shown to her, she pushed past three couples to grab his arm forcefully.

"We are leaving," she announced dragging him toward the girls who she bundled under her other arm. She physically pushed her family toward the edge of the congregation and onward toward their buggy. Everyone made way for them, unprepared to interfere with the mother's authority to bully her own family.

The young woman in yellow glanced back over her shoulder with a nervous smile toward Nelly, who nodded and smiled back.

"I'll do my best to call on her," said Nelly. "I think she could use a friend."

"A wonderful idea," agreed Rita. "I believe you could both benefit from a friendship." George was still standing beside Hamish watching his sister as she and Rita returned to them.

"Still swimming against the tide," he said.

Nelly rolled her eyes.

"What are you planning to do with yourself now that Isaac has passed?"

Hamish thought it insensitive that this was the first thing he had to say to his sister after her being widowed. Why not begin with 'I'm sorry for your loss?'

Nelly didn't seem surprised. "I'll be continuing the business," she said.

"Blacksmithing?" Her brother laughed. "Surely you are joking?"

Nelly blinked slowly at him.

Her brother shook his head. "You are a lost cause," he said. "Remarry. That's your only option."

Rita was becoming irritable now. "Nelly was actually hoping you would know people who might become clients," she said sweetly. "Her work is of a superior quality."

George laughed again. "You do my sister no favours in championing her in this endeavour," he said. To Nelly, he said, "Remarry." He made his way through the remaining parishioners. Rita saw him join his wife.

The congregation was thinning, families returning home for a traditional roast lunch, a meal too heavy in the middle of these sub-tropical summer days.

***

Hamish and Rita returned to the hotel for a lighter meal of sandwiches and freshly made lemonade.

"You said Bellamy wanted to speak to you about something after I left on Friday," said Rita. "What was that about?"

Hamish put down his glass and scraped back his hair. His knee was bouncing, and he knew Rita had noticed.

"The medical examiner has resigned," he said. "Bellamy would like me to take on the position."

Rita sat back in surprise. "That's wonderful," she said. "Isn't it?"

"I don't know," said Hamish. "I don't want to disappoint him. But I'm not sure I want to take on the responsibility. I'm a general practitioner. I have no training."

"You have plenty of experience," said Rita. "Isn't there a course or something?"

"I don't believe so," said Hamish. "A specialisation in pathology is preferred. Other than that, it is a matter of experience."

"There it is then. You have experience."

Hamish was rubbing his hand along his right leg, which was still bouncing.

"I'll stick with my plan," he said, taking another sandwich. "Set up my practice. It's a quiet life I'm after."

Rita also took another sandwich. She rolled her eyes as she tucked it into her mouth.

Chapter Fourteen

"A Paradise for unmarried women: During his stay in San Francisco on his way to England the ex-Premier of New South Wales was interviewed at the Victoria Hotel by a reporter from the Mail.

'The future possibilities of NSW are simply beyond anticipation,' said Sir Alex. 'It's an infant America now and in time will be the haven of millions of people. The population of Australia is now 4,000,000. We pay two-thirds of the passage money for all immigrants except for young girls, who have all their expenses paid.

The country is really in need of more females, women that will make good wives. The situation is somewhat similar to the early days of gold excitement in California when every camp was filled with men and no women. We have room for them all and can furnish the women with fine stalwart husbands within hours of their arrival.'" **The Albury and Wodonga Express Friday 28 May 1886.**

Nelly

Nelly stared into the embers in her forge. They cast a dim glow, struggling to hold on to the last vestiges of warmth. It was this part of the day that she missed Isaac the most. The noise and heat had passed, and the cool lonely silence of evening was about to begin. She watched the embers until well after they had dwindled to a mere whisper, a gentle flickering glow, reminiscent of fading memories and diminished hopes. The ashes made her think about the cyclical nature of life, the ebb and flow of creation and destruction. The cold, silence of night descended in the workshop.

As she sat mesmerized by the transition from light to darkness, a sound startled her. She shifted her head to one side, alert, aware of the slow crunch of footsteps on gravel. She remained still and listened with the attention of an animal sensing danger. No one visited the workshop at this time of the evening.

Nelly turned her head toward the door and registered the silhouette of a man. A small man.

A chill went up her neck. Percival Wellington stood there, hands in his pockets, watching. Only when he was certain his presence had been appreciated, he entered. This was a politeness he had not shown before, and it further unnerved her.

"I've come to update you on the products in question," he said, entering the workshop slowly, hands still casually placed in his pockets.

As long as he keeps them there.

"I have investigated thoroughly, and I can assure you the items were not delivered to Walkers."

Nelly groaned. She looked away from him at the shadow of the anvil and the iron she'd been working on.

He shuffled a few steps closer.

"You must understand, I cannot authorise payment of goods that were never received," he added.

While there was no light to be reflected through them, Nelly's eyes were as dark as the black coals she was staring into. "I expected nothing more," she said in a whisper.

"Nelly..."

She glanced up at him realising she was no longer afraid. Where fear had been there was only disdain in her heart. She contemplated a creature that no longer mattered, an annoyance where once an enemy stood.

"I know those items were delivered," she said. "They were specialised tools that would be of no use to anyone else. The lad could not have sold them, and he would have no use for them himself."

Percival shook his head. His face was contorted in a show of compassion, but his cold eyes said otherwise.

"Why are you doing this?" she breathed.

"Nelly" he said, "Pack up here and sell the house. You'll get a small sum for it, and you can move in with your brother. It will only be for a year while you grieve for Isaac, then..."

"Then what?"

For the first time Nelly witnessed vulnerability in his face.

"You know I will always look after you..."

Nelly reddened. Was this man suggesting...what was he suggesting?

Rage began to replace the numbness. It came in a flood that surprised her.

"I think you should leave," she said, controlling her breathing and her voice.

When Percival continued to stand over her, she added, "Now!"

Percival bowed slightly and left her. It was almost completely dark in the workshop now and he was little more than a shadow as he strode out into the night. But at least he went. She shuddered at the thought of another assault.

Nelly found the energy to close the shop and return to the house where she immediately slumped in her chair at the table. She was hungry after a day of heavy work but didn't have the motivation to prepare a meal. It was pointless. Why was she working? No one was going to buy her goods. And how was she going to pay for coal and iron, let alone feed herself?

She folded her arms on the table and lay down her head on them. She felt adrift in a sea of grief, unable to muster the motivation to carry on. Colour had drained from her world, and she was becoming accustomed to the grey. It felt like a blanket that scratched her skin but the irritation of it was the only thing that reminded her she was alive.

"Isaac," she said quietly, "What am I going to do without you?"

Nelly lay with her head on the table for twenty minutes before shaking herself.

"I have to find my way," she said aloud.

The first step was to let light into the room. To return the colour. Unsure she wanted to, but aware that she needed to go on, she stood up and lit the gas lamp and the fire in the stove. The flood of light brought shadows of contrast to the room, if not colour. She forced herself to make porridge and eat it, and a strong mug of tea.

She had taken the last mouthful and was returning her plate and mug to the basin when she heard a knock on the door. The intrusion of company into her solitude felt unbearable. What if it was Percival Wellington returning? Nelly opened the door tentatively to find her neighbours Mrs Bentley and Mrs Wellington waiting.

The sight of them triggered what may have sounded like a sigh of relief to the two visitors but was actually a groan of acquiescence.

"Come in," she said. "Are you hoping to use the oven?" She thought it was an odd time to do so, but her neighbours had never visited the house for any other reason.

"No," they said collectively as they entered.

"Tea?"

"Thank-you," they agreed as they sat down.

Nelly poured tea from the massive kettle grateful she had lit the fire when she did.

"We came to check on you," said Mrs Bentley, a large woman with a round face. "We didn't want to disturb you at your work during the day."

"That's very kind," said Nelly. She couldn't hide the note of surprise in her voice.

"Have the Police made any progress in the investigation?" asked Mrs Windemere who was smaller, but no less intimidating in her own way.

"No," said Nelly. "I don't believe so."

The women exchanged glances.

"Nelly, dear," said Mrs Bentley, we hear you working away each day out in the shop. We're worried about you."

"Why continue?" cut in Mrs Windemere.

Nelly stared at them.

"It's unseemly, isn't it? That type of thing for a woman?"

Nelly's face reddened.

"We mean, you are a beautiful young woman. It's not as if you need to do hard labour to survive."

"What do you suggest?" said Nelly curtly.

The women looked at one another again.

"Why, remarry, of course."

Nelly laughed.

"You would have plenty of suitors," Mrs Bentley rushed to say.

"What about that fine Mr Wellington? We saw him leaving just now." She rafted a coy glance at her friend and looked back toward Nelly knowingly. "He'd be a welcome catch for any young woman. You could move from here and into a nice house."

"I like this house," said Nelly, her mouth dry.

"We don't mean you should accept an offer immediately. Of course, it is too soon. But move in with your brother and after a decent period, you can begin your life again."

Emotions swirled in Nelly's stomach. She was consumed by grief, struggling to see herself continue in a world without Isaac, and people were asking her to think about remarrying. What was wrong with the world?

The two women must have sensed her discomfort because they swallowed their tea in a hurry and Mrs Bentley stood.

"I think we should leave." She glared at her friend, who also stood.

Mrs Windemere looked back and added, "Think about what we said," as she left.

Nelly slammed her fist on the table and the mug of tea shook. How was she to get through the endless night now?

She lay on her bed staring at the strips of light streaming through the cracks in the unlined timber walls. There was nothing wrong with her house. Her and Isaac had built it together in their first year of marriage. She loved the house and the workshop because it was theirs. Isaac had not been gone a week and everyone was pressuring her to remarry.

Why did no one think she could make it on her own? Why couldn't she sell her own work? She knew she was a good blacksmith, not as good as Isaac, but only because he had more experience. The idea of stepping into his shoes, of preserving the legacy he had built, stirred a quiet determination within her. She would not bow to the weight of tradition and societal expectation; she would prove herself to be more than just a widow seeking refuge in remarriage. She would soon produce items as fine a quality as Isaac. If she were given the chance. But if the people of the town would not buy her goods, then what was the point? She had no clients, only debts. And money owed to her that would never be paid.

Chapter Fifteen

"Our townsman Mr Perry is a much more extensive grower of fruit than anyone would imagine, especially if one judged from the appearance of his trim little shop in Kent Street.

He has built a first class two storied house directly opposite Tiuana Creek on the banks of the Mary River known as Woodman's Gardens. This block is eight acres in extent and is in a high state of cultivation. He does not care for anything beyond oranges, bananas, grapes and pines. He does grow some mangos cherry and strawberry guavas, but these cover a small space of the area. In this area are over 200 fruit bearing trees, some of which are 28 years old and from which a very valuable crop of oranges is a certainty. There are about 200 trees of 3 years old. About 3 acres devoted to bananas. Mr Perry has planted over 20,000 pines off the different areas under his control." **Fruit Growing in Maryborough Sat 26 Feb 1887**

Hamish

Ziggy, dressed in the finest embroidered silk, sashayed into the police station. Hamish caught sight of her through the sergeant's open office door. He also saw Constable Williams drop the papers he was carrying.

"I'd like to speak with Sergeant Bellamy," said Ziggy in her sweetest voice.

Williams turned around to peer through the sergeant's door. Both Bellamy and Hamish gazed out. Bellamy let his chair tip back onto its four legs and Hamish put out his cigarette.

"Ziggy," said Williams. "She would like to speak with you."

Bellamy nodded and looked to Hamish with one eyebrow raised.

Hamish shrugged his shoulders.

Ziggy rounded the counter and entered the office, hips swaying. Arthur asked me to fetch you both," she said. "He can't leave the hotel this morning, but he says it's important."

She pursed her lips to accentuate the word 'important'.

"We had better comply then," said Bellamy as he stood up. Hamish followed close behind and they walked together the short distance to the White Swan.

When they went in through the front door, they found Arthur taking inventory of a large order.

"Sit down," he said.

He handed the pencil and paper to Ziggy instructing her to continue checking the items against the delivery sheet.

Arthur Kane sat down opposite Hamish and Bellamy in the booth along the side wall that had become their 'usual' table. It was out of the way of the main bar where early drinkers sat and they could melt into the dark wallpaper and deep burgundy leather seating.

"Last night," said Arthur "I had a group of men from Walkers in here drinking," He shook his head and chuckled. "That foundry is like a hive of old women for the gossip. Nothing goes unseen or without comment."

Hamish and Bellamy waited while Arthur regained his train of thought. He snorted.

"Anyway," he said, "These men were commenting on a load of items delivered by Isaac's apprentice the week before his death. They heard that Walkers had not paid for the items and Mrs Brown had visited the office with another lady to enquire about it."

Hamish's eyebrows rose upward.

Encouraged Arthur went on. "They also heard that Percival Wellington was insisting the items were never delivered. But the men were adamant that the delivery was made. There was a great deal of conjecture about why he might be avoiding the payment."

"Interesting," said Bellamy, his eyebrows also arched. "And why did they think?"

"Most of them think it is a simple matter. The man is tight-fisted. A couple postulated that he is trying to ruin Nelly, so she'll have to marry him. Everyone knows he has a fixation on her. But no one is impressed by the way Nelly is being treated. They believe she deserves the payment due to her."

"And so, she does," said the sergeant. He turned to Hamish. "This means Nelly is telling the truth. The tools were delivered, and the payment wasn't made."

"Why would Wellington lie about it?" said Hamish, thinking aloud. "The company is successful, there is no business reason for them to refuse to settle the debt."

"Perhaps it is a personal reason, as some of the men suggested," said Bellamy. "Maybe he is trying to force Nelly into giving up her dream of continuing Isaac's business so she will consider his offer of marriage."

Hamish shifted uncomfortably in his chair. "Why would anyone want a union that had been manipulated in that way?"

Arthur sniffed and ran his hand through his beard. "I've seen worse," he said.

Bellamy nodded and rolled his eyes. He sat back in the seat. If it hadn't been a bench built into the wall he would have been balancing on the back legs of the chair. This was his thinking position.

"Is there anything else?" he asked.

"No," said Arthur. "Wait, yes there is one thing. Apparently, Isaac, Ruth and Elijah, the apprentice's father, went to school together."

"Now that is interesting," said Bellamy leaning forward again.

Hamish sat upright. "At last, a connection."

"Who told you this?" asked Bellamy.

"Ziggy," said Arthur. He turned toward the bar and called Ziggy from the back room.

She came out tentatively.

"You're not in trouble," said Arthur, "Get over here woman."

Ziggy cheered up immediately and joined them.

Arthur explained that the detectives wanted to know who told her about Isaac, Ruth and Elijah going to school together.

Ziggy giggled. "No one told me, she said. "I was there with them. I was a couple of years younger of course," she fluttered her substantial eyelashes, "but

Maryborough is a small place, there was only one classroom back then and we were all in it together."

Hamish and Bellamy were still trying to process the new information and what it might mean when Ziggy rushed on, clearly excited to have their attention.

"They were as thick as thieves, those three. Rode together. I was a small...well... boy, then, and I was far too frail for the likes of them. Isaac only stayed at school for a few years. He left at nine or ten to start his apprenticeship."

"Is there anyone else who would know them?" asked Hamish.

Ziggy shook her head and her long earrings jingled. Then her face brightened. "Elijah, Jakob's father, had a brother," she said. "He was older than Elijah, and they weren't close, but he still lives around here. He might remember something."

"Where does he live?" asked Hamish.

"His name is John. Johnno, they call him. He lives near Woodman's Gardens. There's an acreage on the banks of the river near Tinana Creek. Mr Perry grows oranges, bananas, grapes and pineapples there, he has a little shop in Kent Street. Johnno works for him. Apart from that he's a bit of a recluse."

Hamish and Bellamy took the Police cab to Kent Street to enquire after Elijah's brother, Johnno. Mr Perry was in the store taking pineapples from a crate on tracks and piling them in a corner of the shop.

"Johnno doesn't work in the store," he told them. "He does odd jobs for me on the land out at Woodman's. You might find him at his hut, though. He's not working today. It's past the Diggers Arms, and further down the same road."

***

Hamish and Bellamy rattled out of town toward Tinana Creek. They crossed the wooden bridge and guided their horses along the bank. In the golden light of the morning, the water glistened, mirroring the clear blue sky. A gentle current swept lazily over the pebbles. Cries of colourful birds pierced the air. Kookaburras cackled at them as they rode past, while lorikeets flashed green and red through the muted grey of the gums. Wildflowers were dotted in clumps between ancient ferns. This was a place that held memories of a time before European settlement before the intrusion of industry. Old growth forest stood steadfast and defiant along the creek's edge.

When they approached the collection of buildings that made up the emerging township of Tinana, more a suburb of Maryborough than a town on its own, the grandeur of the post-office and the Diggers Arms Hotel seemed like an affront to the senses.

They then came across a large two storey brick house.

"That must be Perry's house," said Bellamy.

"Doing well from growing fruit," said Hamish.

A little further on they came upon a place that was little more than corrugated iron sheets stacked into a kind of lean-to arrangement. There was a man sitting by an extinguished fire, plaiting rope. He stood when their horse and buggy stopped.

"Good morning. I'm Sergeant Bellamy and this is Doctor Hart," called Bellamy climbing down.

The man stood with his hands at his sides and his eyes wary, showing no inclination to greet them. He was at least five feet eight inches tall, but his back was stooped from years of physical work. His face had the deep wrinkles and creases of a lifetime under an unforgiving sun. Hamish noticed his hands were calloused, his fingernails stained the colour of tobacco and his long-sleeved shirt, which might have been white once, was faded yellow and worn. Trousers of canvas were more patches than they were original material. The man looked at them with tired, slightly clouded eyes.

"We're investigating the killing of both Isaac Brown and Ruth Gowan," said Bellamy.

The man continued to stare at them, and Hamish wondered if he could see.

"We know Isaac and your brother were friends as youngsters and we wondered if you could tell us anything about them."

The man blinked in confusion.

It occurred to Bellamy this may not be the man they were looking for.

"What's your name?" he asked.

"What's that got to do with anything?" the man croaked.

His voice was thick and rasping leading Hamish to consider laryngitis or something more permanent. Was he Dutch from the accent?

"I apologise for the intrusion," said Hamish. "We want to find out who murdered Isaac Brown. Are you Johnno, Elijah's brother?"

"I am," said the man, still wary.

"We were hoping you could tell us about Isaac," said Bellamy, "particularly in his school days. We are interested in a connection between Isaac and your brother Elijah."

Johnno sat down and Hamish and Bellamy knelt at the other side of the makeshift hearth.

He poked a stick into the ash as he spoke. "Elijah and Isaac were friends when they were young," he said.

"Ruth Gowan also?" asked Hamish.

Johnno looked at him.

"Not Ruth Gowan then. It was Ruth Flemming. But yes, she was part of the group. They'd ride around the old mines together. Have races, fish in the creek. Ruthie was a 'what- you-call-it? A tomboy. One of the boys."

"Did the three of them have a falling out?" asked Bellamy.

"No. I heard nothing of that kind. Isaac was always old for his age. He started blacksmithing at ten."

"He wasn't even at school for most of the time they were friends. Elijah and Ruth would ride up and collect him after work. They would be riding around all afternoon in the bush."

"How did it end?" asked Hamish.

Johnno pushed a pile of ash one way and then the other creating a series of waves.

"They grew up and went their own ways," he said.

"Ruth married at sixteen. That put an end to the fun and games. They didn't see as much of each other after that."

"I'm struggling to find any connection between Ruth and Isaac that goes beyond their childhood friendship," said Bellamy. "Is there anything you can think of?"

Johnno shook his head slowly. "There was that rumour a while back," he said.

Hamish pricked up his ears. "What rumour?"

"When they were about twelve, Isaac, Ruth and Elijah came across a body in an old dried-up creek bed. They came racing back like they'd been struck with lightening. The police went out there and found an old miner, dead he was. The authorities reckon he must've been heading into town by foot and died of a heart attack. I expected the three of them to be full of themselves for months. They were always telling yarns, tall stories and the like. But they didn't this time. They went quiet after the authorities took the body. They spoke to the Police but wouldn't talk to anyone else. Isaac refused to talk about it the rest of his life. I always wondered what happened out there in that creek bed. But nothing ever came of it. The police were satisfied the old man died of natural causes. He had nothing on him and nothing of note was found at his camp. So that was that. An old miner, down on his luck."

Johnno picked a blade of grass from the edge of the hearth and placed it between his teeth.

He shook his head.

"The three of them changed after that. They kept to themselves more. I always had the feeling that something happened."

"Elijah's wife, Jakob's mother, where is she?"

"She's dead as well," said Johnno. "She left him when Jakob was small. Went back to Sydney to live. When Elijah died, I thought I should let her know, since they were still legally married. But her relatives told me she was dead twelve month, by then."

Hamish and Bellamy thanked the old man for the information and began the ride back to the station. They were both silent pondering the story of the children finding the corpse of a miner in a dry creek bed. Hamish tried to fathom how it might connect with the murders.

It certainly linked Isaac, Ruth, and Elijah, who was already deceased. But it was so long ago.

Chapter Sixteen

"One of the subjects which has of late occupied a good deal of attention is the "subjection of women;" the question of whether her place in human society is merely, and only that of the help-mate of man, whether for one sex, as for the other, we have a right to claim perfect independence of action and equal rights.

Much has been written about women's rights that has been foolish and vulgar. The effect of the establishment of the extreme doctrines would be to diminish her influence on society by making her less womanly. But the question remains whether with perfect consistency with womanliness there may not be properly opened to the weaker sex a much wider sphere of personal action.

The Rev. J.D. Davies writes on the "Advance of Women", by which he means the steps that have been taken in our generation for placing women on an equality with men. Absolute equality is not to be looked for since nature itself has made a difference between the sexes.

If there were no other point on which this difference must continue to exist there is that of physical strength. Women have not a frame capable of enduring the same kind of bodily and mental labour as men. There are also peculiarities in the female constitution unfitting them from at all times bearing with safety the same strain on the nervous system.

But whilst inferior in some qualities, there are others in which they have a naked superiority; for instance, in all occupations requiring fineness of touch and skill in manipulation. The question has of late been discussed with increasing earnestness whether women are to be denied the right of pursuing an independent vocation and career if they choose.

And certainly, the tendency of modern thought and practice has been to enlarge their liberty to recognise the fact that married life is not the only kind of life to which women may look forward; and since there are many women, in fact, who live and die unmarried, to open up to them new avenues by which they may pursue an honourable and useful existence." **South Australian Weekly Chronicle Saturday 26 December 1885.**

Nelly

Nelly hadn't made bread since Isaac's death. She had spent her days in the workshop furiously hammering out metal. For what purpose? She didn't know. There were no customers and no orders. No one had been near the workshop in days, other than the Police and Percival Wellington. But this morning she was in her kitchen thudding a flour, yeast and water mixture on the table with the same force she applied to metal. She knew the bread would be dense and hard as a result of this heavy handedness, but she didn't care. There was no one to eat it anyway, other than herself. When the dough had become so dense it would no longer stretch, she threw it into two loaf pans and put it in the oven. Then she flung herself onto a chair, her face flushed from the effort and an inner rage she had hoped to dispel with the thumping of dough. Her hair was as it had been when she rose from bed, only powdered white with flour. What was she going to do? She brushed the hair from her face with floured hands and spread more of the powder over her cheeks. This was no way to live. Each day was an agony of grief and frustration. She didn't sleep at night, and she was becoming emotionally and physically exhausted.

Her chin rested on her hands, her elbows on the table and numbness overtaking her.

She was afraid if she let go of the rage, if she succumbed to the numbness, she may never feel anything again.

As she contemplated that fear, she became aware of a rapping sound at the front door.

The door was already open, and when she lifted her head, she caught sight of her brother's tall frame standing awkwardly in the doorway.

She groaned. Why wouldn't people leave her alone? He was the second last person she wanted to see. She didn't greet him in the feint hope that if she ignored him, he would go away.

But she knew that was not going to happen. He would come in regardless of whether he was welcomed or not.

Once he was sure she had seen him, he waited for a few seconds politely, then he entered the hall and joined her at the table.

"You are a mess," he said. "You have flour in your hair."

"I know," said Nelly, sitting up with a sigh.

"You can't go on like this, it's not healthy."

"I know," Nelly repeated.

She held her hands together on the table twisting the small gold band around on her finger.

"You're coming home with me," said her brother with authority. "You shouldn't be alone. If I'd known how bad things were, I'd have insisted sooner."

Nelly looked him in the eye.

"I'm staying in my home," she said with determination that equalled his own. "I will make my own living here."

Her brother puffed out his chest and thrust his chin forward, his carefully pointed beard enhancing his attempt at dominance.

Nelly was unmoved by the display.

He stood up and marched from one end of the room and back again.

Another physical display to impart dominance.

"All right," he said at last, when it was clear Nelly was unlikely to concede to his authority. "But at least give yourself time to recover."

He sat back down and spoke in a gentler tone.

"Stay with us for a few weeks, longer if you need it. You'll feel better away from this place. You need people around you. You're going mad with grief here. Look at you!"

Nelly glanced down at her dress. White patches of flour covered the brown cotton. She looked around the room and saw that the white powder was all over the kitchen. Tears began to prick at her eyes. She had cried more in the last few days than she had in her entire life.

She was losing resolve. She leaned one elbow on the table and cradled her head. It would be easy at this point to let go of her pride and simply follow her brother out the front door. She would have no more responsibility, no more worry. She would be fed and cared for. Maybe, in time, she could conceive of a new life away from here.

Tears began to well up behind her eyes again. She took a deep breath. Then she saw a flicker of triumph in her brother's face. It wasn't anything tangible, yet it was undeniable. She instantly felt her strength returning. A life away from her home was not the life she wanted. She wanted to stay in the house she built with Isaac. She wanted to work, to earn her own way. She wanted independence.

She thought about a life dominated by her brother and sister-in-law, forced to sit through ladies' teas and sewing bees, and an acid taste formed in her mouth.

"I'm staying here," she said.

George opened his mouth, but Nelly cut off his protest.

"I'll get myself together, I promise," she said. "But for the Lord's sake give me time. It hasn't been a week since I lost both my husband and my closest friend. I need space."

"I should insist," said her brother.

A hollow laugh escaped Nelly's lips.

"What are you going to do? Physically drag me out of here?"

He looked for a moment as though he intended to do just that. Then the set to his jaw loosened.

"You have always been headstrong Nelly. You know your own mind and you won't be shifted. Know this, though, there is a limit to my patience. I'll be back in a few days to check on you and if I find you like this, I will insist you stay with us. I won't have the town saying I have neglected you."

Nelly smiled. "That's the point, isn't it? You are concerned about what the town is saying about you?"

George's lips twisted.

"Don't be cynical. Jacinta and I care for you. We are responsible for your welfare."

Nelly scoffed.

"Thank you," she said dryly. "But I am responsible for my own welfare."

He decided to take another tack with a lighter tone.

"I believe you are acquainted with Mr Percival Wellington," he said.

Nelly flashed him a venomous glare.

"He's very successful," her brother went on. "He expressed his concern, just yesterday at the Lodge. He was hoping you would move in with Jacinta and I, for a period," he added, then lowered his gaze.

Nelly's blood boiled. That man was trying to manipulate her through her brother now. That the two of them believed they could conspire to decide her future infuriated her.

"I have no interest in Mr Wellington," she said, her voice low and measured.

"I believe he has orchestrated the destruction of my business so that he can control me. I'll not be controlled." She glared at George, defiant and resolute.

George was silent for a moment while he assessed his sister's resolve.

"I suspect you have become paranoid, my dear," he said. "Still, we will put it aside for now." He brushed the flour from his trousers irritably.

"I can see there is no point in pressing the matter. You are quite impossible to talk to in this mood. I will be back in a few days. I expect we'll see you in church on Sunday?"

Nelly shrugged and her brother strode out of the house repeating the word, "impossible."

He hadn't been gone ten minutes when there was another knock at the door. She turned to see a small boy armed with a large bunch of impeccably formed pink roses.

"Mr Wellington said I was to deliver these," the boy said from behind the flowers.

Nelly wanted to shut the door in his face, but that wouldn't be fair to the child. So, she walked over, took the roses, and handed him a penny. She then closed the door and threw the flowers into the hearth. Soot and ash discoloured the petals immediately and she relished the sense of satisfaction that followed. They were too clean, too pale and they represented him.

She shook herself, washed, changed her dress, and combed her hair. She tied the usual bun at the back of her neck, not fashionable, but practical. Then she took the bread from the oven. It was golden brown on the top and smelled inviting.

She knew it would be tough, inedible probably. No matter, she would dunk it in soup later. She couldn't afford to waste the ingredients. There were potatoes and onions ready to harvest behind the workshop and she would have plenty of time to boil them into a sustaining brew.

***

With her face washed, hair tidied and a clean dress on she decided she might as well get out of the house. A walk in the fresh air might do her some good. She had to find a way to function, or her brother would force her into captivity in his household. It occurred to her she might call on Daisy, the Lutheran girl she had caught up with in church. Female company unlikely to tell her to marry Percival Wellington would be welcome. Daisy was young and joyful, her enthusiasm for life had not yet been suffocated by disappointment. Nelly was close to the girl's home when she came upon Daisy accompanying her younger sister from the store.

"Good morning," she said. "I was hoping to tempt you to join me on a walk along the river. But I see you have already taken exercise this morning."

Daisy's eyes lit up. "I'd love to walk with you," she said. She handed the parcels she was carrying to her sister and told her to hurry on home. "Tell mama I met up with friends," she said. "But don't tell her it is Nelly Brown."

Her sister grinned at Nelly and scurried off with the parcels.

They headed away from town winding along the narrow streets toward the riverbank.

Nelly's mood was buoyed by the skip in her young friend's step.

"When I first arrived in Maryborough, the town came as a shock," Nelly said. Daisy agreed.

"The houses aren't finished," she said. "All the exposed timber and open verandas. I thought that everyone was in the process of building houses. I couldn't imagine they were finished."

Nelly laughed. "It does feel as though nothing is permanent. There's no age to anything."

Daisy looked thoughtful. "You know, sometimes I feel disconnected to the ground, as though I might blow away in the next storm, with the dust and the leaves. And they are such strange dry trees."

"I know what you mean."

They enjoyed their shared wonder of this ancient land that was older than time, yet simultaneously shockingly new.

When they came into view of the river, Nelly breathed an audible sigh.

"The river calms me," she said. "It's wide and strong. I come to the riverbank whenever I have that unstable feeling."

Daisy stopped to contemplate the river.

"I like that it continues to flow regardless of the obstacles in its path," she said. "In floods, timber washes down the river, great portions of the bank subside into it, but on it flows, either carrying the debris with it, or tossing bits and pieces to the side."

Nelly realised this young woman was not frivolous though her mother accused her of it, but quite the opposite.

"You're right," she said. "The river doesn't surrender to the forces that oppose it; it adapts and finds a way forward."

Nelly realised the secret to her own dilemmas lay in patience and persistence.

The two women sat watching the movement of the water, gazing on as a steamer weighing many tonnes floated by as if it were a paper boat made by children.

The dappled sun fell on their shoulders through a canopy of trees overhead and Nelly felt the anger fall away.

They were both surprised to hear a man's voice cursing. To their left and back from the riverbank there was a two-story timber house with a well-maintained garden stretching down to the water. A man in a torn, faded military coat was cursing at an iron digging fork, the prongs of which were twisted and broken. He was sweating from the heat and Nelly wondered aloud why he didn't remove his woollen coat.

The man must have sensed people watching him because he stopped to look toward the riverbank.

Nelly and Daisy waved.

The man watched as two beautiful young women stood up from the grass and walked toward him.

"I'm sorry," he said. "Apologies for the language."

"I've heard worse." Nelly leant over to inspect the offending equipment.

"Your garden fork looks like it has given up the ghost."

"It has," said the man. "Hit a tree root. The thing is flimsy anyway."

"I'm Nelly Brown." Nelly held out her hand. "And this is my friend, Daisy."

"Jimbo Jenkins," said the man taking Nelly's hand and nodding to the younger woman. "I'm the gardener here."

Both women looked up at the house. It was whitewashed and gleaming in the shade of a stand of spotted gums. Idyllic. Nelly appreciated its beauty and thought about how it would feel to live in a grand house like this. She shuddered. She wanted to live in her house.

"I can fix it for you," said Nelly, looking at the fork. "Or better yet, make you a decent one."

The man began to laugh, and Daisy looked shocked.

"I'm serious," she said. "I'm a blacksmith. Properly trained. And good at it."

Daisy glanced at her friend in awe. "Mother said you learned your husband's trade," she said. "Although she made it sound like a criticism."

The man was silent. He was considering his broken fork.

"This one is good for nothing," he said. "If you can make me a new one that holds up, I'll have the owners here pay for it. And more besides."

"Will they give business to a woman?" Nelly asked.

"They won't know," said the gardener, grinning from ear to ear.

Daisy squealed in delight. "A customer!" She looked at Nelly with renewed pride.

Nelly suddenly realised that wealthy clients were unlikely to deal directly with the local blacksmith. Their staff would be the ones who knew her.

"That one is too small for you," she said. "You are a tall man you need a longer handle. I'll be back this time tomorrow with a decent garden fork for you Mr. Jenkins."

"Bring me an invoice for the bosses, I'll make sure you are rightly paid."

Nelly and Daisy returned the way they had come along the river, but this time their stride was full of purpose. "I'm so excited for you," said Daisy. "I didn't quite realise what being a 'blacksmith' meant. But now I know you can make ordinary things, like garden tools, I can tell all my friends."

"Please do," said Nelly. "It's not just garden tools though. I can make anything from metal. Pot, pans, fire pokers – anything for the household."

"You'll have all the work you can handle," said Daisy. "I'll make sure of it."

They parted ways and Nelly rushed home to the workshop to set to work on the garden fork. Her first customer.

She would work into the night if she had to. But it only took her a couple of hours and by the time the sun was setting she was finished. She held up a fork that was far sturdier than the gardener's previous one. There was no way it was going to break. It was solid, like her latest loaves of bread, she thought, and laughed heartily for the first time since Isaac's death.

Chapter Seventeen

"The Early History of Gympie Gold-Field: Gympie obtained its majority on October 16, for it was on that day in 1867 that James Hash reported at Maryborough his discovery of this goldfield. The history of the discovery is well-known to the oldest residents, but it may be appropriately related once more. In September 1867, Nash was making his way on foot to Maryborough from Nanango, where he had been digging with poor results, and one evening camped on a little knoll opposite to where the mall gully that takes its rise at the Caledonian Prospectors claim runs into the larger gully, known as Nash's Gully.

Whilst his billy was boiling for his evening meal, he took out his prospector's dish and tried some stuff from the smaller gully and obtained colours of gold. Next morning, he went to the main gully and sunk a small hole, from which he obtained during the day several ounces of gold. Overjoyed by his success, he removed all traces of his prospecting and proceeded to Maryborough, where he obtained rations and tools, returned to Gympie and did some further prospecting with such satisfactory results as to convince him he had found a genuine gold field.

He appears to have gone to Brisbane and sold his gold, returning via Maryborough to Gympie once more, and bringing with him one or more friends and a large supply of rations. After three or four days he travelled back again to Maryborough and formally announced his discovery to the sub-collector of customs. And here it may be remarked it was fortunate that he did so. He might have used the important information he possessed in such a way as to have monopolised the greater part of the area within the treasures of Gympie are contained.

The country was vacant crown land, the owners of adjacent stations not deeming it good enough for pasture, apparently, to include in their holdings.

Nash might have kept the discovery secret, taken up the country as a grazing run, with the aid of a capitalist, and in due time established even a greater monopoly than Mount Morgan. But to his credit, it can be said, he went to Maryborough and gave the alarm. The news was soon followed by the unearthing of the celebratory Curt's Nugget, which had such a magical effect that before the close of the year, between 15,000 and 20,000 people had been attracted from all parts of Australia. The finding of gold at Gympie marked a new era in the progress of Queensland." **The Australian Sketcher Thursday 29 November 1888.**

Hamish

Hamish and Bellamy rode through the heat of mid-morning back toward town. The river was full and blue under the pulsing sun. The sound of crickets filled the air around them to the extent that Hamish could not hear anything else. He was lost in the din and the heady smell of the mangrove swamp. Both were inflated by the searing heat of late summer. Sweat pooled around his collar and the back of his shirt was wet. He wondered if he would ever get used to the humid warmth of the north. Growing up in rural Victoria, with the blistering cold winters and searingly dry summers, he was unaccustomed to the persistence of summer and the heavy moisture in the air. He was attempting to loosen his collar when he became aware of Bellamy speaking to him.

"Do you think Ziggy and Arthur would know anything about the dead miner story?"

Hamish's thoughts returned to the two murders he was supposed to be investigating.

"We can only ask," he said.

By the time they reached the White Swan Inn, the lunch time crowd were leaving, and the hotel had become quiet again. The only patrons were a couple of old miners at the bar drinking.

Arthur brought two tankards of cold beer and settled Hamish and Bellamy at their usual table by the wall. He joined them and they relayed the story told by Elijah's brother.

Arthur nodded and scratched his forehead.

"I didn't know Ruth then," he said thinking through the new information, "or Isaac and Elijah. But I did hear about the old miner they found. Rumour had it that he had struck gold before he died, but no one ever found any so we all gave it up for talk."

One of the old men at the bar turned around.

"Do you want another round?" asked Arthur.

"We couldn't help but overhear your conversation," said the man. "Are you talking about the old fella Ruthie and her mates found out in the creek decades ago?"

"Yes," said Hamish. "Do you know anything about it?"

"Some say the kids found gold on him. Others say they killed him. The gold must've been on him because it weren't nowhere else."

"I've never heard that," said Arthur.

"It's just what they say," repeated the man.

"But where is it then?" asked Arthur defiance in his voice now. "Ruth has never had anything but what she got through her marriage."

His brow furrowed. "And Isaac and Elijah have never been flush with money."

"Aye," said the second man. "Where is it? That's the question."

He raised untidy eyebrows and wiped the beer froth from his beard.

Hamish grimaced then felt ashamed of himself for doing so.

"Do you think there is anything in it?" Bellamy asked Arthur.

He pursed his lips.

"I can't see it. Why wouldn't they have told anyone?"

"Why wouldn't they have cashed in the gold?" asked Hamish.

"If Elijah's wife had known or thought there was any truth in it, she would have demanded the money before she left him. If Arthur doesn't know, then Ruth told no one. What about Nelly? Do you think she knows of the rumour?" asked Hamish.

Rita came down the stairs of the Inn looking refreshed. "I've had a nap," she said. "The excitement of the last few days has quite worn on me."

"Just in time to help us speak to Nelly," said Bellamy. "We're heading over there now."

They arrived as the sun was going down and found Nelly leaving the workshop in a buoyant mood.

"I have a customer," she said.

Rita shrieked with delight. "You see, it will only take time. More work will come from it, I'm sure."

Bellamy was less sure, but he didn't want to be side tracked from his mission.

"We want to ask you some more questions about Isaac," he said.

Nelly led them into the house, and they sat while she lit the fire and set the kettle to boil.

When she joined them, Bellamy relayed the story told by Elijah's brother.

Nelly listened carefully.

"Have you heard this story?" asked Hamish.

"Yes. Isaac did tell me about the old man they found in the creek bed when they were children," she said. "It was a frightening experience for them. They were interviewed by the Police and people wanted to talk about it for days. Isaac didn't like talking about it. When he was a child, the memory gave him nightmares."

Hamish then went on to describe the rumour told by the men at the bar.

"People are saying the old man had gold, but it couldn't be found after his death. Some people say the children found it on his body and took it," Hamish said.

Nelly was shocked.

"Gold? Isaac never mentioned any gold. He would've told me. Where would the money have gone if they found gold?"

"Isaac didn't have any money when I met him. My understanding was that Ruth's money came through the marriage."

"That's what we understand too," said Bellamy. "We just wanted to check with you whether you had heard the rumour."

"No," said Nelly. "And I doubt it is true. The people around here who chase gold are mad. They see conspiracies everywhere."

"Trust me, I know," said Hamish. "My own parents among them. I grew up on the goldfields of Ballarat."

"If the three of them did find gold as children, they seem to be the only three who knew about it. Who would they tell?" said Bellamy.

Nelly said, "Isaac would only tell me."

Rita nodded in agreement. "I think Ruth would have told Arthur, if she told anyone."

Hamish bit his lip. "Arthur Kane says he knows nothing, and you don't know about it," he said to Nelly. "So, who would Elijah tell?"

"Presumably not his wife," said Rita. "If he had, she would have been looking for it after his death."

"What about Jakob?" said Bellamy. "Elijah could have told his son before he died."

They all looked at him with eyes wide as though they all had the same thought at the same time.

"We need to find Jakob," said Hamish.

Rita shook her head uncertainly.

"What's the point of finding him?" she said. "He won't admit to knowing about the gold. He obviously doesn't know where it is, or he would have it by now and be gone with it."

"How do you know he hasn't got it?" said Hamish.

Rita pursed her lips thoughtfully. "It must be a significant find. He would have to cash it in somewhere to obtain the money to get away from here. We would have heard about it. You can't use a nugget of gold to purchase a train ticket, or a ride on a steamer."

"Actually, you can in Maryborough," said Nelly. "But we would have heard about it if he did."

"Maybe we should concentrate on looking for the gold, rather than the lad?" suggested Hamish.

It was Bellamy's turn to look doubtful. "We don't even know there is any gold," he said.

"We can't waste time looking for something that may not exist."

***

Sergeant Bellamy returned to the police station to finish up for the day while Hamish and Rita set off for a walk down to the river front. They were walking past the courthouse when Hamish stopped. He screwed up his eyes to see across the street.

"There's Ryan," he said.

He pointed across the road to an old man waiting to cross behind a large dray carrying timber down to the wharf. The unmistakable scar made it obvious it was the miner they had met in Maryborough. The man scampered across the street toward them just in time to be missed by a buggy. He tripped at the edge of the street and almost fell right into them.

"Ryan," said Rita.

He pulled himself as close to upright as he could manage, not recognising them at first, but clearly knowing he had seen them before.

"Good day," he said, then glanced from Rita to Hamish and back again.

"Oh yes, my friends," he said. "We spent a pleasant couple of hours at the hotel in Gympie. How go you both?"

"We go well," said Hamish. "What are you doing in Maryborough?"

"I've come to see to some banking, financial matters. All done now. I'll return to the mines in the morning."

"Would you like to join us for a drink?" asked Rita.

Hamish wondered what happened to their walk.

The old man became animated at the suggestion of a drink that was to be paid for by anyone other than himself. The three of them entered the closest hotel and found a seat in a private area.

"We've found out more about Elijah," said Rita when they were settled with yet another cold beer each.

"We spoke to his brother, Johnno."

"Ah yes," said Ryan, sipping his beer.

"He told us about the body Elijah and his friends found when they were kids."

Ryan nodded. "Did he know anything more about it?" he asked casually.

"He said there was talk that the old man had found a significant amount of gold. He'd been bragging about it. But there was no gold found so no one knows if it was true."

Ryan sipped on his beer while Hamish silently willed him to keep his beard out of it.

"Did you hear anything about the gold?" said Hamish.

"There was talk," began Ryan slowly. "Elijah had gone about spruiking of a record sized nugget he'd found. Saying he was rich and all that. Mostly when he'd been drinking. But he never produced it. When it wasn't found after his death, some folks did say the kids had taken it. Plenty watched them over the years."

"Did he ever tell you about it?" asked Hamish. "When you saw him before his death, for example?"

Elijah cupped his beard in a gnarled hand and pulled downward smoothing the grey tangled mass.

"He said he'd had one stroke of luck in his life, but because of the way that it happened it were his life's curse instead."

"Did he tell you what it was?" asked Rita.

"Aye, he did. And I've not told a soul until now. But I have an inkling it might have something to do with these murders."

Ryan raised his rheumy eyes to meet theirs.

"He said that old man wasn't dead when they found him. He was close to it – but he weren't dead."

Rita gasped.

"The kids found him in the creek bed gripping that nugget like it was life itself. They took it from his grip. He had little fight left in his body but his mind were sharp. 'Curse you fuckin' little buggers,' he told them, or some such. Apparently, there was quite an argument. Elijah wanted to go for help, but Ruth didn't. She said he was nearly dead anyway. But this is Elijah telling the story, mind. So, who knows. Isaac was the youngest and according to Elijah, he was terrified, shaking and sobbing. Sort of frozen to the spot, like. Regardless, they stayed there watching that old miner until he died. The codger lived for another couples of hours Elijah reckoned, so they could have gone for help. But they didn't. The miner lay there watching them watching him, waiting to pass. Elijah says he had nightmares for years."

"Did he say what happened to the gold?"

"No. Not directly. He said that by the time they reached town, Isaac was unable to speak, Elijah was all jittery like he was possessed, and Ruth had lost her nerve. After answering all the questions from the police, they all spent a sleepless night seeing ghosts everywhere they looked. They were so consumed with guilt and fear they made a pact to hide the gold away and never speak of it again in case they were accused of murder. Isaac never gave Ruth the time of day after that. He wanted no part of it. Elijah blamed his bad luck throughout his life on the miner's revenge, like he was following him from the grave. Anyway, they made a pact, and they kept it. On his own death bed Elijah said he'd sacrificed an easy life to keeping that secret. But then he said that had he not kept it he would have been dead years ago, hung for letting that man die. Can't win in this world, he said, not either way."

Chapter Eighteen

"The Courier supplies the following condensed report of the debate in the Assembly on the employment of barmaids in hotels: -

Mr McFarlane proposed his new clause, which from commencement of the Act would make it unlawful for any license to employ any female, not being his wife or daughter, to sell liquor at any bar or counter, under a penalty not exceeding fifty pounds and the forfeit of the license. In the outset of his speech, the Honourable member made an onslaught on the "upstairs bars" in Brisbane and other towns. Few members were apparently aware of the evils which went on in these bars after hours at night. He had never been in one himself but had derived his information from a special commissioner who had gone through them all.

There were, his friends told him, little liberties in these upstairs bars which were not conducive to the moral or material welfare of the barmaids. His wish for the barmaids was that they be married and comfortably settled in life. He had nothing to say against them, and only desired their good, but he was quite sure no member of Parliament would like any female he had regard for to become a barmaid. The Hon. Member went on to talk of the scarcity of domestic servants and to argue that barmaids would not be thrown out of employment for they would get situations at once as servants." **Toowoomba Chronicle Saturday 10 October 1885.**

Nelly

Nelly watched the gardener as she approached the grand house by the river. He didn't look as old from a distance. His movements were swift and strong as he dug up a new garden bed in clay soil not far from the riverbank.

"Morning," she called as she came close enough for him to hear.

He stood his spade on its edge and looked up.

"Lovely day for it," he said.

Nelly handed over the new fork. The gardener inspected it closely, balanced it in his hands and swung it one way and the other.

"The missus says to order a new set of equipment, if I'm satisfied with the quality," he said.

"And are you satisfied?" asked Nelly.

"Very," he smiled.

The man went on to describe the items he required, and Nelly memorised the dimensions and functions confidently. He placed the new fork to one side of his garden bed and continued digging.

"This is perfect for raking over the soil when I'm done," he said. "Thank-you."

"I'll be back in a week with your order," said Nelly feeling triumphant.

She was smiling with every muscle in her face. This was her first customer without Isaac. She was certain there would be more if she was able to produce high quality work and remained competitive in her prices. Isaac had never pursued this type of domestic work because he had the contract with Walkers, but without that contract she would need to expand her scope. The domestic sphere may well be her market.

Full of new optimism Nelly ruminated on business prospects and ideas for promoting her work as she made her way back along the riverbank toward town. She decided to take the less public track through the trees and enjoy the shaded glimpses of the river as she walked.

She was rounding the bend to see the Mary River widen when she heard a crunch of leaves. Turning to see who was there, she tripped and stumbled. When she righted herself, she peered through the trees in the direction of the sound but saw no one. The trees rustled and whispered overhead but the path back the way she had come was clear.

She remained still and watched while a chill rose at the back of her neck. The familiar sensation of impending doom was creeping through her veins.

An electrical charge spread through her blood from one part of her body to the next until she was reverberating with an acute alertness. Nelly gripped her arms across the front of her body and squeezed. The anxiety that resulted from this sensation was crippling. She didn't experience it often but whenever she did, she knew something unwelcome was about to happen. She was still trying to shake the feeling when a familiar fruity fragrance filled her nostrils. She knew who was there before she turned to look.

"Good Morning," said Percival Wellington. "What a pleasure to run across you on such a beautiful morning."

Fury germinated in her stomach and travelled up her spine. What on earth would bring the insufferable man to this path, at this time of day?

"Are you following me?" she said.

Percival laughed.

"Don't be ridiculous. I've been visiting with Mr Harmon. I believe you sold his gardener some new gardening equipment."

"You have been following me, then," said Nelly.

"No. Dear Lady, I am on my way back to town from my meeting with Mr Harmon. He is a buyer with the State Government Railway Authority. I thought I'd take the river path rather than the road, and here you are."

"How did you know about my agreement with the gardener?"

"My goodness, why all the suspicion? I'm a friend, Nelly. And an admirer. Mr Harmon told me his wife had directed the gardener to place an order if he was happy with the work. Which I knew he would be. You are a sound craftswoman."

Nelly took a breath and willed herself to turn and walk on. She didn't want this man to walk with her, but she couldn't see how she might prevent it. She felt her heart beating in her chest.

"I really don't understand your antagonism toward me," said Percival.

That was too much. Nelly stopped and looked him in the eye.

"You tried to rape me," she said. "Is that not reason enough?"

A sneering laugh issued from somewhere deep within him and his face darkened.

"What an imagination you have," he said. "If you are talking about an incident of misunderstanding that occurred a decade ago, you are very much mistaken."

"There is no mistake," said Nelly quietly.

She turned away from him and began to walk.

"No," said Percival. A dangerous tone had crept into his voice. Nelly acknowledged the unmistakable threat in his demeanour.

"Don't walk away from me," he snarled. "I want this sorted out immediately. Once and for all time."

Nelly stopped again. Her instincts told her to run, but she was tired of pandering to this man and pretending nothing had happened. He was right in one thing. It was time for her to make absolutely clear her feelings toward him and squash any ideas he might harbour of a relationship between them. She was ready to confront him and put this aspect of her life behind her. There would be no clear path forward while the spectre of Percival Wellington and his veiled, and not so veiled, threats haunted her.

"You assaulted me," she said. "When I was young and vulnerable and barely able to defend myself."

"Oh, but you did, defend yourself, as I recall."

"Yes. I did so then, and I will do so even more effectively now," she said.

Her eyes were burning.

Percival Wellington had become a dark shadow as the rage within her burned.

She felt his hand reach out toward her breast and a black cloud descended. She reached back and clenched her fist, then swung her arm forward and punched him in the face with all her strength. She followed through with the momentum long after her fist had made contact with his cheek.

Percival Wellington fell to the ground, his skull making a sickening crunch as it hit a large rock at the side of the path. Nelly looked down at him as she felt the tingle of her blood returning to her arms and legs.

She didn't know what had just happened. For a moment she stared at him. As her senses returned it began to dawn on her what she had done. She leant over him and saw that his head was covered in blood and a red ooze was seeping across the rock. She touched him on the neck and knew with certainty he was dead. She purposely didn't check his eyes. In her mind, she knew they were open. She knew they held the same stunned look that Isaac's eyes had shown when she'd found him. She didn't want to see her own reflection in those cold eyes.

It occurred to her that she should be afraid, and she wondered that she wasn't. She was surprised to realise she didn't feel any emotion. A few moments passed, although it felt a lot longer that she stood staring at his lifeless body. Eventually she realised she was glad he was dead, even though she hadn't intended to kill him, only to repel his advance. She dusted off her dress and walked on toward town. Instead of stopping at her house she went directly to the police station where she found Constable Williams in attendance and told him what she had done.

Williams watched with wide eyes as she spoke.

"I'll need to keep you here," he said when she finished talking. "I need to get the Sergeant."

She followed him calmly to a holding cell. When he opened the door, she walked in and sat down on the narrow bed with her hands in her lap.

Williams locked her in and ran off to find Sergeant Bellamy.

Nelly waited calmly, surprised by her own lack of emotion. It can't have been more than ten minutes before Williams returned with Bellamy, Hamish, and Rita.

Bellamy separated Williams from the others to question the constable about the exact words Nelly had used in her confession while Rita and Hamish ran directly to Nelly's cell.

When they saw her sitting quietly on the bed, hands clasped and eyes as wide as saucers they stopped in their tracks.

"I'm not sorry," she said.

"Quiet," said Hamish looking around for prying ears.

"Tell us what happened," said Rita gently through the bars.

Nelly stayed where she was.

"I killed him," she said firmly.

Rita whistled a small breath of air through her lips.

"Did he try to assault you again?"

Nelly nodded.

"I had to put an end to it," she said.

Rita felt her cheeks burn. "I'll make sure they hear your side of the story," she said.

Rita looked pleadingly at Hamish, who was white with shock and fear for what might follow for the blacksmith's widow.

Nelly nodded almost imperceptibly.

Hamish

They returned to the Sergeant's office where Bellamy was organising for a team of men to go to the murder site.

"We need to go too," he said. "You'll need to see the body in situ."

"What about Nelly?" said Rita.

"She'll be safe until we get back."

They all climbed into the police cab and travelled to the beginning of the river path. "We'll have to walk, the rest of the way," said Bellamy. "The cab won't be able to traverse the path."

When they arrived at the site, Williams was there with three other men. They were guarding the body but had remembered not to tread too closely with their big boots.

"Good work," said Bellamy.

Hamish and Rita stepped lightly over to the body and saw that Wellington had a massive bruise on one cheek and a split in his skull where it made impact with a rock. Blood covered the rock and the ground around it. When they were satisfied, they nodded toward Williams and the men came together to carry the body to the road where a carriage was waiting to transfer him to the morgue.

Bellamy, Hamish and Rita returned to the police station in silence. No one wanted to think about what this would mean for Nelly.

Less than two hours after she had entered the police station, Nelly was brought into the Sergeant's office where he, Hamish and Rita waited.

Rita sat beside her and took her hand.

"Just tell us what happened, all of it, from the beginning," said Bellamy.

Nelly took a deep breath and began. "I think he followed me from the Harmon's House," she said. "I went there to deliver an order and decided to walk back along the river path. It's shorter than the road, and prettier."

She blinked and looked at Rita for encouragement.

Rita nodded for her to go on.

"He said he didn't follow me, but I believe he did. He must have seen me with the gardener. Anyway, he came up behind me, quite startling me. He said he didn't understand why I disliked him so. I reminded him he had assaulted me in the past. He laughed."

Nelly looked up at Rita. Hamish knew his friend would be seething with indignation on behalf of the young woman.

"He pretended it didn't happen," she went on. "He implied I was making it up." Her voice was pleading.

"I tried to walk away but he insisted we have it out."

Nelly watched her fingers as she twisted the gold ring Isaac had placed there during their wedding ceremony.

She spoke quietly but distinctly. "He put his hand out toward me...he has done so before and I knew he intended no good, so I punched him. I hardly remember it. I just took a swing and punched him as hard as I could in the face. I shouldn't have hit him that hard, but I was angry. I was so outraged that he felt he could do it again. Again, and again. Like it was his right. Like he was somehow entitled..."

Rita took her hand and squeezed it.

"That's it," she said. "He fell and hit his head. And now he's dead. I wish I could say I'm sorry. But I'm not."

Bellamy and Hamish looked at one another.

"I understand," said Bellamy. "You were defending yourself. But there will need to be an inquiry and a trial. Mr Wellington was an important man. The town will expect to know what happened. They'll expect a trial. But I think you'll be alright if you tell the truth."

Nelly was sent back to her cell and Williams was instructed to make her as comfortable as possible.

A few minutes later, Daisy ran into the station gasping for breath. "I came as soon as I heard," she said. "Can I see her?"

Hamish looked imploringly at Bellamy.

"I suppose so. For a moment."

Williams led her to Nelly's cell.

Chapter Nineteen

"Maryborough has many things which are of great interest. She is the proud possessor of the most extensive and complete foundry in the colony where molten iron runs in brilliant streams from fearful furnaces, where mighty hammers pound, pound, pound all day long, and where swarthy men ceaselessly move in and out of the bewildering maze of machinery with which the gigantic building is closely packed. She has also a mammoth sash and door factory which covers, I forget how many acres, and where a lady can obtain a collar wondrously cut out in the fashion of lace work from the sweet-smelling cedar by a machine as delicately and finely constructed as the work of her watch.

Maryborough has big sawmills where the musical whim of the saw is heard week in week out all year round. She has gardens in abundance and noble men and fine buildings. The town is cleanly kept and the Mayor is able to save the ratepayers money by turning out the gas in the public lamps shortly after midnight. The stream of life runs along very placidly in this town, and I am inclined to believe it is perfectly free from sin and scandal. The residents are respectable and their propriety of conduct worthy of emulation. The cablemen are truthful, the omnibuses are clean and the horses sleek and well fed. The hot pies sold are hot! There is an air of peace and tranquillity and of repose in Maryborough which is particularly gratifying."
The Brisbane Courier Thursday 16 October 1890.

Hamish

The Black Swan Inn was alive with chatter when Hamish and Rita entered the dining room. Hamish was convinced of a distinct drop in the noise when he and

Rita entered. Ziggy cleared their usual table for them by the wall, poured beer for all, and joined them. Arthur finished with the table he had been waiting and sat down as well.

"Is it true?" Ziggy breathed as she tucked her bustle out of the way to sit.

Hamish brushed the fringe from his eyes. "If you mean Percival Wellington is dead, then yes, it is true."

"I never liked him," said Arthur.

"What happened?" squealed Ziggy.

"Apparently, he followed Nelly onto the river path and tried to assault her. She punched him, then he fell and hit his head on a rock."

Arthur and Ziggy looked aghast.

"Assault?" said Arthur.

Ziggy pursed her glossy lips. "I wouldn't put it past him," she said.

"He has done it before," said Rita. "Nelly told me he almost raped her ten years ago when her and Isaac were first married."

An audible gasp came from Ziggy as she placed her hands over her mouth.

"She told Ruth about it, but no one else," Rita went on.

"Isaac would have killed him long before this, had he known," said Arthur.

"There was another incident not long ago. Then this approach on the river path. I imagine Nelly had had enough."

"I don't blame her," said Ziggy. "Men!" She threw her head back in disgust.

Hamish fiddled uncomfortably with his collar. He didn't want to be lumped in with this category of "men". And how did Ziggy identify so thoroughly with being female? Rita, on the other hand, accepted him as one of her own without question.

"I know," she responded with a conspiratorial wink.

Hamish was perplexed. What was this secret language that women used, a silent language that unified them through half-smiles, winks, nods, and flicks of the hair? And how is it that Ziggy could be included?

"How does this event link to the two murders?" asked Arthur, oblivious to the surreptitious asides of his companion.

"If Nelly told Ruth about the assault, she would not have remained silent, no matter how much Nelly asked her to. She might have confronted Percival, threatened to tell Isaac. I would be surprised if she didn't tell him."

"Yes," agreed Hamish. "There would have been a motive for Percival to kill both Ruth and Isaac to save his reputation."

"But why would he go ahead and threaten Nelly again?" said Rita.

Arthur scoffed. "That man thinks he is entitled to whatever he desires. He tormented the poor fellow who previously held his position at Walkers until he had a heart attack."

Ziggy leaned forward eagerly. "Percival was obsessed with Nelly. He killed Ruth so she wouldn't expose him, killed Isaac to get him out of the way. And then went after Nelly. It didn't occur to him that she'd reject his advances."

"I think he was sabotaging the blacksmith business," said Rita. "Nelly is convinced the order was delivered by Jakob prior to Isaac's death, but Percival insists it was not."

"The workers have confirmed to us that the order was delivered. But none of them had the courage to stand up to Percival."

"Is that the solution?" said Hamish looking at Rita. Percival killed Ruth and Isaac."

"It would be a tidy solution," said Rita.

"It would make it easier to clear Nelly's actions," added Hamish. "If Percival was known to be a murderer, people would be less inclined to convict Nelly for killing him. Easier for people to believe it was self-defence."

"It was self-defence," said Rita glaring at him.

"We know that" said Hamish "but will the town believe it?"

"We don't have any evidence to link Percival to either crime." Hamish was tentative, fearful of another scathing stare from Rita.

"We need to find some," she said. "Let's look around that shed again. I still don't understand what Ruth was doing out there in the middle of the night. We know the acid was stored in the shed, maybe the killer left something behind that can identify them. Or maybe Ruth left something that would indicate why she was out there."

"I'll woman the bar," said Ziggy. "You go help them. She shoved Arthur toward the door.

Hamish, Rita and Arthur walked down the lane beside the inn to the shed, where Arthur unlocked the padlock.

"This shed was never locked before the murder," he said. "I didn't think there was anything of value in here."

"There probably isn't," said Hamish.

They threw the doors open to let in what light they could. Even so, it was too dark to see all the items piled in the shed clearly. They each took a quarter to concentrate on. Hamish was responsible for the corner with the hay and the acid container. He carefully swept the fallen hay aside with his hands to see if there was anything other than acid on the ground. He lifted the leather harness and the riding crop and examined them, releasing into the air a pungent scent of dust and oil. He sneezed.

"Bless you," said Rita from the other side of the shed.

"Anything?" Hamish said.

Rita shook her head. "A pile of old trunks stacked into one another. I'm pulling them out one by one to look."

"Nothing here," said Arthur. "The parts for that old buggy are scattered around. It looks like Ruth's husband was working on it before he died. He pulled it apart but didn't get a chance to put it back together."

"What's this?" Rita said quietly.

Hamish came over to her to see.

She placed the last of the cases on the ground. Beneath the crates a wooden pallet became visible.

"That would have been put down to protect the cases from moisture on the ground," said Hamish.

"Help me lift it," said Rita. "I think there's something underneath."

Hamish was about to ask if that was necessary when Rita lurched one end of the pallet off the dirt. A hole in the rough shape of a square was revealed.

Hamish dragged the other end away from the hole and the three of them stared into it.

There was something dark at the bottom, at a depth of about two feet.

Hamish and Arthur reached in and felt the cold surface of a metal box. With some shuffling of the box, they managed to lift it out of the hole and place it on the ground.

"A metal box," said Hamish, "It's pretty beat up." He brushed away the dirt. A metal strap wound around the box, secured with a crude weld to keep it shut. Hamish shook it and was assured by the clatter that there was something inside.

They looked around for something they could use to cut the strap.

"What about this?" said Rita, handing Hamish a chisel she found on the seat of the old carriage.

Arthur handed him a hammer and he used it to belt his way through the metal strap. It gave in easily.

Their eyes met nervously, no one quite ready to open the lid.

"Could it be the gold?" whispered Rita, even though there wasn't another soul in earshot. She stared back at the box. "It couldn't be...I mean it could be anything..."

"Or it could be gold," said Hamish. "Think about it. Three children find something valuable on an old man. They're afraid to tell anyone because they might be accused of stealing, or worse killing the man. They might hide it until later when the fuss dies down."

Rita swallowed.

"So, this box might contain the legendary gold nugget?"

"It might," said Hamish.

He looked at Arthur for a decision.

"Open it."

Hamish carefully lifted the lid to reveal the largest nugget he had ever seen.

The three of them gasped out loud.

Hamish's hands were trembling.

"What do we do now?" said Arthur.

Hamish thought about it. "This might still be the reason behind the murders of Ruth and Isaac," he said. "We'll remove the nugget for safe keeping but put the box back as it was. We need to think this through. We might be able to use it to lure the killer."

Hamish pocketed the nugget while Arthur put the box back in its nest and replaced the wooden pallet and the cases on top of it. They made sure they left no sign of having moved anything. Rita scattered more dirt onto the pallet where she had disturbed it. Arthur carefully locked the shed behind them.

"Not a word to anyone," warned Hamish.

Rita stopped. "We need to tell Bellamy."

"Of course, we will. We'll have to give him the nugget to lock in the police safe." Hamish took her arm gently and led her forward. "Let's talk on the way. We need to talk this through beyond any listening ears."

"Could Percival have known about the gold?" asked Rita.

"I doubt it," said Hamish. "None of the three who knew had any reason to confide in him."

"That's disappointing," said Rita. "I wanted him to be the murderer."

"Percival was a bully, but I don't believe he was a murderer," said Hamish.

"Arthur was genuinely surprised when we found the box."

"Yes. I don't believe he knew of its existence, or that the gold was anything more than a legend. But we can use this to our advantage. If we were to let it get out that we had a tip there was an old box somewhere in the barn that might contain the missing gold, maybe the killer would come looking for it."

"Do you believe the gold is the link between the murders?" said Rita.

"I do. I think the killer tried to get Isaac to reveal its location. When he refused, he killed him. Then Ruth was the only one left who knew about it. He probably lured her to the shed to pressure her into telling him where the gold was hidden. Obviously, she refused to tell him, and he took the only thing to hand to torture her into revealing the secret. He probably didn't expect her to die. He wanted to break her resolve."

"Who would have known about the gold at all?" asked Rita.

"I can think of two people immediately," said Hamish. "His son, Jakob for one, and that old miner Ryan for another. They both visited Elijah shortly before his death."

"We have to tell Bellamy," said Rita.

"I agree. The more I think about it, the more it fits. We'll tell Bellamy and establish a plan."

***

By the time they made it to Bellamy's office, Nelly's brother George was waiting there.

He threw his hands in the air. "What the devil is going on? I've heard that Wellington is dead, and my sister is in custody."

Bellamy flashed a sidelong glance at Williams who had the decency to blush.

"I thought he should know, sir," he said.

Bellamy sighed resignedly.

"You heard correctly," he said. "Your sister has confessed to killing Mr Wellington."

George slumped into a chair looking at the sergeant with a mixture of desperation and confusion.

"How?" he said. "Why?"

Bellamy sat down behind his desk and gave an account of the assaults. He relayed Nelly's confession using words as close as possible to her own.

George's lower lip trembled. "I don't believe it," he breathed.

"Which part?" asked Hamish. "The part about the string of assaults? Or the part about killing Wellington?"

George held his hair back from his face with both hands. "Any of it," he said. How could any of this be happening? I know my sister is head-strong, but she wouldn't kill anyone."

"Not even in self-defence?" said Rita.

"I'm afraid there is no doubt," said Bellamy. "She came to the station of her own will and confessed."

George shook his head. "Can I speak with her?"

Bellamy glanced at Hamish and Rita.

Hamish shrugged.

"I think not," said Bellamy at last. "Not for now. Let me investigate further and get back to you. Perhaps you can see her tomorrow."

George put his palms forcefully down on the desk. "I want her released into my custody," he said. "She can stay under my care until a trial – or whatever happens next. Nelly is no murderer. She shouldn't be here in a cell." His face was contorted.

"That won't be possible at this stage," said Bellamy. He stood holding the door open indicating to the man that it was time for him to leave. "Go home and return tomorrow when we know more."

George rose reluctantly and walked out in silence.

"I don't think Nelly will want to be released into his custody," said Rita.

"Maybe she will after a night in the cell," suggested Bellamy.

Rita's head tilted to one side. "I don't know, she is pretty tough."

Bellamy scratched his head. "You two go to the morgue and examine the body. See if there is any evidence at all that could shine light on the incident one way or the other. I'll meet you at the White Swan for dinner tonight."

Hamish hesitated.

"What is it?" asked Bellamy. "It's not like you to be slow to take up a trip to the morgue."

Hamish pursed his lips but decided to let the jibe slide.

"This morning Arthur, Rita and I decided to take another look in the shed behind the inn," he began.

Bellamy put down his pencil and sat up straight.

"We found something," said Rita.

Hamish took the nugget from the carpet bag he was carrying it in and put it on the sergeant's desk.

Bellamy's eyes lit up. "Good Lord! Where was it?"

"In a metal box hidden under a stack of rubbish. The box was at the bottom of a deep hole covered with wooden pallets," said Rita.

"I've been thinking we might use the rumour of the gold to flush out the suspect for Isaac and Ruth's murders," said Hamish.

Rita and Bellamy listened while Hamish shared his plan.

"We'll have Ziggy gossip with the patrons at the White Swan Inn about how she has been told the three children did steal gold from the old miner years ago and they hid it in the shed somewhere. Then we wait for the killer to come looking for the gold."

Sergeant Bellamy nodded thoughtfully. "We'll wind up with half the town in the shed looking for the gold. How will we know if we have the killer?"

"They will have to have known about the existence of the gold beforehand to have committed the murders. We eliminate anyone who couldn't have known Isaac and Ruth. Also, they needed to have the opportunity to carry out the killings. After that we'll need a confession, I suppose."

"For my money, the only two people who Elijah is likely to have confided in are Ryan and Jakob, both of whom saw him in the days prior to his death."

Rita gasped. "The killer may well have scars on their hands," she said.

The others stared at her. "Chances are good they will have been burned at least minimally by the acid."

They agreed they would wait twenty-four hours before setting the trap to give them time to establish enough officers to keep an eye on the shed. Hamish and Rita left Bellamy securing the gold nugget in the station safe.

***

At seven that evening, Bellamy, Hamish and Rita were seated in the dining area of the White Swan Inn. Ziggy served three plates of piping hot roast lamb to the table. Ravenous, they tucked in, while several coy glances from Ziggy alerted them that she was keen for information about what had happened that day. The rumour mill had clearly been working and most of the town knew the basic facts about the death of Percival Wellington by this time.

Bellamy avoided Ziggy's glances and Hamish kept his eyes on his plate.

Rita nodded and winked.

Eventually, Ziggy got the message that there would be no gossip that evening and busied herself with her other customers.

It wasn't until the meal was finished that Bellamy wiped his chin and brought up the question of the autopsy.

"What did you find?"

"Nothing," said Hamish.

Bellamy waited.

"Nothing new," he corrected himself. "The engineer died from blunt trauma to the skull caused by a fall and hitting his head on a rock. The rock remains in situ at the site, and examination of the site confirms that Nelly did not pick the rock up to strike him."

"He indeed fell and hit it as she says. He did sustain a significant blow to his face, though. She packed quite a punch."

"She has strong arms," said Bellamy "from a decade of hammering iron. I'm sure she punched him hard, particularly if she was afraid."

"There is no evidence that she meant to kill him or did anything more than repel his advances," said Hamish.

Bellamy listened carefully.

"It clearly wasn't murder," said Rita. "How could she have known he would hit his idiot head on a rock?"

Bellamy poured himself a glass of red wine from a carafe Ziggy had brought to the table unasked. Though she had accepted that they weren't ready to willingly share information about the killing of Percival Wellington with her, it didn't stop her from finding every excuse possible to come to the table to listen in on the conversation.

When their plates were empty, Arthur came to the table to clear them. He leant over Bellamy's shoulder.

He said in a conspiratorial tone, "Three workers from Walkers came in this afternoon. They said they witnessed Wellington's assault on Nelly at the New Year's Eve celebration. They're prepared to testify in court."

Rita swallowed a large mouthful of wine. "I'll testify in court," she said. "I'll repeat the story she told me and the fact that she told the same story to Ruth Gowan before her death."

Arthur cleared the table and returned to the kitchen.

"I'll talk to the magistrate in the morning," said Bellamy folding the napkin on his lap. "It's not for us to decide what she should be charged with, or indeed whether she should be charged with anything. Your testimony will be of great value in court," he said to Rita. "Let's hope it doesn't come to that."

Bellamy stood up. "Have a good night's sleep," he said, and headed upstairs to his room.

"Do you think there's a chance Nelly could be given a lesser charge than murder?" Rita asked.

"I hope so," said Hamish. "I don't know enough about the law to say. But a man's common sense tells him that there was no intent to kill."

Hamish and Rita finished the last of the wine and followed the sergeant's lead.

***

The following morning Hamish and Rita arrived at the police station to the sound of raised voices. Bellamy was in his office arguing with Nelly's brother, George.

"I've spoken to the magistrate," George was saying. "He has agreed that Nelly is to be released into my custody."

"I understand that, but Nelly is refusing the arrangement."

"Is there anything we can do to help?" said Hamish interrupting the two men whose voices had become strained.

Bellamy sat down at his desk and tried to take control of the situation from there. "A lot has happened this morning," he said. "The magistrate has agreed that Nelly is not a danger to the public at large and ought to be released into her brother's custody awaiting charges and a trial."

"That's excellent news. Isn't it?" said Hamish.

Bellamy threw his head back in frustration. "It would be, except that Nelly is refusing to go. She insists on staying in the watch house unless she is free to return to her own home."

Hamish looked to Rita.

"I'll talk to her," she said.

"For pity's sake, talk some sense into her," said Bellamy.

"I don't understand why this is necessary," said George. "The magistrate made a ruling and Nelly must abide by it. Unlock the cell and I'll take her with me."

"You intend to drag her out of here?" said Rita.

"If necessary," replied George.

Rita dismissed him with a wave of her hand and pushed past the men. She looked to the back of the room for Constable Williams. "Let me in," she said.

Williams immediately did as he was bid and allowed Rita entry to the cell. Hamish followed her.

Rita sat on the bed by Nelly's side, while Hamish leant against the cell door.

Nelly's skin was pale and her eyes dull. She looked as though she hadn't slept.

"Talk to me," said Rita.

Nelly turned her face toward Rita. "I don't want to go with George," she said. "If I can't return to my home I'll stay here."

"But why? George seems genuinely concerned about you. Surely you will be more comfortable at his home than you are here in this cell."

Nelly's eyes brimmed with tears.

"If I go with him now, I'm afraid I will never be free of him."

Rita hesitated while she thought about that.

"Is he cruel to you?"

Nelly shook her head vigorously. "No," she said. "He isn't cruel. But he doesn't understand my desire to live independently. He won't allow me to work. He will be bringing home matches to marry me off before long.

She made a small noise like a chuckle.

"Although that might be a challenge even for him, now."

Rita nodded and glanced across at Hamish. He gave a slight nod to his head to indicate he understood the irony.

"Even if I am acquitted of this killing, I'll never be able to fit into George's idea of society," Nelly went on.

Hamish heard footsteps approaching and turned around to see Mr Hawking, the Walkers Director, walking toward them. Williams was one step behind. He shifted past the director to unlatch the gate.

"You have another visitor Mrs Brown," he said. He kept his head down as he moved out of the way so the Walkers Director could enter. Williams nodded to Hamish and left them. It was becoming crowded in the tiny cell.

Nelly looked alarmed.

Hamish wondered what Mr Hawking wanted to say to the woman who killed his Senior Engineer.

"Sergeant Bellamy has told me the circumstances of the incident yesterday," he said.

"I want you to know that I will support you through this ordeal. The men have informed me of Mr Wellington's attempt to defraud you out of the money owed to you, and they've also told me they have knowledge of his advances. Several men witnessed his actions at the New Year's Eve celebration and Bellamy tells me there have been more significant attempts at assault in the past. Mr Wellington had no legitimate reason to be on that path, other than to torment you. I will stand in court and say so."

Nelly looked stunned for a moment then said, "Thank you."

"I've always had the deepest respect for Isaac, and for you, Nelly," he said, and bowed his head slightly before leaving them.

Hamish, Rita and Nelly sat in stunned silence for a moment, then Bellamy approached the cell.

"On discussion with Mr Hawking, the magistrate has agreed to let you return home while charges are being considered, Bellamy explained. The magistrate is reluctant to have you charged with murder, but manslaughter is being considered."

Nelly bowed her head.

"However," Bellamy continued, "for manslaughter to be charged, the act that caused the death must breach the law."

"It is not clear that punching a man who is trying to assault a woman is a criminal act, in and of itself. In any event, the magistrate does not believe you are likely to run, so you may return home awaiting charges and a trial."

"How has my brother taken the news?" asked Nelly.

Bellamy hesitated. "He's not happy," he said at last.

He stood beside the cell holding the door open for Nelly to leave, while Rita assisted her to stand up. Rita walked with her arm in arm, to steady her as they made their way past the office where George stood watching. She gave him a weak smile on her way past. He stood upright and stiff, his jaw tight.

Hamish and Rita stayed with Nelly all the way to the house.

"Take the evening to let events sink in," said Rita when Nelly was settled. "Are you all right alone?"

"I prefer it," said Nelly.

Rita didn't question the truth in her claim.

"I honestly didn't want to kill him," she murmured. "I just wanted him to know I would not tolerate his advances another second."

"I know," said Rita.

Hamish and Rita left Nelly to take in her new reality. There was a lot to process.

"Do you think there will be a backlash?" asked Hamish when he and Rita were alone. "Remember how the town reacted when the plantation manager was killed in Logan a couple of years ago?"

Rita shook her head. "This is different," she said. This concerns a white woman, not a South Sea Island labourer."

"I hope you're right. Bellamy has arranged for a constable to keep an eye on the house overnight. In case of trouble."

***

Hamish and Rita returned to Nelly's house the next morning to check on her. When they arrived, they heard the familiar tapping from the workshop. Nelly was already at work.

They went through to the workshop to find her at the anvil.

"I have this order to complete," she said when she saw the look of surprise on their faces.

"We won't keep you from your work," said Rita. "We wanted to check you have recovered. And we see that you have."

They left her heating metal in the forge.

Chapter Twenty

"'I'm off to Pialba,' was the usual answer to the query frequently uttered last week, 'where are you going to spend the Christmas Holidays?' On Saturday afternoon and early Sunday morning the long procession of buggies and horsemen down the Pialba Road proved that very few had failed to carry out their intention, and from its dull and sleepy quietude of the preceding weeks, our excellent watering place woke up on Sunday morning to find a large and lively population temporarily settled all along the esplanade from Urangan to Point Vernon.

The weather during the holidays was most eccentric in its peculiar changes. The exodus from Maryborough was made in bad weather with sloppy and boggy roads. It cleared up at Pialba on Saturday morning and rain did not fall again until Tuesday afternoon just as the majority of people were returning home, and the result was that, with the heavy traffic, the roads were cut up to such an extent they were impassable in some places, and the long miserable ride home took much of the pleasure off the whole trip.

Every house on the Bay was crowded and the two Hotels, Hunter's and Antcliffe's were in the same condition, while here and there in the paddocks adjoining were pitched a number of tents principally occupied by parties of young men enjoying the novelty of 'roughing it.'

During the stay there was no lack of pleasant pastimes. Programmes of horse and foot races were drawn up and carried out on the beach at low tide. Plenty of fun and no small amount of betting resulted therefrom. A number of members of the town band visited Pialba and serenaded along the esplanade, also playing for a number of dances at Antcliffe's on Boxing Night. A number of bonfires were lighted on Christmas Eve at different spots along the Bay and produced a very pretty effect. Amongst numerous other sources of pleasure were fishing parties, riding parties, and delightful swimming in which the majority engaged at every high tide.

The one great feature which all were prepared for-either to support or studiously avoid-was the bazaar held in the Nondenominational Church in aid of that building. Inside the building a pretty sight was disclosed. The walls were prettily decorated, and the stalls were heavily laden with an indescribable array of fancy articles, bric-a-brac and toys. The public were soon surrounded by a bevy of young ladies whose object it was to plunder their victims by inducing them to go in for this or that raffle at extortionate amounts. Any tendency on the part of the poor subject to wince at the demand, or back out of the raffle was quickly overcome by a winning smile and a little coaxing. **Maryborough Chronicle, Thursday 29 December 1887**

Hamish

Hamish and Rita returned to the White Swan Inn and settled into their usual table. Ziggy offered tea, but it was a hot walk from the Blacksmith Shop. "Freshly made lemonade?" she suggested, and they nodded enthusiastically. They drank quietly watching Ziggy flounce across the room with a jug of beer and flop herself down among a group of miners in town to refurbish supplies.

She participated in playful banter and sideways comments at her expense for some time before easing into her task. Leaning over the table, she spoke in a secretive tone and immediately caught the attention of the men.

"We had an old miner in last night," she whispered, "he was asking questions about the inn, like how long the building has been here."

The men all leaned in to listen.

"I told him it was farming land prior," she said.

"Aye, that it was," said one of the men.

"But he was particularly interested in the shed at the end of the lane."

"Aye, the shed outback predates the Inn," said another of the men.

Ziggy sat in one of the vacant chairs and leaned in even closer. The men did likewise.

"The miner said there is talk of hidden gold at the inn somewhere, they say it is in the old shed. He says his friend Elijah told him about it before his death."

Ziggy's eyes grew large, and she glanced around the room as if to ensure no one was listening. "We've had a quick look in the shed this morning, but we couldn't find anything." She looked around the room again.

"The gold will be there," she said. "When we have more time, we're going to go through that shed with a fine-tooth comb."

She picked up one of the men's drinks and took a sip, watching the others over the top of the glass.

Their eyes were bright with curiosity.

"Bellamy's right, half of Maryborough will be pulling that shed apart," Hamish whispered to Rita.

"It won't do them any good," she smiled. "Let's hope one of them is the killer."

Hamish swallowed the last of his sherry.

"How long do you think we'll have to keep watch?"

Rita tapped her glass.

"I don't imagine it will take long for the gossip to reach Ryan's ears. Jakob, I'm less sure about. Who knows where he is."

"We should go back to the station and see if Bellamy has organised the watch for tonight," said Hamish placing his empty glass on the table.

As they were about to stand up, two strangers came into the bar and took a second glance at Ziggy. One of the men was tall and slim with lanky hair down to his shoulders. The other was stocky and bald, without eyebrows or any hint of hair on his face, he had a permanent startled expression. The strangers bought drinks and joined the table where Ziggy and the local men sat. They pulled chairs from an adjacent table and pushed themselves into the group.

"What have we here?" said the tall stranger.

Everyone at the table was silent.

"It's not a woman at all, is it? It's one of those queers, you hear about."

Ziggy kept her eyes down.

Hamish and Rita could feel the tension emanating from the table.

"What's yer name queer?"

Ziggy kept her head down and stood, ready to leave them.

"Wait on," said the second man grabbing her by the wrist. "Where do you think you're going?"

Ziggy froze.

He tugged her hard and she fell into his lap. Ziggy strained to pull away from him, but he wrapped his arms around her waist and tightened his hold.

Hamish stood up and approached the table. At the same time the local men at Ziggy's table also stood.

"Let her go," said one of the local men, his voice low and steady.

The stranger further tightened his grip while Ziggy struggled.

"Want the queer for yerself, do yer?"

Just as Hamish registered the sneering scowl on the newcomer's face, a fist appeared seemingly from nowhere and smashed into it, knocking the stranger backward and releasing two of his teeth. Freed of her captor, Ziggy darted behind the bar.

Arthur, who had swung the surprise punch stood his ground as the stranger stumbled to his feet wiping blood from his mouth. His bald companion helped him to his feet then looked ready to belt Arthur. But the four men at the table and Hamish moved forward. The strangers, the tall one already nursing his jaw, weighed their chances in a fight against five men and decided they didn't like the odds. They left the inn, upsetting empty chairs as they did so.

Rita helped Hamish set the chairs right and then went to the bar to check on Ziggy. Her hands trembled as she wiped glasses that were already clean.

Rita's eyes softened.

"You would think I'd get used to it," Ziggy said with a weak smile.

Arthur put his arm around her shoulder. "You'll be right, girl. Those blokes as have known you all your life won't let any harm come to you."

***

That night Hamish lay awake on his bed thinking of Williams and the other constables assigned the task of watching the shed. He tossed and turned listening for every sound of disturbance outside. Williams had been instructed to blow a whistle if Ryan or Jakob showed up. Anyone else, they were to watch and wait.

By three in the morning, Hamish fell into a deep sleep, nonetheless by six he was awake again. There had been no activity through the night, but Bellamy was pounding on his door, calling out his name. Hamish had slept in his clothes so he would be ready for any action that might occur in the shed. He stumbled to the door rubbing the sleep from his eyes.

"What's going on? Is someone searching for the gold at this time of the morning?"

"No," said Bellamy. "I've heard from the police station at Pialba that Jakob was seen drinking at the hotel there last night. He's been asking around for work out that way. I've asked them to bring him into the Pialba station and I need you and Rita to go out to the bay to interview him. The coach leaves in half an hour."

Hamish struggled to take in the information this soon after being woken from a deep sleep.

"Pialba? Isn't that miles away?"

"It's not that far. You'll be there by lunchtime, but you need to get ready to leave. The coach is waiting. I've arranged accommodation for the night at Antcliffe's Hotel."

"Overnight? But what about the plans here?"

"Don't worry. I have several constables watching the shed. If anyone turns up here, we'll be waiting. I need you two in Pialba."

At that point Rita's head appeared over Bellamy's shoulder.

"Are you ready, Hamish?" she said.

"I've already filled Rita in," said Bellamy.

Hamish shook off his reluctance and grabbed his coat.

"I suppose we should go then."

A carriage and four horses waited for them outside. Hamish couldn't help feeling excited about being off on another adventure with Rita. As the carriage rattled along the rough road toward the coast, it jolted over corrugations and slipped through boggy gullies. The rain from a week earlier coupled with the week-end traffic had impacted the road badly. The trip was slow, but Hamish and Rita's mood soared as they travelled across the landscape toward a place they'd never been. They enjoyed nothing more than new experiences, in the company of one another.

"Have you thought more about Bellamy's offer?" asked Rita as they passed Scrub Hill.

"I told you. I'm going to build my general practice," said Hamish.

Rita stared at him until his skin tingled.

"Are you, though?" she said.

Hamish shifted in the seat as they hit a deep gully.

"It's what I came to Brisbane to do," he said.

"Yes, but you have been doing more running around investigating murder, than you have general practice," she said.

"I didn't choose to be a medical investigator. It chose me in some ways."

"Perhaps you should go with it," suggested Rita. "Have you given Bellamy your decision?"

"I told him I'd let him know at the end of this case."

"It must be playing on your mind, though."

Hamish could no longer hide the frustration from his voice.

"Actually, I wasn't thinking about it all until you brought it up."

Rita smiled and watched the tangled scrub from her window. They didn't speak again as the carriage rattled and jostled along through mile after mile of bush. The clacking of crickets and the oppressive heat filled the space within the carriage. Warmth, the rhythmic movement of the carriage and the monotony of the landscape threatened to put Hamish to sleep.

When they finally saw the first glimpse of the bay glimmering against the horizon, Hamish realised he had indeed, nodded off. As the scrubland opened out onto the most exquisite bay Hamish had ever seen, all sense of sleepiness disappeared, and the excitement returned. Now that they were closer to the coast the landscape was defined by sugar cane for as far as the eye could see. The carriage carved through the tall cane on either side almost up to the coastline.

When they finally stopped, it was in front of a small cottage stood on ground that was completely devoid of grass. The cottage was pretty, but the land around it was barren, in contrast to the lush paddocks of green in the distance.

"This is the police station," said the driver. "I'll take your bags on to the hotel."

It was clear that Hamish and Rita were expected to leave the coach, so they climbed out, surprised by the strange feeling of solid ground under their feet after the bumpy ride. A young man of similar age to Constable Williams greeted them.

"I apologise for the state of the garden," he said. "We have had a plague of caterpillars."

"Caterpillars?" said Ria looking around at the bare earth.

"Yes," he said. "They've carried off every blade of grass."

"I'm astounded that such tiny creatures can execute such havoc," said Hamish.

"Come in, doctors."

They followed him into the cottage which consisted of a drawing room at the centre and two additional rooms either side. At the back there was a kitchen and outside two substantial cells in a single block.

The place was pleasant. It was clear that the constable lived there.

"I have men out picking up Jakob now," he said. "He has been staying with acquaintances near Polson."

Hamish and Rita nodded. They sat down in the drawing room and accepted the tea offered, while chatting amiably about the area. The constable told them that a new mail service had begun only recently, so that now there was horse mail from Pialba, via Torquay, Urangan, Booral, the Old Telegraph Line, Doolong Hill and Chapel Road then back to Pialba. A round trip of about twenty miles. Hamish and Rita made sounds to indicate they were impressed. As the clock ticked over, it became apparent that there was some delay in bringing Jakob in for questioning.

"I might ride out and find out what is holding events up," said the constable at last. "Why don't you take a stroll down the esplanade. It's quiet now being late in the season, but there are still some holiday makers about. The view is superb."

He looked at the clock on the mantle.

"It should be high tide. There will be swimmers out."

Hamish and Rita were glad to get out of the room and stretch their legs.

***

It only took a few minutes to walk to the esplanade and they followed it north along the bay. The water was clear and inviting, with many swimmers taking advantage of the cooling effect of the sea. A light breeze took off the edge of the worst of the heat as Hamish and Rita enjoyed the view. There were a few impressive terrace houses along the beach front, and they could see a hotel in the distance that they assumed would be their accommodation for the evening.

Further along the esplanade they noticed a small gathering of women, all dressed splendidly in white gowns of cotton and lace, two of them holding pretty parasols perfect for a beach stroll. As they came closer, they saw that there was a photographer in their midst. His large camara apparatus was balanced on a tripod and he was trying to arrange the women into a group pose. They giggled and held one another as they attempted to follow his instructions. Hamish and Rita watched on fascinated. The photographer maintained an exterior impression of patience, but it was clear to Hamish that his frustration was growing as he found it increasingly difficult to convince the young ladies to remain still while he established focus and captured the image.

"I've always wanted to learn about the new science of photography," said Hamish. "I can see endless possibilities in medicine. The images can provide an objective view of the human anatomy, rather than relying on the interpretation of illustrators."

Rita wrinkled her nose. "Surely you are not referring to the images taken of mental health patients in asylums to ascertain the physiological signs of mental illness?" she said.

"I won't condone that level of objectification of the vulnerable. Thirty-five emotions, indeed."

Hamish tilted his head back and scratched at his temple.

"No," he said. "The popular idea that we can objectify emotions in that way and narrow them down to thirty-five expressions that transverse cultural and racial boundaries is ludicrous. That's not what I'm saying at all. I'm talking about physiology – skin conditions, and tumours, lumps and abnormalities. Teeth, bones, eyes. The possibilities are endless. Think of how useful it will be to have realistic images to compare?"

"Do you think the images would have sufficient contrast to make meaningful interpretations?" asked Rita.

"The science is progressing at a rapid pace. I believe the best photographers are already there."

"I purchased a copy of The Photographic Review of Medicine and Surgery when I was in Melbourne. It's published in the United States and is full of competent 'before' and 'after' photographs."

They watched as the photographer bid good day to his giggling subjects and they floated away like a white cloud.

"We should have our portraits taken," suggested Rita.

Hamish looked startled. "We're not here on holiday."

Rita pursed her lips. "Still."

But Hamish remained steadfast in his refusal to be drawn into the idea.

"I'm getting hungry," said Rita as they gazed back at the caerulean sea.

"I can agree with that," said Hamish. "We missed breakfast when Bellamy herded us out at dawn's light."

The sound of the constable's horse plodding up to the esplanade disturbed them. He pulled on the reins and stopped.

"Jakob seems to have slipped from our grasp, momentarily," he said.

"But don't worry, we'll soon catch up with him. Would you join me back at the station for lunch? Mrs Bloom has created a spread for us, in your honour. Her homemade quince jam needs to be tried to be believed."

Hamish and Rita agreed eagerly. Hamish was an enthusiast of home-made jams. He immediately thought of Wallace's strawberry jam and his mouth watered. They followed the constable on his horse back to the station eager to try Mrs Bloom's fare. They found a banquet waiting for them. Laid out on the table were freshly made ham sandwiches, scones with quince jam and fresh cream, pineapple peeled and cut into delicious triangles and freshly squeezed orange juice. There was enough food for ten and they were only six at the table. All of it fresh and refreshing on such a humid day.

"Jakob was last seen visiting Polson looking for work, this morning," explained the constable. "Perhaps after lunch we should ride out there. I'll have the stableboy ready horses for you, if you agree to the ride."

"Of course," said Hamish. "Perhaps we should hurry," he began, anxious that the lad was going to get away again.

"No hurry," said the constable. "He won't go far."

When they finished their meal, Hamish and Rita climbed onto two fine horses and followed the constable along the coast toward Point Vernon. They rode through forest land until they reached an acreage of cultivated fruit gardens. The block was divided into about two acres of productive kitchen garden and seven acres or more of fruit trees including orange trees, custard apple, common apple, date, plum, Chinese peach, mangoes and the rare gooseberry guava. All the trees were in a healthy state and flourishing. When they reached the house, the owner, Mr Thompson appeared to welcome them.

"Has my officer been here this morning?" asked the constable after he introduced Hamish and Rita.

"He has," said Mr Thompson. "He was looking for the young blacksmith apprentice. He missed him, though. He stayed here overnight but left early this morning. Unfortunately, we had no work for him at this point in the season. Is the lad in trouble?"

"No," said the constable. "We need to talk to him, that's all."

Hamish sighed audibly. Jakob had alluded them again. He hoped the long trip had not been a waste.

"Would you like to join my wife and I for afternoon tea?" asked Mr Thomson.

Hamish was eager to get back to the station to await further news of Jakob's whereabouts, but the constable accepted immediately. They followed him into the house, where Mrs Thompson was preparing a platter of citrus cake and tea. Hamish wondered if he could possibly eat any more, but Rita tucked in heartily. Her appreciation of the cake was so obvious, Hamish found room for some himself.

They were beginning to enjoy the cheerful company of their hosts when one of the garden workers ran into the house shouting something unintelligible.

Mr Thompson stood up immediately. "What do you mean by barging in...?"

"It's Jack," cried the man immediately. "They've dragged him from the creek."

"Jack?" Mrs Thompson was standing now. "What's happened?"

"Jack is the Thompson's son," the constable whispered. "He's about seven, I think."

Hamish and Rita instantly became alert.

"He was swimming in the dam," said the man, "come quickly."

"Mrs Thompson cried out a sound indistinguishable from the fear it expressed.

They all ran from the house and across the paddock toward the dam. There on the grass, lay a small boy, with one of the female gardeners bent over him.

Rita carefully but firmly moved the woman away from the little boy.

"Let us examine him," said Hamish.

He put his fingers at the boy's neck and watched his chest. There was the slightest rise and fall and Hamish felt a weak pulse at his neck.

"What happened?" demanded Mr Thompson, shaking uncontrollably.

"He was swimming, like he often does when its warm," said the gardener. "I kept an eye on him, but I turned away for a moment to dig out some roots and when I looked back, I couldn't see his head bobbing. I ran over to check, and he was underwater. I went in as quick as I could and dragged him out. But I don't know how long he was under." She begun to sob. "I got to him as soon as I could missus. I swear it."

"Mrs Thompson threw herself over the boy crying out his name and weeping as she brushed the wet hair from his face. "Wake up my darling boy, wake up."

Jack's eyes remained firmly closed and a blue shadow made them seem hollow.

Rita gently lifted the child's mother gently but firmly, while she struggled to keep a physical connection between herself and the boy, as though touch alone would keep his soul from leaving her.

Hamish scooped the boy into his arms and sat him upright. At first his head lolled against his chest, then he coughed and spluttered and opened his eyes. A collective gasp of relief spread through the small group watching. Jack continued to cough up water for a few minutes while Hamish held him. Then he signalled to the boy's mother to take the lad. Hamish slipped Jack into his mother's arms.

Mrs Thompson gathered the child to her breast and rocked. The boy snuggled there stunned but breathing.

"He'll be all right," said Hamish. "But make him rest. Watch him for twenty-four hours. He's taken in a lot of water. There are rarely complications but watch him anyway. If he has trouble breathing, or doesn't seem right in any way, send for us."

Mr and Mrs Thompson thanked the doctors profusely then focussed their attention on getting the small boy back to the house.

"We should leave them to it," said the constable and both Hamish and Rita agreed. They collected their horses and set off back to the police station.

There was silence among the small group as they rode, each contemplating the close call it had been for the Thompsons. Though they didn't want to think about it, they couldn't help acknowledging that the afternoon could have ended differently.

When they reached the station, the constable checked with his men for news of Jakob.

"There is no sign of him," he reported back to Hamish and Rita. "He seems to have vanished. I'm sorry you may have come all this way for nothing." The constable sounded appropriately embarrassed.

"He might still turn up," said Rita. "Besides, we have seen your beautiful part of the country."

"Worth the trip," said Hamish not believing his own words even as he said them. In truth, he was frustrated that they'd missed Jakob again and will have been away from Maryborough for a day and a night when there may well have been progress there.

Still, the hotel was well appointed and comfortable, and Hamish fell asleep easily with the sea breeze wafting through his window. The sun had not long come up when he heard a knock at the door.

"Not again," he said out loud. He had once again slept in his clothes, this time too weary to bother changing, but he did think it might be worth making it a habit if people were going to continually wake him in the early hours.

When he opened the door, the constable was waiting.

"Jakob?" said Hamish hopefully.

"No. The Thompson boy, Jack. He's ill. He can't breathe."

Hamish grabbed his coat and banged on Rita's door. She came immediately in her night gown.

"Get dressed," said Hamish. "Jack can't breathe."

"Respiratory oedema," said Rita pulling a skirt over her night gown. She put on a jacket and buttoned it quickly, slipped into her riding boots and followed Hamish and the constable down to the horses. They rode as quickly as they could to the Thompson property.

Jack was lying on his bed coughing and choking when they reached him. His lips were blue and there were dark circles under his eyes. Hamish pulled him up while Rita packed pillows behind his back. "He needs to be propped up to help his breathing," said Hamish. But Jack continued to cough.

"How long has he been like this?" asked Hamish.

"He has been getting worse through the night," said Mrs Thompson. "He hasn't slept."

"He has water on his lungs," Rita explained to his parents. "It happens to children sometimes after a near drowning. The water inflames the lungs."

"He needs oxygen," said Hamish. Even as he said the words, he saw a picture of the oxygen therapy apparatus at Maryborough in his mind. "If we can get him to the hospital, we can help him."

He looked at the constable, "Will the carriage pick us up here?"

"I think in such an emergency, it will," he said.

"We don't have much time, if we hope to save your son," said Hamish. "Will you allow us to take him to the hospital in Maryborough?"

"Yes," the boy's mother croaked, looking desperately toward her husband. He nodded.

The constable rushed away to bring the carriage and driver.

It was less than half an hour until the carriage was waiting at the front of the Thompson's house.

Nonetheless, it felt like an age to Hamish and Rita, who knew it must have been torture for Mr and Mrs Thompson.

When the carriage arrived, Hamish and Rita bundled the child in. He sat curled up on Rita's lap, his head resting against her chest.

"Keep his head up to facilitate his breathing," said Hamish.

Rita shot him a look that suggested, I know as much about this as you do.

The driver moved the horses forward as quickly as possible along the road back to Maryborough. With every bump and gully, the boy coughed and rasped. He moaned quietly in between coughing fits. "My chest hurts," he complained.

"We know," said Rita, holding him close. "Try to stay calm."

***

They managed to get back to Maryborough in half the time it had taken to reach Pialba. Having received notice by telegraph from the Pialba police station, the hospital staff were waiting for them as they carefully bundled the lad into the surgery. The oxygen apparatus was already set up and an orderly was on hand to pump the oxygen. Rita settled Jack onto the bed, propped up on pillows, while Hamish placed the glass facemask over his nose and mouth.

"Breathe normally," said Rita gently, coaxing the lad by gently patting his hair.

Jack took a few breathes of pure oxygen and retched, then he settled into laboured breathing. Soon he began to breathe more normally.

"That's enough," said Hamish after some time. "We'll give him time to rest before we provide oxygen again."

"How do you know the correct dose and frequency?" asked Rita.

"I don't," said Hamish. "I'm making it up."

Hamish's face was contorted with anxiety. He had never used this procedure and he had no evidence it would work. But he did know the child's lungs weren't working effectively and he would die without oxygen.

While they were waiting for the second treatment, Mr Thompson ran into the surgery. He had ridden from Polson after them.

"He seems calmer," he said as he put his hand on Jack's chest.

"He has had one treatment of the oxygen," said Hamish. "We are about to give him another. We'll keep this up until he can breathe by himself again."

"He looks a better colour," said Mr Thompson hopefully.

"Yes," agreed Rita. "He does."

By six that evening, Hamish and Rita were exhausted. It had been a long, stressful day. Jack was breathing easier, and they were confident he would continue to improve.

They demonstrated the process to the doctor on shift at the hospital and left him to care for their patient overnight. Mr Thompson was settled in beside his son and vowed not to leave him.

***

When they returned to the White Swan Inn, Hamish and Rita went immediately to their rooms. Arthur and Ziggy saw the exhaustion in their faces. They let them go without asking questions.

Once in his room alone, Hamish breathed a sigh of relief. He hadn't known how the treatment would go and he was desperately afraid he was going to suggest hope when there wasn't any by rushing the lad to Maryborough. But as it turned out, Jack was clearly improving, and Hamish was reasonably sure he would live. The experience of working with the oxygen apparatus was exhilarating. He had a clear idea of how it worked now and would lobby to have a similar set of equipment installed at the hospital in Brisbane. He knew there were oxygen rooms in Europe, which were easier on the patient because they avoided the use of the mask, but he couldn't work out how they could be as effective, because most of the oxygen would be dissipated into the air, rather than going to the patient.

He had been in the same clothes for three days. He washed and changed into a clean pair of trousers and shirt. Even though he was going straight to bed, he put on clean day clothes in the expectation that he could be awake at any hour if the police caught someone going into the shed.

Hamish slept as soon as his head hit the pillow.

Chapter Twenty One

"The official returns of the exports and productions removed coastwise from the port of Maryborough, as representative of last year's industries of the Wide Bay District, have been published at this early date. The facts and figures therein enumerated are suggestive of the growing importance of our district. The total value of products coming within the knowledge of the Custom House authorities amounts to 896,800 pounds, an increase of 50,102 pounds over the year 1880.

Gold from Gympie occupies, of course the premier position with a value of 235,062 pounds; timber shows well at 53,407 pounds; and sugar, molasses and rum with the sum of 73,559 pounds proves the large importance of that class of agricultural products. It is noteworthy, however, that no other farming product has a place in our exports. Pastoral pursuits at 22,470 pounds reveals the comparative insignificance of sheep and cattle pasturage." **The Queenslander 14 January 1882.**

Hamish

A shrill whistle pierced Hamish's sleep. Almost as though he had been waiting for it, he leapt from his bed and ran downstairs, bumping into Rita on the way.

"It's just after one, I heard the clock chime downstairs," she said.

Hamish took her arm and propelled her forward. "It's the signal from Williams. We need to hurry."

They rushed out of the inn, skirted the front of the building and turned into the lane. They fought their way through the thickness of the night, the shed not visible until they were almost on top of it. Using the sounds of struggle at the end of the lane to orient them in the right direction, they managed to find Williams and another constable grappling to hold on to a young man, who was doing his best to wrestle free of their grip.

"It's Jakob," Williams called when he saw Hamish and Rita running toward them.

But while Williams was distracted, the apprentice took the opportunity to wrench himself free and disappear into the stables.

The constables, Hamish and Rita ran after him. Hamish saw Jakob untie the first horse he came to and throw himself onto its back. Hamish quickly untied a second horse and did the same. Jakob whipped his horse into a gallop and headed down the street with Hamish following. Hamish was a less experienced rider and hung on to the horses' mane with both hands. He had rarely ridden without a saddle.

Jakob charged ahead increasing the space between himself and Hamish as he headed out of town. The space between them made it impossible for Hamish to see the apprentice on the road ahead, but he heard the horse's hooves on the gravel and the grunt of his breathing, so he knew he wasn't far behind. Once they had travelled beyond the limits of the town, Jakob turned off the road and into the bushland. Hamish heard the change in direction, but it wouldn't have mattered if he hadn't, his horse knew he was tasked with following his mate, so he shifted sideways and scurried off the road at the exact spot Jakob's horse had done so.

Within moments Hamish detected movement in the dense scrubland and knew Jakob wasn't far ahead of him. He ducked under low branches as the horse made its own path through the bush, more fully aware of where their prey travelled than was Hamish. He wasn't in control of the animal, he was ducking tree branches and hanging on for his life.

Every so often Jakob's head would appear between the trees, or the glossy coat of his horse would flash between bushes.

As long as he could maintain glimpses of Jakob, Hamish was convinced someone would eventually catch up to them and take over the chase. Hopefully a more competent rider than himself.

When he learned to trust the horse's ability to navigate between the tangled gums and follow his prey, he was lulled into a sense of rhythm, moving easily with the horse's movements.

Then he realised he hadn't seen Jakob crashing through the scrub in some minutes. He couldn't register exactly how long it had been. Had it been minutes? Or was it an instant? Hamish was trying to decide when he felt a jerk to his body, and he could no longer feel the movement of his horse beneath him. He was overcome by the sensation of flying, followed by the kind of free-falling he had only experienced in dreams.

He had no time to make sense of the situation before he felt the crushing thud of his bones on a stony creek bed. Out of the corner of his eye, he saw his horse stumble, regain its footing, and gallop off. Hamish lay in the creek bed holding his head. A quick check of his limbs assured him that nothing was broken. Everything ached, but he could move his feet and hands. He tried to sit but the world swirled around him. He lay back down and stared at the handful of stars that had broken free of the clouds.

"Damn," he thought.

Then he heard horse hooves on the ground beneath his head and soon the scuttle of a horse pulled to a halt over him. He looked up to see Ryan looking down at him from the back of his horse."

"Are you injured?" he said.

"I don't think so," said Hamish.

"I'll keep after the scoundrel, then," Ryan said. "The constable is behind me." He galloped off.

Seconds later, Constable Williams and his partner stopped their horses by the creek bed.

"You stay with him," said Williams as he galloped off after the others.

The Constable tied his horse to a gum and helped Hamish sit up.

"They'll catch up to him," he said. "Williams knows this land better than most. And old Ryan, better than anyone."

"Why was Ryan here?" asked Hamish.

"He must have been watching like us," he said. "I suppose he heard the word Ziggy put out and was watching the shed."

Hamish held his head in his hands. He was still dizzy from the fall.

"When you're ready I'll take you back to town," said the Constable.

"Give me a minute," said Hamish.

Hamish sat for a few moments with his head in his hands. The ground was swirling around him. But he knew he had to get on the horse with the constable and get back to town. He needed to be ready to question Jakob when they found him. He allowed the constable to assist him to his feet and climbed groggily onto the back of the horse behind him.

"I'll keep the ride as steady as possible," said the constable patting the horse's neck.

Hamish was grateful. He found, to his surprise, that he could hold his head up without too much effort and soon his body was synchronised with the movement of the horse.

They were travelling along the creek bed rather than back to the road.

"This will be shorter, and a smoother ride than through the bush," said the constable.

Hamish thought how much he preferred short and smooth.

He was rocking gently in a state of semiconsciousness when the constable suddenly pulled the horse to a stop. Hamish's head fell against the constable's back, jolting him awake.

"What is it?" he whispered.

"There's a horse up ahead," he said. "I caught a glimpse through the trees. Someone else is following the creek back to town."

"Is it Bellamy or Williams? Bellamy must have come out after us."

"Shush," said the constable.

Hamish tried to peer around his frame.

He saw the flash of a light grey horse through the gums, about two hundred yards ahead of them. It was only the pale coat that made the horse visible, catching any small sliver of light from the stars.

They both remained still and silent while they decided what to do next.

"We need to keep going," said Hamish. "But carefully. It's not one of us, it might be someone out for a ride."

"It might be Jakob," said the constable.

"Why would Jakob be heading back to town? I would've thought him well gone by now."

Then Hamish realised his mistake. "Unless he's going back for the gold," he said. "While everyone is occupied."

They moved along the creek as quietly as they could. The rider ahead was keeping up a decent pace and they tried to match him, but without getting close enough to alert the rider.

The sound of every twig cracking beneath the horse's hooves was amplified and they thought the horse and rider ahead would bolt. They stayed just close enough to keep occasional sight of grey in the distance.

Eventually, the horse came out onto the road where a small wooden bridge traversed the creek. They had closed some of the distance between them and they could see clearly that the rider was a young man.

"Jakob," said the constable.

"Keep back," instructed Hamish. "I don't think he is aware of us."

Jakob looked to the left and right when he reached the road and proceeded out when he could see no sign of his pursuers.

The constable kept his horse in the creek until Jakob was well ahead before climbing the horse up and over the bank onto the road.

"It won't matter if he rides out of sight," said Hamish. "I know where he is going."

They arrived back at the White Swan Inn with no sign of Jakob. They tied the horse at the front of the building and skirted the shadows along the wall down the lane toward the shed. They pressed themselves against the walls each side of the door and listened to the shuffling inside.

Hamish took a deep, steadying breath, his pulse thudding in his ears as he stepped into the doorway. There, crouched in the gloom, Jakob was furiously ripping away at the pallet, exposing the dirt beneath. The cases had been tossed aside carelessly, and with both of Jakob's hands occupied, Hamish seized his chance. He slipped from the shadows and, with a surge of adrenaline, lunged.

Jakob spun at the sound of Hamish's feet, a wild cry escaping his lips as he swung blindly. His fist missed its mark by inches as Hamish slammed into him, wrapping his arms tight around the lad's waist. Jakob let out a strangled snarl, twisting and clawing at Hamish's arms, fighting like a cornered animal. Hamish gritted his teeth, his arms burning as he tightened his hold, refusing to let go.

They hit the dirt hard. Jakob landed on top of Hamish, the impact knocking the wind out of the doctor's lungs. Pain shot through Hamish's back, but he clung on. Jakob kicked wildly, his legs a blur of frantic movement as he tried to break free. Somehow, Hamish managed to sit up, tightening his grip as he flung Jakob onto his stomach, pinning him with his weight.

But Jakob was relentless. His body buzzed with desperation, his hands clawing at the ground as he thrashed beneath Hamish's hold. With a sudden, wild reach, Jakob's fingers found a riding crop lying by the hay bales. In an instant, he swung it over his head, the leather cutting through the air with a vicious crack.

Hamish's back exploded with pain as the crop lashed across him. He cried out, his grip loosening just enough for Jakob to slither out from under him. Before Hamish could regain his senses, Jakob was on his feet, standing over him with the crop raised high, his eyes blazing with madness.

For a split second, Hamish saw a flicker of something unhinged in Jakob's face, a spark of danger that sent a cold shiver down his spine. He scrambled to his feet, his legs shaky, his breath coming in ragged gasps. Jakob's chest heaved, his lips curled into a feral snarl as he raised the crop again, this time aiming straight for Hamish's skull.

Time seemed to slow. Hamish braced himself, knowing he couldn't dodge in time. The crop began its deadly descent—

Crack.

The gunshot echoed through the barn like thunder. Hamish's breath hitched as the sound tore through the moment, and Jakob's eyes widened in shock. The riding crop slipped from his grasp as his legs buckled beneath him. He hit the ground hard, a groan of agony escaping his lips as he clutched at his leg, blood seeping through his fingers.

Hamish turned, his heart pounding in his chest. Rita stood in the doorway, the colt revolver in her trembling hands, her eyes wide with shock.

"I couldn't let him hit you," she whispered, her voice shaking. Her face was pale, as if she couldn't quite believe what she had done.

Hamish staggered a few steps toward her, his vision blurring from the exertion and the adrenaline crash. His body felt heavy, his limbs sluggish. He fell to his knees, clutching his head as the world seemed to spin around him.

"Where's the constable?" Hamish rasped, trying to gather his thoughts through the fog. "I thought he was right behind me when I went after Jakob."

Rita's voice was thin, uncertain. "I... I think he went for backup."

Hamish let out a bitter laugh, the sound rough and tired. "He was the backup." He collapsed onto the dirt floor, sitting there with his head in his hands, too drained to care about the pain that throbbed through his body. He closed his eyes, letting the tension drain from his limbs as the fight finally left him.

Five minutes passed before Hamish heard the heavy boots of constables approaching. He opened his eyes to see them rushing in, a blur of dark uniforms and concerned faces. Jakob lay writhing on the ground, his groans of pain filling the air as they slapped handcuffs onto his wrists. The apprentice's leg was soaked with blood, but the fire in his eyes had dimmed, replaced by a dull, exhausted pain.

Hamish was helped to his feet, his body protesting every movement as they led him to the Inn. He barely registered the pain in his back or the ache in his head. He only knew that it was finally over.

Twenty minutes later, Sergeant Bellamy stormed into the room with Williams at his side.

"We've lost him," Bellamy growled, shaking his head.

Hamish almost laughed at the absurdity of it all.

"He's in the watch house," he said.

Chapter Twenty Two

"It is perhaps too early in the life of the Australian colonies to expect that any special type of native Australian will have been evolved from the parent stock which supplied the original settlers. Or that the Anglo-Saxon, or rather the British race should be in its physique or in its moral and intellectual qualities display any distinctly marked modifications caused by the climate or other influencing agent of the new habitat.

The brief period that has already elapsed since the foundation of this new nation and the constant accessions of new blood from the mother country are, no doubt, reasons why at present the Australian youth – male or female in all essential particulars is practically indistinguishable from his or her British counterpart. In Australia, the Anglo-Saxon with his Celtic fellow subjects played, so to speak, a lone hand In the establishment of the colonies, and the immigrants of nations other than the British have been too few in number to have had any material influence upon the general mass of the population.

There are very few persons, other than mere children, who are the offspring of 'Native Australians'. There will be a time, however, when the Briton in Australia will develop in his figure and disposition certain changes wrought by the changed conditions of existence in his new home, and these characteristics will become known in men as 'Australian'. The agencies whereby these modifications may be expected to be affected are soil, climate, food, and new habits of life; and to these may be added, in the case of Australia, the obliteration of class distinctions and the extinction of national prejudices." **Euroa Advertiser Fri 24 December 1886.**

Bellamy

The sun was rising, casting a yellow haze across the town by the time Hamish, Rita and Bellamy gathered at the police station. Constable Williams was bleary eyed and dishevelled. "Bring Jakob into my office," said Bellamy, "and then go home and get some sleep."

The young officer hesitated. "What about you, sir?" he said.

"I'll sleep when this is over. You go. We'll be travelling back to Brisbane soon, judging by this turn of events. You're going to be in charge again. You need a clear head."

Constable Williams screwed up his face at the thought, but he did as he was instructed.

When Jakob was seated before them, Bellamy leaned forward, his eyes narrowing. The room closed in on them, the air thick with unspoken accusations.

"Tell us, Jakob," Bellamy's voice dropped to a low growl, "what were you looking for in the shed?"

Jakob's lip curled into a mocking smirk. The silence was deafening, as if the walls were waiting for his response.

"We know about the gold," Bellamy continued, each word cutting through the tension like a knife.

"Is that what you were after?"

Hamish's voice, softer but no less piercing, followed. "Was it the gold, Jakob? Did you think you could just take it?"

Jakob's eyes lifted slowly, meeting Hamish's gaze with a cold defiance. "What if I was? It belonged to my father."

Bellamy's smile was tight, predatory. "Did it? Or did your father steal it—along with his friends—from the miner who found it?"

Jakob's smirk faltered for a fraction of a second before returning, sharper. "I was only looking for what was rightfully mine. There's no crime in that."

Hamish's eyes darkened. "But there is a crime in murder."

Jakob shot him a look so hard it could cut stone. "Who says I murdered anyone?" His voice was icy, measured. "I was just looking for the gold. That's all."

Rita, who had been watching Jakob intently, spoke with quiet authority. "How did you get those scars on your hands?"

Jakob instantly tucked his hands behind his back, a flicker of something, fear? Crossing his face.

"They look recent," Rita continued, her voice as calm as a predator stalking its prey. "Burns, aren't they? Must be painful."

"Burnt meself in the forge," Jakob muttered, though the words came out too quickly, too rehearsed.

Hamish's voice dropped an octave. "You haven't been near a forge in over a week."

Bellamy, now standing, barked the command with sudden fury. "Show the doctors your hands."

Jakob's eyes flashed, but he didn't move. Bellamy's voice cracked like a whip. "Show them!"

Reluctantly, Jakob extended his hands, palms up, the skin blistered and raw. Rita stepped forward, gripping his wrists with the careful precision of someone who knew exactly what they were looking for.

Hamish and Rita exchanged a glance. The burns were unmistakable.

"These burns," Rita said, her tone deadly serious, "are consistent with acid burns. Exposure like this would worsen over days."

Bellamy's voice was a razor blade as he leaned in closer. "So tell me, Jakob—how did you get acid on your hands?"

Jakob's lips pressed into a tight, thin line. His silence was louder than any confession.

Bellamy moved to his desk and perched on its edge, swinging his legs casually, but his eyes remained fixed on Jakob, unblinking. "You see, there are only two people who saw Elijah in the week before his death. One of them is you, Jakob. And you—of the two—are the most likely candidate. It makes sense, doesn't it? Elijah would want to pass on his secret to you, his son. A legacy of sorts."

Jakob shifted, the defiance in his eyes flickering with uncertainty.

"And now," Bellamy continued, his voice softening to a dangerous whisper, "here you are—with burns you can't explain, a history you can't hide, and a story that's quickly unravelling."

The silence hung heavy in the air, Jakob's defiance crumbling under the weight of Bellamy's logic.

"You had access to Isaac and Ruth Gowan. No one knows where you were when they were murdered. And those burns? The same ones found on Ruth's body." Bellamy stood, looming over Jakob like a shadow. "We have enough to charge you with murder."

Hamish's eyes flicked over to Bellamy, uncertain. Did they really have enough? But Jakob's next words were venomous, laced with desperation.

"That gold belonged to my father," Jakob hissed, his voice shaking with barely contained rage. "It's mine now."

Bellamy raised an eyebrow, his voice cool, composed. "But it didn't belong to them, did it? Your father, Ruth, Isaac—they let the old miner die and took what wasn't theirs."

Jakob's face twisted in fury. "Anyone would have done the same!"

"I'm not sure anyone would, Bellamy replied, his tone icy. "But what about you, Jakob? What did you do?"

Jakob's façade cracked. His eyes darted between Bellamy and Hamish, his hands trembling slightly. Then, as if compelled by the need to unburden his soul, the words spilled out.

"Pa told me about the gold before he died. Said it was my inheritance, my way out." His voice was strained, the veneer of calm peeling away to reveal something raw beneath. "He said it was mine by right."

Hamish's jaw clenched. "And what gave him the right to that gold?'

Jakob sneered. "It was his! He found it!"

"Did he?" Hamish pressed, leaning forward. "Did he really find it, or did he let the miner die with it in his hands?"

Jakob's face went ashen. His voice dropped to a whisper, barely audible. "They could have saved him... but they didn't."

The room fell deathly silent, the truth hanging in the air like a noose tightening around Jakob's neck.

"Pa said it was my turn to claim it," Jakob muttered, almost to himself. "Said I could take my share, make a life... but Ruth and Isaac wouldn't tell me where it was hidden. They kept it from me, all these years. I didn't want any of this to happen, I just wanted what was mine..."

His voice broke, the words collapsing under the weight of guilt, of something far darker than mere greed.

"And now?" Bellamy asked softly, yet the question cut like a blade.

Jakob's eyes filled with a mixture of regret and fury. "Now... I have nothing."

The blacksmith's apprentice kept his eyes down.

"It doesn't matter what happened out there," he muttered, his voice trembling with a mix of defiance and regret. "Pa wanted me to have what was mine." He paused, as though waiting for some kind of understanding, but none came.

"They hid the nugget," Jakob continued, his tone growing heavier, "and didn't talk to anyone about it. Except Pa... Pa got drunk sometimes and let it slip." His face twisted. "There were whispers—rumours, but nothing more."

Bellamy and Hamish exchanged a look, the weight of confirmation settling in the room, pressing against Jakob's already fragile composure.

"Dad thought... he thought I should know. So, when the time came, I could go to Isaac and Ruth and ask for my share." Jakob's voice wavered, his eyes darting between them, searching for some kind of relief from his growing anxiety. "He thought we could get it together, retrieve the nugget. I could take it down south—pretend I found it while fossicking—and then send them their share. No one would ever have to know about... the old man's death." His voice cracked, the weight of that secret almost too much to bear. "But I couldn't do it without them."

"Pa never told me where it was hidden. He said only one of them knew. And... and he didn't know if it was Ruth or Isaac. He'd tried asking, but neither of them would tell him."

Hamish brushed back his hair, his eyes sharp. "And, of course, you fully intended to give them their share when you cashed in the gold?"

"I bloody did!" Jakob shouted suddenly, his chair scraping the floor as he almost leaped up, his fists clenched in fury and desperation. His face flushed red; his voice strained to the breaking point. "I did!"

"Sit down," Bellamy ordered, his voice calm but firm. Jakob froze, and slowly sank back into his seat, his body rigid with tension.

"I didn't want this!" Jakob screeched, the words spilling out, jagged and raw. "I didn't want any of this to happen! I just wanted what was mine—what was fair and square!" He was panting now, his hands shaking uncontrollably as he wiped the sweat from his brow.

Bellamy didn't flinch. "Go on," he said, picking up his pencil again, the scratch of it against paper the only sound in the tense room. "Tell us how you came to murder your father's two oldest friends."

Jakob's face twisted, his teeth grinding together as he slammed his fist down on the desk with a hollow thud. "They weren't no friends!" he spat; his voice filled with bitterness. "They went on with their lives, made something of themselves, while my father... he was left behind, stuck, knowing he could've been rich. It ate him alive." Jakob's eyes blazed with fury, the resentment choking his words.

Bellamy leaned forward, his gaze unrelenting. "Tell us what happened to Isaac and Ruth."

Jakob's body slumped back in the chair, the fire in his eyes replaced with something darker, something more broken. "I went to Isaac first," he admitted, his voice hollow. "Told him what Pa said... that I wanted my share. Isaac told me to leave it alone. He said it was no good opening up old wounds, that if we went public with the gold, it would be taken from us anyway. But I had a plan. If they helped me get down south, I could claim it—pretend I found it. I'd send them their share, and no one would ever know. It could've worked!" Jakob's voice trembled, his belief in that lie unravelling before their eyes.

"But Isaac... he wasn't having it. He wouldn't budge. I thought if I could just get him to tell me where it was hidden, I could take the gold myself. I'd figure out a way to get to Brisbane... or even Sydney. I could've stolen a horse, lived rough—anything to get out of that life." His voice cracked, the desperation bleeding through. "I told him I needed the day off, and he agreed. So I went to the workshop, early, thinking maybe the gold was there, where Isaac spent most of his time."

Jakob's eyes filled with a wild panic as he relived the moment. "It was dark... I could barely see anything, searching by candlelight. Then I heard him. Isaac. He came in, and I panicked. My heart was racing, my head spinning. He saw me in the dark, and for a second... I swear, it was like he'd seen a ghost."

Jakob's voice grew frantic, the memory clawing at him. "I pretended I'd just arrived, started cleaning up the mess I'd made, but Isaac... he knew. He knew what

I was after. He said, 'You were looking for the nugget.' And I saw red. I screamed at him—told him to tell me where it was, that we could be free of this shit life!"

Jakob's breath was coming in ragged gasps now, his voice cracking with raw emotion. "But he didn't care. He just said, 'I like my life.' He turned away, like none of it mattered. Like my father... like me didn't matter." Jakob's eyes brimmed with tears of rage, his hands shaking uncontrollably.

"I didn't mean to kill him," Jakob choked, his voice barely a whisper. "I just... I wanted him to listen. I picked up the hammer, and I hit him. I didn't even think. I didn't mean to... but when I heard the crack, I knew. I knew he was gone. I didn't even give him a chance to say anything. His skull..." Jakob's voice broke, and he buried his face in his hands, his body shaking with silent sobs.

He took a shuddering breath and continued, his voice hollow. "I ran. I ran to Ruth. Sent her a message, telling her I knew about the gold, that I wanted my share. Told her to meet me at the shed or I'd tell the press everything. I threatened to expose them... tell the world how they killed the miner and stole the gold."

Jakob's voice turned hollow again as he recounted the meeting with Ruth. "She came. But she wouldn't tell me. She figured out I'd killed Isaac—I saw it in her eyes. She knew. And when she turned her back on me, I knew she wasn't going to help. She was going to leave me to rot, just like Isaac."

He swallowed hard, his hands twisting together. "I followed her. I didn't mean to kill her. I just wanted to scare her. I saw the acid, and I grabbed it. I thought... if I could hurt her, maybe she'd tell me where the gold was hidden. I didn't think it would... I didn't think it would kill her." Jakob's voice trembled, the guilt wrapping around his throat. "But when I threw it... she screamed, and she fell, and I ran."

Tears welled up in Jakob's eyes, his voice breaking into a sob. "I didn't mean for any of this to happen. I just... I just wanted what was mine." Jakob twisted his blistered hands.

"I didn't even know I'd got some on my hands for a bit. Then the pain came. It was bad. Then the blisters. I had to stay out of sight."

"You need to stop rubbing them," said Rita, "You're making it worse for yourself."

"You went to Gympie?" asked Hamish.

"I went to Gympie and asked around for work a bit, they wouldn't think anything of a blacksmith's apprentice with burnt hands. And I went to Pialba. But really, I've just been waiting. I knew there was too much attention on the inn and the shed after Ruth died. I wouldn't be able to search for the gold unnoticed. But when I heard it muttered around that word of the gold being in the shed was out, I knew I had to act fast."

Hamish and Rita exchanged satisfied glances.

"I'll charge him with the murders of Isaac Brown and Ruth Gowan," said Bellamy.

"Then, I'll take him back to his cell."

Chapter Twenty Three

"The Wide Bay News of the third instant says: Rumours upon rumours in connection with the gold discovery by Le Blower have been flying about ever since the specimens of stone brought down by the prospector have been shown to the acquisitive and inquisitive public. Some of the rumours are quite absurd and have set numbers of people all agog – to use a mining phrase, they have gone "off their head." A syndicate was formed off-hand and thirty-four people clubbed together and put a half-sovereign each in the pool to acquire the right of accepting dividends out of this champion El Dorado. Subsequently shares were sold at the rate of four hundred pounds, one-eights readily finding buyers at fifty pounds. All of this was done before anything was definitely known of the prospector, the real extent of the stone, or the tenure by which the ground was held. At every corner groups of excited "brokers" are congregated discussing the matter and any prominent citizen has to run the gauntlet of answering excited questions as to the whereabouts of the Mount Martha phantom and how much she is worth.

Why the locality of the new find should be kept secret is a mystery, but it cannot now be very long before the matter is cleared up. The latest report is that the stone which has caused the flutter comes from the vicinity of Drummer's Creek, near Mount Perry, and a large number of Maryborough's mining adventurers left by train yesterday to take up some of the golden gully before it's all snavelled. May their golden dreams be realised." **The Telegraph Thursday 8 March 1888.**

Hamish

Bellamy took the gold nugget from the safe and placed it on his desk.

"I've never seen a nugget this size," he said. "I can see why the three of them were worried, even once they became adults. A nugget of this size could not be cashed in without a great deal of attention."

"The rumours would certainly have surfaced, and they'd have had a lot of explaining to do. They would have had to swear blind the old miner was dead when they found him – and if that were the case, why hide the nugget for so long?"

"What happens now?" whispered Rita.

Bellamy placed the rock back into a simple box and lifted the whole package. "This will go into evidence," he said. "But after that, I don't know."

"Word of this will get out fast. It'll be in all the newspapers," said Hamish.

"I imagine relatives of the old miner will start appearing out of the woodwork to claim the nugget," said Rita.

"I expect it will be declared the possession of the government," said Bellamy.

Hamish shrugged.

"Personally, I think a find like this should be held in a museum."

"Now that the three children who found it on the old man have passed away, I think it should go to their beneficiaries," said Rita.

"The courts will decide the fate of the nugget," said Bellamy. "In the meantime, our job here is done."

Hamish glanced toward Rita.

"Time to go back to the inn and pack for our return home."

Bellamy stopped them. "I forgot to tell you, in all the confusion. The little boy, Jack, has been released from hospital and has returned home with his parents. He is quite recovered from his ordeal."

Hamish and Rita beamed. "Wonderful news," said Rita.

Hamish took Rita's arm, and they left the shed for the warmth and light of the day.

"About my proposal," Bellamy called to them. "We'll discuss it on the train."

"Yes," Hamish called back. "We'll have the opportunity to discuss it on the train."

Rita was still watching him when they were outside in the lane and on the way back to the inn.

"I thought your mind was made up," she said.

"It is," said Hamish.

"Then why didn't you tell the Sergeant?"

Hamish sighed.

When it was clear he was not going to answer her question, Rita smiled, and let it go.

"I'm going to walk on and visit Nelly first," she said. "I want her to know I will be back to testify in court when her case comes up. Do you want to come and say good-bye?"

Hamish confirmed that he did so they walked past the inn and on to the blacksmith's workshop where Nelly was tapping away out back.

She stopped and rubbed her hands on her leather apron when she saw them.

"Busy?" asked Rita.

"Yes," she said. "I have quite a few domestic orders to fill. It seems the people of Maryborough are beginning to come round. I don't have the industrial and agricultural work that Isaac had, but I'm happy with my new niche."

"Have you had word about your case?" asked Hamish.

"I had a visit from the magistrate himself, this morning," she said. "It seems that Mr Hawking has been pleading my case. With his testimony and that of the workers, the magistrate has decided that Mr Wellington's death was accidental. In the act of trying to repel his advance, I punched him, but the magistrate agrees that I couldn't have expected that act to result in his death."

"That's marvellous," cried Rita. "Does that mean there are no charges?"

"I believe so," said Nelly.

"Congratulations," said Hamish. "A decision well made!"

Nelly beamed. "I heard Jakob has been arrested," she said. "I can't get used to the idea that he killed both Isaac and Ruth."

"Gold can have a terrible effect on people," said Hamish.

"That's another thing I'm having trouble understanding. Why would Isaac have kept that secret from me all these years?"

Rita bit her bottom lip. "Because he knew the awful effect greed for gold has on people," she suggested.

"All three of the children were wracked with shame about not going for help for the old man and I imagine, as children, they thought they would be suspected of murder if they told. When they grew up, they probably just didn't want to face the interrogations and suspicions," said Hamish.

Rita nodded.

"Though it seems clear that Elijah resented their decision to keep it hidden,"

Nelly shook her head.

"I didn't know Elijah, but he strikes me as a coward. He was bitter about keeping the gold hidden during his life but when he was on his deathbed he passed the problem onto his son."

"We'll stay in touch," said Rita curling around Nelly in a tight hug.

Hamish held out his hand to shake hers, but Nelly reached in and kissed him on the cheek. He blushed.

***

That evening Hamish, Rita and Bellamy were on the train on their way back to Brisbane. They were all eager to return to their routine lives.

"I'm looking forward to being back with Wallace and Red," said Hamish. "I miss Wallace's cooking."

"I miss them too," agreed Rita.

"Have you thought anymore about my offer?" said Bellamy wasting no time.

Hamish brushed his fringe back from his face. Bellamy and Rita were both staring at him.

"I have," he said.

"And...? asked Bellamy.

"I came to Brisbane to establish a general practice," Hamish said.

"I know you did. But you haven't done so, effectively."

Hamish shot him a wounded glare.

"Well, you haven't, have you?"

Hamish looked to Rita for support.

"He's right," she said. "Either you have to choose general practice and give up swanning around Queensland investigating murders, or you choose to be a medical investigator and be done with it."

Hamish felt trapped, both physically and emotionally crushed in between them on the train.

The sound of the wheels rattled along on the track.

Why did he find it so difficult to settle down to general practice? He thought of Mrs Grisham and her bunions. The medicine was pedestrian. His clients were middle-class and entitled. Within seconds, a million reasons for his difficulty came rushing into his head. He was cut out for more than general practice.

"I like research," he said.

"You're introducing a third option?" said Rita astounded.

"Not necessarily," said Bellamy. "Forensic medicine is a growing field. You'll find there are plenty of opportunities for research in the job."

Hamish blinked. He hadn't considered that.

Rita nudged him with her elbow.

He looked at her and drank in that smile.

"Medical Examiner, it is, then."

Bellamy and Rita clapped.

When the three of them stepped off the train onto the platform at Roma Street, they were happily chatting about the future, despite the limited amount of sleep they'd had over the past few days.

Hamish saw Wallace standing near the platform gates with the red terrier bundled in his arms. When the dog recognised Hamish and Rita, he wriggled free and jumped to the ground, his paws hardly touching the platform as he ran toward them and leapt into Rita's arms. He nuzzled her neck, and she kissed him on the head.

"It's good to see you too, Red," said Hamish drily. He took a paw and shook it.

Wallace was collecting their bags.

On the road there was a cab waiting for Sergeant Bellamy and another for Hamish, Rita and Wallace. They shook hands and said their good-byes.

"I'll need a couple of weeks to tidy things up with the practice," said Hamish.

"See you in two weeks, then," said Bellamy.

"There's a letter from your mother waiting," said Wallace as they climbed into their cab.

Hamish groaned.

They dropped Rita off at her home and travelled on to Wickham Terrace. When Hamish saw the convict-built windmill on the hill he felt a pang of homesickness. He hadn't realised how much he had longed for his own smart terrace house. Wallace opened the door with one hand while carrying his bag in the other. On the side table near the door sat the letter. Hamish picked it up immediately and went to his favourite blue velvet armchair, the one Rita insisted on draping her legs over, rather than sitting on like a normal woman.

He opened the envelope and unfolded the paper inside, recognising the fluid handwriting of his mother.

" *Dearest Hamish,*

I trust you are well. I am writing to notify you of a change in your father's condition, only because you insisted that I do so."

"*He has become more unsteady on his feet of late and has developed a shuffling gait. He refuses to wear anything other than his worn-out slippers and I fear he is about to fall at every moment. It has become unsafe for him to go to the track every day as he used to. He needs someone to watch him, and I suspect the staff have grown tired of doing so. He did upend the bookmakers table with an accompanying rant about corruption, something akin to that of our Lord and the Jewish moneylenders, I am told. I suppose I can't blame them for wanting him out of their way. But it does mean he is home with me all the time and he can be quite intolerable.*

He has also begun wandering at night. The stableboy found him in the stables last night trying to saddle up a horse. Fortunately, the horse was having none of it and made an unholy fuss. The boy brought him into the house and put him to bed in his room, so no harm done. I didn't even wake up as I had a powder before bed. I am at my wit's end. But don't worry, I only write to keep you updated, as you instructed me to do so.

Your mother"

Hamish took in a deep breath to settle the nervous energy twisting his gut. When he was in Melbourne, he had advised his mother to allow the doctor to admit him into full time care. But she wouldn't hear of it. He had offered to come back home to assist with his father's care. But his father had ordered him out of the house and his mother made it clear she didn't want him there either. He didn't know what else he could do.

His first instinct was to pack up and return to Victoria. But there was his new job to consider. And the fact remained that his parents didn't want him to help.

Wallace had provided a plate of scones with his homemade rosella jam and was sitting on the sofa with Red curled up comfortably in his lap. Hamish began from the beginning and read the letter aloud to Wallace.

"Tea?" asked the older man, holding up the teapot.

Hamish nodded.

Wallace poured the tea slowly and carefully.

"In my opinion your mother simply wants to vent her frustration," he said. "I don't believe her position has changed. I don't think either of them would appreciate you rushing down there to speed up progress of the inevitable. They will realise in their own time that your father requires full time care. She will come to terms with her inability to manage."

He passed Hamish his cup of steaming tea, and a plate of scones.

"I feel so helpless," said Hamish.

"It's part of their story together. It's not your story, they don't want you to be part of it. Allow them their privacy. Write back to your mother and convey your sympathy and your love."

"Doesn't that make me incredibly selfish?"

Wallace laughed. "My friend, racing down there to place your father in care against both their wishes, would make you selfish. Allow the story to play out. That's the selfless thing to do."

Hamish drank his tea incredibly thankful for the old Cook's advice. The weight of an indescribable burden fell from his shoulders. He admitted to himself for the first time he was looking forward to the beginning his new career, officially, as a medical investigator. Woe betide anyone who interfered with his corpses or murder scenes now!

Epilogue

Nelly was taking a perfectly formed, golden loaf from her oven when there was a knock at the door. It was still early in the morning. She had been up at four to bake the day's bread so she could put in a full day in the workshop. She had several orders to fill for domestic items, but it wasn't enough for a comfortable living. She had committed in her mind to giving herself six months to build up her business. If she was frugal, she could live until then on the money that had been paid by Walker's.

She would re-evaluate her position then. She hoped desperately that she could stay in her home and make her living at the work she loved.

Nelly opened the door to a boy holding out a letter. She took it from him and gave him a coin from the pocket of her apron. When she was inside, she saw that the letter was from the magistrate. Her heart skipped a beat. Had there been a change to his decision about the death of Percival Wellington?

Nelly opened the letter with trembling fingers.

" Dear Mrs Brown,

I am writing to inform you that a decision has been made in regard to the ownership of the gold nugget found by Ruth Gowan, Elijah Jennings and your husband, Isaac Brown. As the nugget was in the possession of these three individuals at the time of its recent emergence, and no record can be found of ownership by the deceased with whom the children found it, it has been decided that ownership can be legally assigned to the abovementioned individuals: Mrs Gowan, Mr Jennings and Mr Brown. Since their passing, the nugget will be transferred to the ownership of Arthur Kane and yourself, as beneficiaries of their estate. Mr Jakob Jennings has forfeited his legal claim to the nugget through the murders of Ruth Gowan and

Isaac Brown. The nugget is currently being held at the Royal Bank of Queensland in Kent Street Maryborough. Please confer with Mr Kane in regard to what you would like to do with it next.

Congratulations on your fortunate windfall.

Yours, etc."

Nelly sat down with a thud. She felt oddly feint.

***

At the same time, Arthur Kane was reading a similar letter.

"What?" cried Ziggy.

Seconds later they were dancing around the bar.

Author Notes

The muse must muse on Blacksmith Joe,
Who used his arms like flails.
But talk of blowing – Joe could blow
And blowed his nose and nails.
And though he was an honest man
As any man could be,
The story through his neighbours ran
He lived for forgery.
And still, one might think it odd,
He had a righteous soul,
And while he oft would steel a rod
Tis true he never stole.
And Joe was strong and brave and tall,
And good as he was nice,
And though he had no faults at all
Yet he did possess one vice,
No stauncher friend could ever be,
No secret he divulged,
But though a kindly fellow, he
In irony indulged.
Melbourne Punch Thursday 13 May 1886

***

My husband is a blacksmith. I can hear the tap tap tapping from the workshop at the end of the garden as I write. Today he's making coat hooks. He screws them onto weathered wood with new old stock screws from the turn of the century. Customers renovating their homes in industrial chic can't get enough of them.

Some days he holds workshops with groups of three or four tapping away at fired metal which they twist and turn it into beautiful objects. He has as many female students as he does male. The therapeutic effects of hammering malleable iron work as well for women as for men.

The idea for this story came from a chance comment from my husband. "You know when a blacksmith dies, his wife is allowed to take over the trade," he said.

"Good to know," said I, raising a sceptical brow. While the alchemical characteristics of transmuting raw iron into intricate scrollwork appeals, the physical effort required is a deal breaker for me. But my eldest daughter, who is tiny, but strong, loves it. Nonetheless, the thought of the blacksmith's widow played on my mind until the story line developed.

***

Most of my stories begin with a place. The town of Maryborough was a mecca of industrialisation in the 1880's and with no less than nine blacksmiths trading in the area it seemed a perfect setting for my story. I must also admit to a personal fascination with the town as the place where my ancestors landed in 1848. As some of the earliest free settlers in Queensland, two brothers, Nicholas and George Thurecht established themselves in Maryborough where the family grew and flourished. The story about holding Lutheran services in the household of my ancestor Nicholas Thurecht prior to the establishment of a church is true, according to family folklore.

But this story is not about me or my family. It is about women who dare to be different and the growth of an industrial town alongside a valley of gold.

The rich history of gold mining in Queensland and its impact on mining towns such as Gympie and the adjacent growth of Maryborough is fascinating, and that story provides the rich background for this book. But a story less well known is the essential nature of blacksmithing to the growth of industrialisation and colonial settlement.

Even more interesting than the contribution to economic growth is the relationship between blacksmithing and European cultural identity. Today, the blacksmith reminds us of a quaint past characterised by cottage industry and craftsmanship, but throughout history the blacksmith was central to any settlement, often not only a skilled craftsman but magical, the stuff of myth and legend, the flag bearer of alchemy.

***

From the iron age through to the late Victorian industrial age of Hamish's time, the blacksmith played a central role in shaping cultural identity. We know this because of the vast array of ancient myths, symbols, stories and poems about blacksmiths.

Some of our earliest archaeological records of blacksmithing date back to the Hittites, a civilization from the 14th century BCE in the area we know today as Turkey. The Hittites mastery of blacksmithing played a pivotal role in their society. They were among the first to smelt iron ore revolutionizing the production of weaponry. They used clay cubicles and advanced furnaces to reach temperatures high enough for iron smelting allowing for the manufacture of steel weapons (iron with carbon) that were harder and more durable than bronze.

Hittite blacksmiths also developed advanced techniques for alloying metals. They created various bronze alloys combining copper with tin, arsenic, or other metals to produce materials with specific properties. These alloys were used to create a wide range of tools and weapons, each tailored to a purpose. Iron weapons were not only more durable than bronze but easier to produce in large quantities. This gave them an advantage over other contemporary civilizations.

Blacksmithing was also essential for crafting everyday tools and implements used in agriculture, construction, and domestic life. The Hittites advanced metalworking allowed them to improve their agricultural practices, which in turn, supported a growing population. Blacksmithing skills were highly sought after, leading to extensive trade networks. The Hittites exported metal products, including weapons and tools to neighbouring regions strengthening diplomatic ties and their economy.

But Blacksmithing was not only a practical skill, even then. It also had cultural significance for the Hittites. Mythology and religious practices featured deities associated with metal work. The Hittite sun goddess Arinniti, for example was often depicted alongside a metal working forge.

By the time of the ancient Greeks (around the sixth century BCE) the supernatural had become a major element of Blacksmith folklore. In the pantheon of Greek gods and goddesses Hephaestus, known in Roman mythology as Vulcan, held a unique role as the god of fire, craftsmanship and ingenuity. His significance in Greek mythology reflects the Greek's reverence for the art of blacksmithing and the transformative power of fire. Hephaestus was born to Hera, Queen of the gods, but his birth was unusual and tragic. He was born lame or deformed, and in some versions of the myth, she cast him out of Olympus. Hephaestus rose above these hardships to become one of the most skilled and respected gods of Olympus.

He was a master blacksmith and metal worker, creating incredible objects and weapons for both gods and mortals. His workshop, located beneath a volcano was said to be a place of extraordinary craftsmanship where he used the transformative power of fire to shape metals into magnificent creations.

One of Hephaestus's most famous creations was the shield of Achilles, as described in Homer's 'Iliad'. This shield was a masterpiece of artistry, with intricate scenes depicting various aspects of life and the cosmos.

In ancient Greece, blacksmiths revered Hephaestus as their patron deity. His association with craftsmanship and fire underscored the importance of these skills in Greek society, where metalworking played a pivotal role in both warfare and daily life.

The Norse god of thunder Thor also had a close relationship with blacksmithing. One of the most iconic aspects of this association is his possession of Mjolnir, a powerful hammer forged by the dwarf brothers Brokkr and Ivaldi. This hammer is not only a symbol of Thor's might, but a testament to the skills of the blacksmiths who created it.

It was Loki, the trickster god, who had two sets of dwarves compete to create items more extraordinary than any others. This competition led to the creation of a series of remarkable artefacts with Mjolnir being the most famous. The hammer was not just a weapon; it was imbued with the power to protect the gods from the giants and served as a tool of Thor's thunderous wrath.

As the god responsible for defending the gods and humanity from the chaotic forces of the giants, Thor's protective role extended to safeguarding the skills of blacksmiths. In Norse society, blacksmiths were highly regarded for their ability to forge weapons and tools necessary for survival. Thor, as their patron deity was believed to watch over and bless their work.

Thor's character embodies the qualities that were highly valued: strength, courage, protection and loyalty. These attributes resonated with the blacksmiths who depended upon the god's favour to excel in their craft.

Another legendary figure found in various Norse and Germanic traditions is Wayland the Smith. His narrative is one of craftsmanship, captivity, and vengeance. He is depicted as a master blacksmith and craftsman renowned for his unparalleled skills in forging weapons and creating intricate works of art.

Wayland's story typically follows a tragic trajectory. He was captured by the Swedish King Nidud and forced into servitude as a blacksmith. During his captivity he was cruelly maimed, with his tendons cut to prevent him from escaping. However, Wayland's spirit remained strong. He crafted a magical set of wings and managed to escape his captors. He took flight, soaring above the earth and leaving behind his prison, representing triumph over oppression.

Wayland settled on an Island where he forged extraordinary weapons and artefacts, including a sword known as "Mistletoe". He then sought revenge against the King's sons who had wronged him as well as the King himself.

The story of Wayland's captivity and subsequent escape resonated with a society that valued freedom and self-reliance. His cunning and resourcefulness in overcoming his captors became emblematic of the human spirit's ability to triumph over adversity.

By the medieval period blacksmiths were central to every village. Their techniques seemed to many so mysterious they were considered magical.

During the time of Charlemagne, smiths produced the swords, armour and chainmail that constituted a person's value at death. Blacksmiths had the skills and knowledge that Nobles required to set themselves up as future leaders. They also had the skills to produce all the tools and equipment needed to sustain everyday life.

During this period the smith learnt his trade from a Master, who often employed several apprentices. Only the most talented would rise to become Masters. This regulated the number of tradesmen and preserved the prestige of the industry. The development of Guilds provided further regulation. The Elite of the trade were admitted to positions of authority within the region, such as town councils. This cemented the blacksmith as an important asset in both international trade and civic development. The blacksmith produced wrought iron into agricultural implements, cooking utensils, tools, chains, gates and weapons. In some communities, blacksmiths earned more than physicians.

***

"The Smith and the Devil" is a widespread and enduring legend that has variations in folklore from various cultures around the world. The core narrative typically revolves around a skilled blacksmith who encounters the devil in some form and engages in a high stakes contest. The legend highlights themes of cleverness, human ingenuity, and the tension between good and evil.

In its most common form, the legend tells a story of a blacksmith, known for his exceptional skills and craftsmanship. One day, the devil in disguise approaches the blacksmith and challenges him to a competition. The nature of the challenge varies in the stories from different regions but usually involves a contest of skill, strength, and wit. The devil's intent is to win the blacksmith's soul in exchange for extraordinary abilities or rewards.

The blacksmith, aware of the supernatural nature of his opponent, agrees to the challenge but uses his intelligence and cunning to outwit the devil. Through a series of clever tricks or loopholes the blacksmith manages to fulfill the terms of the contest without losing his soul, and in exchange gains extraordinary abilities.

The blacksmith's triumph over the devil illustrates themes of human resourcefulness and resilience in the face of temptation and malevolent forces.

***

While most legends of blacksmithing involve men and male strength, there are also female blacksmiths in the historical record. Elizabeth Hager (1755-1843) was not only a blacksmith during a time when the trade was predominantly male, but she also made significant contributions to the American revolution. She exhibited a strong interest in blacksmithing from a young age and began her training under her father, a skilled blacksmith himself.

During the Revolutionary War, blacksmiths held a crucial role in supporting the American cause. They were responsible for crafting essential tools, weapons, and equipment for both soldiers and civilians. Blacksmiths also repaired muskets, forged ammunition, and maintained the transportation infrastructure, ensuring the military's mobility and readiness.

Elizabeth Hager's involvement in blacksmithing included her actively participating in crafting and repairing weapons and tools for American troops. Her skills were particularly valuable given the shortage of male blacksmiths due to the high demand for their services on the front lines. Hager's dedication made her a respected figure in the community.

Hager's blacksmith forge became a centre of patriotism. It served as a gathering place for locals who sought to contribute to the war effort. She not only worked tirelessly at the anvil but also encouraged others to join her in supporting the cause, fostering a sense of unity and purpose among her neighbours.

Hager did encounter scepticism and prejudice from some who doubted her abilities due to her gender. Nevertheless, her determination and skill gradually earned her respect.

After the war, Hager continued her blacksmithing work and contributed to her community's growth.

***

In the early days of colonial Australia, the blacksmith held a pivotal role that was instrumental in the survival of the settlements. The blacksmith's skills were highly sought after, and their work was crucial in shaping the physical, economic, and social landscape of colonial Australia.

One of the primary roles of the blacksmith was the production and repair of tools and equipment. Blacksmiths were responsible for crafting a wide range of essential items, including axes, ploughs, hoes, nails, and horseshoes. These tools were indispensable for agriculture, construction, transportation, and without them the settlers would have struggled to establish their communities.

Colonial Australia's success was heavily reliant on agriculture. Blacksmiths played a key role in improving the efficiency of farming practices by producing better tools and equipment. For example, they forged durable ploughs that could break through the tough soil, leading to increased production.

Blacksmiths were often skilled wheelwrights as well. They crafted wheels for wagons and carts, and the ability to repair these vehicles was crucial as the harsh terrain took its toll. Blacksmiths were also involved in buildings and infrastructure. They forged nails, hinges, and other metal components needed for construction. Their expertise in metalwork was essential for creating locks and security features for homes and businesses.

As Australia's mineral resources were discovered and exploited, blacksmiths played a significant role in supporting the mining industry. They crafted tools for prospectors, miners, and smelters, contributing to the development of the mining towns and industries that would later become vital to Australia's economy.

Beyond their practical contributions, blacksmiths also engaged in artistry. They created decorative ironwork, such as gates, railings, and ornamental pieces for homes and public buildings adding an aesthetic element to growing towns.

The blacksmith's workshop often served as a central point of the community. People would gather there not only for metalwork services but also for news, conversation, and social interaction. The blacksmith became a respected figure within the community, often consulted for advice and assistance.

While it is clear that the blacksmith played an essential role in the economic development of human societies from the iron age through to late Victorian industrialization, it is also evident that there was a religious, or spiritual element to the trade. Blacksmiths were long believed to hold special powers and to operate at the borders of light and darkness, good and evil. In its purest form the craft takes raw material from the ground and transforms it through the use of fire into something beautiful, functional, often powerful. This process of transformation is central to the relationship between blacksmithing and spiritual change.

The blacksmiths forge, a place where raw, shapeless metal is heated, hammered, and transformed into functional often beautiful objects serves as a powerful metaphor for ideas of spiritual transformation and rebirth. Across cultures and throughout history, the blacksmith's craft has been intertwined with symbolism and rituals that reflect the human quest for inner change and renewal. There exists throughout the ages, a rich symbolism of the blacksmiths forge and its profane connection to spiritual transformation and rebirth.

By the turn of the 20th century, blacksmithing as a trade began to decline. Innovations in manufacturing and transportation made the town blacksmith all but obsolete. The rise of the factory system meant that iron products could be manufactured cheaply and in quantities the local smithy couldn't match. Then, steel became available cheaply and the demand for wrought iron dwindled. As the motor car replaced the horse and carriage even the farrier side of the business disappeared.

Today there is something of a resurgence of interest in cottage industries, and consequently in blacksmithing. This interest is embedded in nostalgia for a simpler past. The magic of creating something from raw materials with nothing more than your strength, tools you have created yourself, and fire, is a magic that lingers in our psyche. A place of which we dream.

Bibliography

Bishop, Catherine. Minding Her Own Business: Colonial Business Women in Sydney (2015) University of NSW Press.

Dickens, Charles. Great Expectations: (1867) London: Chapman and Hall.

Elliott, Elizabeth. (1980) Women, class and history: feminist perspectives on Australia, 1788-1978. Sydney: Fontana/Collins.

Hentzschel, G. R., Reynaud, D., & Jackson, W. (2019) A Salvation Army commencement narrative: An investigation of the literature focused on the Army. in Queensland. The Australasian Journal of Salvation Army History, 4(2), 15-26.

Lynch, D. & G. Lunney. Maryborough: A Rare Old Town. (1996) Maryborough: True Blue Books.

Maryborough, Wide Bay and Burnett Historical Society. (1998). A history of Maryborough, Queensland, 1842-1997.

Stanford, J. How the Queensland Deposit Bank Shaped Suburbs in the 1880's: Queensland History Journal Vol 23(10) August 2018.

Theile, F. Otto & United Evangelical Lutheran Church in Australia. Queensland District. Publication Committee. (1938) One hundred years of the Lutheran Church in Queensland: Retrieved April 5, 2023.

Watson, A. The Blacksmith. (1977) New York: WW Norton and Company.

Newspaper Articles

www.ingramcontent.com/pod-product-compliance
Lightning Source LLC
Chambersburg PA
CBHW030821210726
48290CB00002B/706